Water Memory

Lyrical, Satirical, Genre-defying

And that's the funny thing about the end of the world, they never tell you how long it's going to take. Too bad they couldn't be more specific.

The earth's magnetic poles have reversed and civilization has just had its clock reset to the great cosmic flashing 12:00am from almost a million years ago, and humanity, and everybody in it, is pretty much forgetting everything it learned since the last time. Everybody except Hertell Daggett, who remembers pretty much everything because he'd once been shot in the head—the doctors got the bullet out, but missed a few tiny specks of copper that remained, floating inside his brain, connecting him to the things everybody else on earth is slowly forgetting. Hertell sees an opportunity to start civilization all over again, and maybe even get it right this time. What could possibly go wrong?

Praise for the Author

"... at once thoughtful, engaging and unsettling, but more than anything, wickedly funny... Strelich's profane, irreverent vision of a realignment of human sensibilities to save an undeserving world serves up a rewarding read—Virginia Brackett, author of *In the Company of Patriots*

"...Satirical? Yes, you will laugh out loud. Pure satire? No. Water Memory is much richer and purer than that. Strelich has concocted a familiar semi-sci-fi setting with industrious, damaged, absorbing inhabitants who have a dazzling, terrifying gift thrust upon them: The chance to start over."—RG Halleck, author of *Evade the Dark* and *The Search for Macadamia*

"... close enough to real life to bring you in, but far enough to the side you have to use your peripheral vision... a reader's roller coaster... If you can survive the whiplash, you will be richly rewarded" —Tom Lederle, author of *Digital Surrealism*

"... laughed out loud many times... fun and witty... written in an intelligent and sarcastic tone that is so unique and refreshing... Will definitely be reading Strelich again! "—Ashley Dunston, author of *The Strange*

"The hysterical-realism that characterized Strelich's first novel finds new life in a speculative, near-future, plausible sci-fi apocalypse story that's as funny as it is beatific... the redemption of existentialism, a smiling Sisyphus... The inherent humanism of it cuts through the satire like a knife. Like Dog Logic before it, Water Memory is richly conceived, compulsively entertaining, and thoroughly brilliant."—Alex Lee, Stoner/Web Developer

"What a JOY to read ... Poignant, humorous, timely and rich, it held me hostage from the melodic Prologue to the final imagery envisioned in the last sentence.... I have a message for Kurt Vonnegut and Richard Bach, housed in my personal Writer Hall of Fame: Make room for Tom Strelich" -- Michael R. Simmons, Managing Artistic Director - Carolina Actors Studio Theatre (CAST)

Water Memory

A Novel

Tom Strelich

Owl Canyon Press

Owl Canyon Press

Copyright

Library of Congress Cataloging-in-Publication Data

Strelich Tom.

Water Memory -- 1st Ed.

p. cm.

ISBN: 978-1-952085-22-2 (Paperback)

ISBN: 978-1-952085-26-0 (Hardcover)

2022948773

Owl Canyon Press

Boulder, Colorado

Invitation

Free Audiobook

I hope you enjoy reading *Water Memory*, and if you'd like a free audiobook edition of *Dog Logic* (the first book in the Dog Logic Triptych) for those long drives, walks, bike rides, or airline flights, just point your smartphone or tablet camera at the QR Code below to download a copy...

Audiobook

To Wynn Handman. He was very kind.

Prologue

The Mustard Seed National Cemetery didn't look like a normal National Cemetery: no expanse of green grass studded with endless ranks and rows of uniform white headstones, no flags, no flowers, no cannons, no plaques, no statues, no trees, no fountains, not even a gate to get inside. Just a 10-foot-high cyclone fence topped with razor wire surrounding 10 square miles of barren, bleached foothills on the outskirts of Bakersfield. The final resting place for the lost civilization of Mustard Seed.

It wasn't an ancient civilization lost to some environmental calamity, but was instead a fairly fresh one, dating back to the Kennedy administration. Its destruction wasn't a dystopian affair, the civilization crushed beneath the heel of an oppressive police state, or a fundamentalist theocracy purging a heretical cult, or a techno-utopia enforcing perfection, it was just an unfortunate and regrettable misunderstanding in the normal course of civic events. Nobody to blame for it really. Nevertheless, nearly a thousand souls had once lived beneath the cemetery in a massive underground complex due to some bad information they got back in 1963 about the end of the world. There they had lived contentedly for over half a century until their discovery and emergence, but complications ensued and now they all lay dead beneath the silent hills behind the ugly fence.

The only indication that it was a National anything-at-all were the numerous warning signs posted at regular intervals along the fence:

"RESTRICTED AREA, U.S. GOVERNMENT PROPERTY, NO TRESPASSING"

Almost every day at sunset, a lone bagpiper would stand on a hilltop at the edge of the Mustard Seed National Cemetery. Doug knew all of the dead, some better than others, but all of them to some degree. And he also knew that he was directly responsible for their fate.

Not directly responsible like he literally dropped the bunker buster bomb on them, or that he gave the order to drop it, but directly responsible in that he failed so miserably as an impromptu hostage negotiator. He didn't beg the people of Mustard Seed to surrender to the swarm of SWAT teams, Humvees, MRAPs, Strykers, APCs, and helicopters that had, once upon a time, dotted the hillsides and darkened the skies over the future Mustard Seed National Cemetery.

He didn't plead, or urge, or advise, or even suggest that they surrender to the authorities. Quite the opposite in fact. He advised the people of Mustard Seed to shelter in place and tell the assembled SWAT teams to fuck off, which, while it may have been emotionally satisfying at the time, nevertheless had the unintended side effect of resulting in the death of the entire Mustard Seed population.

Playing the pipes at the fence line was a way of coping. It didn't absolve, but it did help. Day by day, and week by week, and month by month he'd play whatever tune came into his head in remembrance of the person he was honoring, "Amazing Grace," "La Cucaracha," "Happy Trails," "Aloha Oe," etc. Until today, when he played the final farewell to the most extraordinary, yet seemingly ordinary, man he'd ever known, Hertell Daggett. The man who'd accidentally discovered the Mustard Seed civilization living beneath his Li'l Pal Heaven pet cemetery, brought them up into our surface world, and tried to protect them as best he could, to the very end.

And while Doug knew every man, woman, and child below, what he didn't know was that just a few hundred feet beneath where he now stood, Hertell and the others were still alive.

Chapter One

The End of The World

It started out simply enough, a non-event, just a random question.

"What's this for?"

Hertell looked down at the object in question. He was older now and wise around the eyes. On the whole he was a fairly average looking man, the kind you'd never expect to save the world. He was probably no more than six feet tall, but for some reason always seemed taller to most people. His hair was still thick and mostly black like it was before, but it now had a spattering of gray that suggested Harris Tweed. He was handsome in his own way, a way that women appreciate and men respect. He was standing on some scaffolding near the top of a broad passageway painting some clouds over the Grand Canyon when the question was asked.

He put down his paint brush and knelt on the scaffold deck to get a better look. "It's a compass."

The inquisitor was a thirtyish math and physics teacher named Lox, so named because his eyes were said to be the color of liquid oxygen. He always wore a white short-sleeve shirt and a narrow tie and had the look of a Kennedy-era NASA engineer. He rubbed his crew cut thoughtfully, "Yeah I know it's a magnetic compass, but what does it do, what do you use it for?" He proceeded to perform an awkward pirouette, pivoting on one foot, turning several full revolutions while looking at the compass, "A student asked me if it was broken. I didn't know what to tell her. No matter what you do, it keeps pointing the same way."

Hertell held out his hand, and accepted the compass in his open palm, "It's a thing you use when you wanna know which way you're heading relative to magnetic north." Hertell made a small level arc with his hand. "See how even when I change the way the compass is facing, like you did when you were doing the Curley thing, the little needle always points in the same direction?"

Lox watched the demonstration, "Okay, so that's why it doesn't move, it's always pointing toward the magnetic north pole, that makes sense."

"Yeah, so if you wanted to go to the north pole, you'd walk the way the needle is pointing, and if you wanted to go south to Mexico or LA or someplace down there, you'd walk the opposite way."

"North is that way now?"

Lox was pointing the same direction as the needle, down an enormous and beautifully lit passageway leading the wrong way, south, toward Mexico.

Hertell climbed down from the scaffolding and took some steps away from it. "I think the scaffolding might be messing up the compass." He watched the compass as he crossed toward the middle of the large domed hall.

"The scaffolding is ferrous, iron, so that might be what's making it point the..."

"Thank you, but I know what ferrous means." Lox also taught Chemistry and Latin, and followed along behind Hertell, "And also ferric and the various oxidation states of iron."

Hertell knew that Lox would continue on with the rest of the periodic table if left to his own instincts, "Yeah, well it's not the scaffolding then, it still says north is down that way, so maybe it's just a bad compass."

Lox shrugged, "Possibly, unless north really is down that way now."

Hertell started to laugh, but then stopped, "Do you mind if I keep this?"

"Keep what?"

"The compass."

Lox nodded, "Sure, we don't need'm down here anyway. It's no wonder I forgot what it was for."

Hertell watched as Lox strode purposefully down the muraled passageway toward Mexico.

This had been happening more and more lately: people asking what things were, or what they were for, simple things, self-describing things, like doorstops, and music stands, and cannon balls, and now a magnetic compass. He had to admit that people living underground don't use magnetic compasses much anyway since travel opportunities beneath the surface are limited, so forgetting what they were called, and what they were for, was understandable.

But for some reason he felt compelled to establish with some finality that the compass was indeed defective. Perhaps the rock formation of the chamber they were in had some magnetic properties that could be influencing the compass, even if the scaffolding didn't.

He proceeded north toward Alaska, passing through broad cornfields, a bright gymnasium where a volleyball game was in progress, a dim cathedral where the choir was practicing, a miniature golf course where someone was having a birthday party, all the while with the compass stubbornly insisting that he was headed south toward Mexico.

At length, he found himself on Main Street, which looked like a cross between Disneyland's Main Street USA and a Norman Rockwell painting. It was a timeless small-town square from some mythical past complete with a flagpole and a cannon and a pyramid of cannon balls, a bell and bandstand, ringed with stores and offices and streetlights and park benches, and a movie theatre with "The Nutty Professor" on the marquee. He could hear faint clonking from the bowling alley in the distance and some Duane Eddy drifting out of the malt shop.

At the center of the town square was a 10-foot compass rose, a concrete circle with large brass letters identifying the four cardinal directions "N", "E", "W", and "S", but Hertell was primarily interested in what stood at the center of the circle: a large nautical binnacle housing a massive gimbaled compass. The compass served no useful purpose since Mustard Seed was underground and therefore stationary, but had been placed at the very center of the settlement at its founding, to symbolize Mustard Seed's role as the vessel to safely navigate and ultimately deliver humanity and civilization into the post-apocalyptic future.

The binnacle had become less of a symbol and more of a fixture over time, so he pulled out his shirttail and rubbed the dust from the brass hood and the clouded, dinner plate sized glass view port. He could see the big nautical compass clearly now and where its needle pointed. He looked over the binnacle at the large brass "N" embedded in the ground five feet directly in front of him. He thumped on the hood with his palm to see if anything moved, but nothing did. The needle was motionless and pointing directly at his belly. The symbolic compass, which had always pointed true north, into the bright post-apocalyptic future, was now saying that north was south and south was north.

Hertell ran a hand through his Harris Tweed hair and leaned on the massive compass, because he knew what it meant, and in fact had been expecting it, but not in his lifetime, and not in the lifetime of anyone he knew. It didn't seem to demand much attention though, and if it hadn't been for Lox's random question, Hertell would have never known.

Nevertheless, here it was.

The end of the world.

Chapter Two

Timing is Everything

U p in the surface world, it started out mostly as a kind of curiosity, south becoming north and north becoming south, and mostly stayed one until everybody simply forgot that it happened.

People don't use compasses much anymore anyway, except for airplane pilots or sea captains or Boy Scouts since they're the only ones who really care which way is north or south, and even then, they've got GPS, so it's not even something they really need at all. So when Earth's magnetic poles reversed, it didn't get that much attention.

When it first happened, it got a bold red headline on *Drudge* with a rotating beacon animated .gif because a lot of people were expecting something noticeable, like WiFi not working anymore. Or like they have in the movies with tidal waves and buildings falling down and the earth opening up and swallowing shopping malls, and people being shitty to each other because they're scared. Except for the hero, who's usually a scientist that nobody listened to, even though he kept telling them that his research and his instruments and computer simulations were predicting it the whole time. And he's usually divorced and dealing with a deeply conflicted kid, or two sometimes, that he's got to save, only they're clear on the opposite side of town with the ex-wife, that he still loves. And then complications ensue and he finally learns the true meaning of Christmas, or gets his wife back, or a full professorship, or whatever it was he was angling for when the movie started.

Only none of that actually happened. Not even close. So, the story lost the rotating beacon animated .gif on *Drudge* and eventually the bold red font, and ultimately drifted down the webpage to a normal size font and typeface, with links to experts explaining how it's really no big deal and that it's happened lots of times over the last few billion years or so. Just routine. Nothing to see here. Move along, but first... *Remember this child actor? You won't believe what she looks like now!*

The experts were correct as far as it went, as you'd expect them to be. They were experts after all. The detailed and exhaustive Brunhes–Matuyama study of the most recent reversal almost a million years ago indicated that there was no massive extinction event, and not even a noticeable impact on climate or plant life or animal life, though there was some scholarly conjecture that there may have been some confusion among migratory bird species.

But that reversal happened almost a million years ago, before civilization and culture, and alphabets and money, and numbers and God, and atom bombs and X-Box. So, this time it wouldn't be like all the other magnetic pole reversals, back when the world only had saber tooth tigers and wooly mammoths running around eating each other all day.

It would be different this time, not enough to notice, only enough to sense. Like when you walk into a room and then realize you can't remember why you walked in there in the first place. You can retrace your steps and try to remember what you were thinking to conjure up your original intent. That works sometimes, but not usually, and you're eventually left with the vague sense that you once had a reason and a direction, but now have no idea what it was. It would be like that for people of Earth, little things at first, like the name of that thing you open cans with, or what a compass is for, and why it points at anything. At all.

And that's the funny thing about the end of the world that they never tell you: not the crazy people on late night AM radio, and not the people in the movies, and not the Jesus freaks, and not the heroes and not the scientists and not the prophets. They'll tell you about the end of the world, that it's just around the corner, or that it's finally here.

But they never tell you how long it's going to take. Too bad they couldn't be more specific.

Does the world end in a day, or does it just take its time?

Chapter Three

The Answer is a Question

After chancing upon the end of the world, Hertell remained at the compass rose for a time. The sun was setting. It wasn't the real sun, just the massive planetarium projector that was turning day into night.

The actual configuration of Main Street and the massive dome in which it was nestled, always reminded Hertell of the big atrium hotels lurking at the edges of Disneyland. He'd once spoken at a conference in one of them back when he was a physicist. It had a hectare-sized central courtyard complete with creeks and bridges and Koi ponds and waterfalls and a mechanical lion up on a rock that would roar at the top and bottom of the hour. Above it all rose a twenty-story box canyon of hotel rooms overlooking the courtyard and the people and the lion and the Koi fish far below, with glass elevators full of families and businessmen sliding silently up and down the canyon walls.

But Hertell wasn't a physicist anymore and he wasn't in a hotel. He was beneath the earth, in a massive complex of ancient lava tubes, the walls, ceilings, and floors of which had been smoothed by a few million years of a torrential water flow giving the broad passageways and great halls a natural cove quality, gently curving domelike overhead, horizonless and seemingly infinite, and lit for the illusion of day and night. It was like an enormous ride at Disneyland, only you weren't in a boat with pirates shooting cannons over your head, you were walking past storefronts on Main Street USA and *Leave It To Beaver*'s house and looking up side streets that stretched into the distance—they didn't actually go into the distance, but just a few arm's lengths or so. It was all an illusion and palpably artificial, yet fascinating and strangely, but undeniably, comforting, like an intricately detailed train set or doll's house or Nativity Scene.

He watched the mechanical sun set and the mechanical stars rise and considered the implications of the emerging pattern. He kept trying to collect his thoughts and formulate rational, alternative explanations for what the compass was telling him.

Perhaps it wasn't the end of the world, perhaps the old binnacle compass was improperly installed. He'd never actually looked at it before, so it may have been pointing the wrong way the whole time. Perhaps it was simply defective or possibly it was an irregular or a factory second which would explain why it was just a symbolic fixture in a setting where it didn't really matter which way it pointed. Perhaps there had been a stealthy but nevertheless massive tectonic event that had not only escaped everyone's notice but had also rotated the entirety of their underground world exactly 180 degrees.

But each logical explanation yielded to various logical counter-arguments and ultimately to rejection: a defective binnacle compass would have been destroyed at the factory and never found its way onto a ship much less salvaged; earthquakes result from faults that either go up and down or side to side, but there's no such thing as a rotational fault.

At length, he finally accepted what had so obviously and undeniably happened.

And it was all starting to make sense now. The odd questions and mystifying behaviors that he'd noted with some amusement initially, had been slowly, almost imperceptibly increasing in frequency until now, when almost every day there was an off-axis incident, like Lox's question about the compass. The poles reversed and people were forgetting stuff, not everybody perhaps, and not everything either, and not all at once, just an odd, random assortment. But there were two issues troubling Hertell.

One, when did the reversal happen? Hertell had only been asked the compass question a few hours before, and had just accepted the fact that the poles had indeed reversed, but he had no idea when the reversal had actually happened. It may have been a week or it could have been a month, or it could have been a year, or more. How long had people been forgetting things?

Two, what if he was forgetting things too, but was unaware that he'd forgotten them, or that he'd even ever known them in the first place? Does it count as forgetting if you've forgotten something that you didn't even know you knew in the first place? This issue sent Hertell into a rigorous self-assessment.

He crisscrossed the town square touching and confirming that he knew the name and purpose of everything within reach or in sight, causing several people to come out of the bowling alley, and a few more from the malt shop, to see what Hertell was up to as he performed the role of museum docent describing the Main Street diorama to an invisible or otherwise imaginary group of tourists.

"...This is a bandstand where musicians can give concerts. A musician is someone who can play a musical instrument, there are three, no four main kinds of musical instruments: string, brass, woodwind, and percussion. A musician can also be a singer, but singers don't really count as musicians unless they can actually play an instrument, and tambourines don't count as an instrument, even if you put scarves on'm, or on the microphone stand, like some of the old rockers used to do back in the '80s..."

"...This is a Zeiss Model II planetarium projector, and it is a key element of an extensive and sophisticated studio lighting system that was set up many decades ago to provide the illusion of day and night for all the inhabitants of Mustard Seed and to preserve their circadian rhythms..."

"The lighting system, and all of Mustard Seed, is powered by by O-S-C-N, Orthogonal Symmetric Collimated Normalized Toroid reactors, or Oceanoid reactors for short, that use the weak nuclear force to produce basically infinite energy without the Chernobyl downside of ionizing gamma radiation and nasty nuclear waste by-products. In addition to the heat for driving steam turbines for electricity, there

15

is also a significant amount of gold, and lesser amounts of other Platinum group metals, generated as a byproduct of the complex reaction sequence..."

Sanford and Dannon ran the bowling alley, they were also visibly excited, and they always finished each other sentences, "Hey Hertell are you working on that... gameshow thing you told us about?"

Hertell had once regaled them with the story about his experience on *Jeopardy* when he was in college in LA, but that he forgot to answer as a question on the last big question and lost all the money.

"But don't forget to answer as a question this time, so you don't... mess up like you did on TV."

"What? No, not doing the game show thing..." But then Hertell pivoted and took the opportunity to see how much they were forgetting, "Yes, yeah actually, I am, so the category is 'Patriotic Artifacts' for $500, and here's the answer, "I am a pole and at the top of me flutters Old Glory, what am I?"

Sanford and Dannon looked at each other and then laughed, "What is an old glory... pole?... Yeah glory pole, what is a glory pole?"

Hertell warmed to the role of gameshow host, "Close, but it's actually a flag pole, what is a flag pole, flag pole." Sanford and Dannon nodded and shrugged, "Oh yeah, that's right, I almost... said that too."

Hertell pointed to the flag, "Bonus round."

Sanford and Dannon brightened and were joined by Tristan and Trevor from the Malt Shop.

"This next answer is about that flag on the flagpole, so look at the flag for a moment and then I'll give you the answer. And remember the answer is a question."

The group looked up at the flag. There was never any wind underground, so the flag had a stiffener in it so that it stood straight out as if in a bracing 30-knot wind, like the flag at the Apollo 11 Tranquility Base, only without a bug-like lunar lander in the background or a saluting Neil Armstrong.

Tristan folded his arms in appraisal, "You know it just seems kind of busy to me, don't you think?" Trevor agreed, "It's trying to do too much, and the stripes don't go with the stars at all, and..."

"The American flag has thirteen, alternating red and white stripes to represent the original thirteen colonies, and has fifty stars to represent what?"

Tristan and Trevor blurted, "Outer space."

Sanford and Dannon corrected, "What is... outer space?"

"I'm sorry, but it's actually the fifty states, the fifty stars represent the fifty states, what are the fifty states."

Sanford slapped his thigh, "Dang, I was thinking that, but outer space just made a lot more sense."

Tristan was unimpressed, "It's still too busy."

A crowd had gathered around Hertell by this point, "This is really good, you guys are really helping me work up stuff for Mustard Seed Jeopardy, so one last question."

He wanted them to get at least one question right, so he came up with one so obvious that they couldn't get it wrong. He gestured toward the old cannon and the pyramid of cannon balls.

"A kind of ball you shoot out of a cannon, and you use the cannon to shoot these balls at people you want to kill or blow their heads off and so forth..."

Hertell trailed off, since he now knew why he didn't seem to be as affected by the pole reversal as were the others in Mustard Seed. He'd been shot in the head once. Not with a cannonball though, just a 9mm, back when he was still a physicist. The doctors got the bullet out, but some microscopic specks of copper eluded them, and since he was expected to die anyway, they left them floating inside his brain. Only he didn't die, and evidently now that north was south and south was north, those copper specks allowed Hertell to remember things that everybody else in Mustard Seed seemed to be forgetting.

"What is a cannon ... ball?"

He turned to Dannon, "That is correct, what is a cannon ball. Now will you go find President Higgs, I think he's in the bowling alley, and ask him to..."

"Yeah, he's in there with his league," Sanford laughed, "What is a gutter ball?"

"Tell him we need to have an emergency meeting of the National Security Council in the gym in ten minutes."

Hertell gave similar instructions to Trevor and Tristan to inform the cabinet of the emergency meeting. He then took one last look at the rising moon as it touched one of the clouds he'd painted on the smooth rock sky and wondered what people were forgetting in the real world above.

Chapter Four

Note to Self

"**M**usic stand, right?" Doug was looking at a rickety little metal music stand.

His wife called in from the kitchen, "That spidery looking metal thing you put your music on?"

"Yeah, that."

Doug was on the north side of middle age, but still active and fit, even though his memory wasn't what it used to be. He was the same basic size he was in high school, though softer around the middle now. His wife said that he resembled a movie star from the '50s whose name she could never quite recall.

The conversation continued between the kitchen and the den.

"No that's a defibrillator."

Doug was confused for a moment, then laughed, "Hey, kiss my ass!"

It had become something of a playful game between Doug and Audrey; they'd both been coming up short on the names and purposes of various things and would go to ridiculous lengths when coming up with answers, partly because it was

TOM STRELICH

funny, but mainly because it was a way of coping with the terrifying sense that their worlds were progressively getting both smaller and increasingly hazy.

"It's a music stand, dumb ass!"

He could hear her laughing. They were empty nesters, and it was kind of fun to banter in foul language that they never would have used when their daughter was living with them.

Doug wrote on a sticky note, "Muzic Stand". He knew it didn't look quite right, but he shrugged it off, "Well at least I still know the... the..." He thought for a moment, searching. He knew that the Phoenicians had invented it, and that there were several different kinds, Greek, Latin, Cyrillic, Chinese, and so on, but he just couldn't think of the actual name until he eventually had a eureka moment, "Alphabet!"

"What?"

"Nothing, just a word that came back to me."

He put the sticky note on the music stand, and then surveyed the room where a scattering of colored notes labeled various household items, furniture, and fixtures. It reminded him of something he'd once read in a book many years before by some Mexican writer about an Indian village someplace where everybody had terrible insomnia and forgot the names of everything and wrote little notes to themselves to remind them of what things were called.

And this is what frustrated Doug the most, that he could remember a minor incident in some nameless book he'd read 40 years before, but that he couldn't remember something as simple as the name of that metal stand you put music on.

He'd recently had an MRI, as had Audrey some weeks later. The neurologist determined that both of their brains were

20

fine and that they didn't have that disease that makes you forget stuff, but that they should cut down on sodium. It had taken them many months to schedule their MRIs due to both a huge spike in demand for MRIs and also because there was a shortage of doctors who still remembered how to interpret them; nevertheless, they were comforted by the doctor's diagnosis and content to live with the minor inconvenience of a few gaps in their working vocabulary.

It was something of a miracle that they'd managed to get an MRI at all since the waiting list was nearly two years long and growing. However, forgetfulness seemed to be permeating the entire population, so a lot of people were simply forgetting that they had MRI appointments and were constantly missing them. The scheduler sent Doug the MRI FastPass App that would alert him when a slot was predicted to be available because she recognized his face and voice from his podcast and YouTube series that had gone viral a few years before and made him famous.

Doug had been a psychologist before he'd gotten famous, and he was only famous because of Mustard Seed. It had all started out innocently enough, at a bagpipe funeral for a police dog because, in addition to being a psychologist, Doug was also a bagpiper. It was a graveside service with full honors including speeches, testimonials, a volley of gunfire, and it concluded with "Amazing Grace" with Doug on the bagpipes, after which he first met Hertell.

He'd had a pleasant and wide-ranging conversation with Hertell that day on a variety of topics: Doug's profession, Hertell's head injury, theories about parallel universes and the reversal of Earth's magnetic poles. And then, only a few days later, Hertell discovered a civilization living beneath the hills of his Li'l Pal Heaven and brought them to the surface, and the world's attention, resulting in the complications that brought Doug into the picture as the psychologist for the people of Mustard Seed.

He recognized the importance of the event, which he considered the equivalent of the discovery of Pompeii. Only these people weren't entombed in lava in contorted death poses but very much alive when discovered, though confused by the modern world in which pretty much everything they knew, believed, and valued was completely inverted.

If it hadn't been for their chance bagpipe and police dog funeral meeting, Doug would have just been another passive witness, a mere member of the studio audience rather than a featured performer, participating and chronicling the epic events, technological disruptions, and cultural aftershocks arising from the Mustard Seed discovery and their eventual destruction when the modern world, or more accurately, certain elements of local, county, state, and federal governments determined that Mustard Seed, rather than being a mere archeological curiosity, was actually, literally, a menace to society.

Such a menace in fact that a siege ensued, and when the various federal, state, and local enforcement actions failed to coax the people of Mustard Seed from their subterranean stronghold, Doug was brought in as a kind of hostage negotiator, even though there weren't any hostages, and ordered to talk them out of their burrow to face whatever charges were being conjured from the penumbra of the sovereign state.

Due to his poor performance as a hostage negotiator, he was stripped of his license, denounced, smeared, vilified, charged, prosecuted, and jailed for aiding and abetting a terrorist organization, as Mustard Seed was subsequently declared after it had been destroyed and all of its inhabitants killed.

And it was while serving 18 months in Lompoc Federal Prison followed by another 18 months under house arrest with his anklet, that he began chronicling the epic saga of Mustard Seed from its inception back in the Truman administration, its construction in the Eisenhower administration, its activation in the Kennedy administration, its discovery by Hertell, and its eventual destruction. He started with yellow legal pads while at Lompoc and then after he got web access while under house arrest, he started a blog, complete with extraordinary photos of all the people and places below.

The success of the blog led to the podcast series that went viral. Doug had one of those voices and faces that people just seemed to intuitively trust and a very engaging style of speaking. Celebrity and fortune followed with a multi-year binge-worthy series on Amazon, and even a Broadway show with astounding sets, and the music was good too—nothing you could whistle but nevertheless a pester of insidious tune weevils that would burrow into your head just before you went to bed and torture you into a fitful sleep like an old radio jingle.

The fame was nice, but the money was better. It allowed Doug to buy the old Merle Haggard estate near the mouth of Kern Canyon and adjoining the former Li'l Pal Heaven

Pet Cemetery, where he would continue to honor the people of Mustard Seed by playing the pipes at sunset in their memory, long after the public had moved on to other blogs and podcasts and binge series and Broadway shows.

In addition to Doug, several other featured performers in the saga of Mustard Seed found fame as well: the most notable two being the Kern County Sheriff's deputy who'd helped Hertell bring them to the surface and then went on to start what eventually became a massive global megachurch based on the book of Revelation. The other was a disillusioned Federal investigator who created a Mustard Seed Duck-and-Cover MMORPG game that had over three billion downloads worldwide and then went on to create a Silicon Valley tech empire and launch the asteroid mining industry.

The fate of Mustard Seed had been something of an embarrassment to the authorities at the time, so the Li'l Pal itself had long since been condemned, fenced off as federal property, bulldozed and cleared of all traces of Hertell, the Li'l Pal, and Mustard Seed. Since it was federal property, they even took down the old wooden cross that had been on one of the more prominent hills on the Li'l Pal. Doug however, managed to buy the old rugged cross from the demolition contractor and then planted it on top of the tallest hill on his own property right next to the cyclone fence of the Mustard Seed National Cemetery, where it now stood looking down upon its former home on the Li'l Pal.

Doug could see the old rugged cross from the living room where he now stood with the sticky notes on his hand. He looked at the sticky note he'd just put on the music stand. He then took it off. He took some sheets of bagpipe music off the floor and placed them on the stand, and then stood back and looked at it, "Well what'dya know, it still does what it's supposed to do whether I know what to call it or not."

Fuck it, he thought, things will still do whatever it is they do, give you something to sit on, or step over, or put music on, so it doesn't really matter what you called them. It wouldn't even be frustrating if you didn't fight it like that story about the oak tree and the reeds in a big storm or something, or like fighting a rip tide, since you'll only end up exhausting yourself anyway and then drowning.

He proceeded to take the sticky notes off of everything and crumple them into a ball. "Audrey, I'm taking the notes off everything."

"What?"

"I said I'm taking the notes off everything!"

"The defibrillator too?" Audrey had been a cardiac nurse before they got rich and famous.

"Yeah, that too!" He looked at the wad of colorful sticky notes in his hand, "I mean, what the hell, this is bull..." He was searching for the word, and called out toward the kitchen "Hey what's that thing that comes out of a bull's butt when it goes number two?"

"That would be shit?"

He plucked a post-it from a lamp shade, "Yeah, this is bullshit!"

Chapter Five

Soldering Iron

I t wasn't going well.

Kaye, the acting Secretary of State, was sitting in the bleachers with the President, the National Security Council, congressional leadership, and the rest of the cabinet. The bonsai US Government seated in the spacious gymnasium was being addressed by Hertell, who was informing the leadership of Mustard Seed that Earth's magnetic poles had reversed, and that there were subtle but nevertheless definite neurological effects causing people to forget stuff.

Kaye had been married to Hertell, on and off, for well over twenty years. He wasn't the sweet boy she married anymore, neither was he the cold man she divorced. He was nowhere in between either. He was beyond both. He'd become something else entirely. She was never quite sure what. Whatever it was, she saw him as something more than a man somehow, but still childlike in many ways, the best ways. He could be excitable and obsessive about things sometimes, like now for instance about some fucking compass and forgetting stuff.

"It's not just about the compass, and that's the thing about this, you won't realize that it's happening, because you won't even know that you're forgetting stuff, because you're forgetting that you even knew the stuff in the first place."

President Higgs was shaking his head, "Well, so what if we are forgetting stuff? As long as we're all forgetting stuff together. I don't see a problem with that, it'll be the new normal. You're forgetting stuff too, aren't you?"

"Well, actually no, I'm not forgetting stuff like the rest of you because I got shot in the head once."

Which Kaye knew to be true, and that it had contributed in some way to the gradual but significant improvement in the man she'd divorced, enough to make marrying him again unavoidable. She also knew that Hertell was probably a special case, but if it could be made to work consistently, that there were a lot of men, and women too, possibly even herself, who would benefit from a bullet in the head.

"It was back when I was living on the surface, before I found you all down here, and before the big dust-up we had with the county a few years back." He noticed a few blank stares. "Where they blew up the whole western pressure buffer complex? You all remember that, yes?"

Most nodded, but some shook their heads.

He wasn't prepared for that. "Some of us got killed too, remember? Virginia, Tommy, Barbara and Jack..." He paused and swallowed. His throat was aching, so he just trailed off unable to continue with the sad roster. A few more nodded, but there were still a few that shook their heads.

"But you all remember that I got shot in the head once?"

Everybody was nodding now with a chorus of affirmations... "Yeah, you just told us that... yep, just a second ago..." Hertell was nodding too. Okay, this was progress. He sensed that they could remember new stuff, so maybe it was just old stuff people were forgetting.

"Who shot you?"

Hertell rubbed the top of his head, "Well nobody, exactly, and besides that's not why I bring this up."

"Well somebody must have pulled the trigger to make the gun go off..." Lox took a keen interest since he also served part-time as Secretary of Defense.

Lox's assertion was followed by a flurry of supporting arguments from the bleachers, "Guns just sit there... it's just a piece of metal with some wood attached... it can't do anything by itself... a car can't drive itself... an airplane can't fly itself... a gun can't shoot itself... did you shoot yourself?"

Kaye interjected, "It was an accident, nobody shot him in the head on purpose."

Hertell held up his hand to restore order, "To clarify, yes, it was an accident, and who pulled the trigger is irrelevant to the discussion at hand. My point is that I got shot in the head once, and there's still some tiny specks of copper that are still floating around in there, connecting things that aren't connected in the rest of you, which is why I'm not forgetting stuff like the rest of you."

"Does it hurt?" Twila, the Senior Senator from California and also director of the bell choir, had asked the question.

"Forgetting stuff? No, I don't think so, no more than learning stuff in the first place..."

"No, getting shot in the head."

Hertell saw an opportunity. "Well it turns out the brain doesn't have any pain receptors at all, unlike the whole rest of us, where we've got pain receptors all over the place, but none in the brain at all. So you could lift off the top of a person's head, and start poking their brain with a red-hot soldering iron, and they wouldn't feel a thing, they'd just wonder who was frying up the SPAM."

He looked at the assembled crowd, "Now, who remembers what a soldering iron is?"

A random scattering of men and women nodded their heads, smiled, and raised their hands, but the remainder stared back from the bleachers with blank faces as if confused by the question.

Hertell stood below an ancient man in the 3rd row, "Mister Tate, you taught metal shop to everybody here when they went through your 7th grade class, yes?"

Mr. Tate looked back over his shoulder at the people sitting in the bleachers. "Yeah, started with a biscuit cutter and then a threaded hammer and then on from there."

"Mrs. McAtee, you taught basic electronics to everybody in here when they went through your 8th grade class?"

Mrs. McAtee looked down from the top rank of bleachers, "Yes I think so, series and parallel circuits, ohms law, and all that."

"So, every one of you have held a soldering iron in your hand, even if it was a long time ago. Whether it was a cookie cutter or a circuit, everybody has used a soldering iron. And yet a number of you, enough of you, have forgotten that there even is such a thing as a soldering iron. Enough of you so that I think it proves that something is going on."

The Secretary of Agriculture arched his back and cracked his knuckles, "People don't have to remember everything. There's plenty of crap worth forgetting and even more crap not worth remembering, and just because you forget something, doesn't mean you're gonna forget everything. This I believe is an over-reaction on your part, I mean you've been shot in the head, you said so yourself, that it messed up your brain. Just saying. I simply don't think this is a real issue for anybody, besides you, I mean. I'm not forgetting anything."

Hertell nodded, "Yeah, you may be right. Maybe it's just me." He fished something out of his pocket and held it up for inspection, "What's this thing for?"

Kaye was losing patience. "It's a compass Hertell, everybody knows that."

"Yes, that's correct, it's a compass. What's it for, what does it do?"

Kaye laughed, "Oh for hell's sake, it's for... uh... you know... measuring... stuff...or..." For some reason the answer was eluding her.

Hertell held it up for the bleachers to see, "Anybody? Anybody remember what a compass is for?"

Only Lox raised his hand.

Chapter Six

Flashing 12:OO AM

"**W**ell fuck me dead."

Hillary was looking at a 3D model of the brain, and the data made absolutely no sense at all: the voxels were the right color in the wrong place and the wrong color in the right place, and this was going to totally knock her off the tenure track. She folded her arms and stared at the visually compelling but obviously erroneous display.

She was somewhat surprised by her salty vocalization as she typically internalized such things, but then attributed the utterance both to the popularity of the expression in various video games, viral memes, and her own personal growth as she'd been working on herself to acknowledge and express her feelings.

Hillary had bounced around several post-doc research gigs in fly-over country, wasted several years as a GS-13 reviewing research proposals at the CDC, and then conceived, proposed, and secured a post-doc research beachhead at UCSB, writing research proposals for the CDC and other three lettered tentacles of the federal government that wasted money on scientific stuff rather than agricultural subsidies, retirees, and stealth submarines and such.

She would never be mistaken for a button-nosed anime heroine or chinless Disney Princess. She had the cheekbones and blue eyes of a Basque peasant, a jaw that would make Hepburn proud, soot black hair, and an aquiline nose that looked like it had been broken, even though it hadn't. She had dimples when she smiled, but more pronounced on the right than on the left, so in her youth she would always chew on the smaller side in pursuit of dimple symmetry – a practice she would eventually and laughably dismiss, although she would pursue other forms of symmetry and order for the rest of her life.

She was a post-doc in her prime, although that term had undergone something of a transformation over time to now include anyone beyond the age of teen pregnancy and before the onset of dementia. She was definitely beyond teen pregnancy and comfortably far from dementia. She considered herself average in every conceivable way, height, weight, intelligence, every way but her instinctive grasp of math, which she didn't count toward intelligence at all. She thought of it as more of an aptitude, like hand-eye coordination, or sense of direction, or perfect pitch, like an idiot savant only without the idiot part.

She also couldn't recognize faces. There was a fancy Greek word for it, but basically, she was blind to faces, even her own. She'd once been in a bar with some friends, noticed a girl staring at her, and asked a friend standing beside her who the girl was that was checking her out. The friend cracked up laughing and asked the rest of the group who the saucy tart was that was ogling Hillary in the mirror behind the bar, more laughter. She then noticed that the girl was wearing the same clothes and had the same pixie haircut, and eventually realized that it was in fact her, and then laughed herself.

As an adult, when she'd meet someone at a party, she'd mention that she had face-blindness and that they shouldn't take it personally if she didn't recognize them a few minutes after meeting them. Although as a kid, and before she'd been diagnosed, she'd presumed her inability to recognize people and remember their names was simply because she wasn't very smart, which undoubtedly contributed to her considering herself of average intelligence, when in fact she was three sigma above average.

She'd grown up in the Central Valley, only 70 miles and several mountain ranges north of Santa Barbara. However, the baby boomers that burned the banks in Isla Vista back in the '70s were all in their 80s and 90s now, and thanks to nanotech and biotech and 3D bioprinting, were still skiing and cycling and surfing and clinging to their professorships well past their best-if-used-by date.

She'd established her tenure track research beachhead by riding the "Fake Science" strawman that loomed into view late in Trump's 1st term. The strawman eventually turned into a well-funded bipartisan piñata that showered money on any academic or corporate R&D department that promised to replicate, and thus either confirm or refute, an assortment of politically contentious scientific studies and experiments.

There were the usual suspects of course, global warming, global cooling, is red wine really good for you, evolution, and so on, all categorized as settled science and all still viciously debated depending on whose sacred cow was being gored or whose market was affected. But Hillary deftly threaded the needle by proposing to replicate some landmark and grudgingly accepted social psychology studies and experiments. She would combine not only advanced statistical and data analytic methods, but also advanced brain imaging techniques to demonstrate and validate a totally transparent and unbiased methodology that could then be uniformly and impartially applied to any and all of the viciously contested studies and experiments. And they bought it.

She was awash in funding from the NSF, CDC, DHS, DOE, HHS, Fish & Game, plus some floor sweepings from several lesser agencies, duchies, and pork barrel constituencies which made her a source of pride, and a profit center, for her department. And her methodology would make her the go-to quant diva for every fake-science replication study, and guarantee her co-authorship on a steady stream of peer-reviewed academic publications. She wouldn't need to worry about publish or perish no matter who got pissed off, and she could keep the gravy train flowing indefinitely as long as the politicians were willing to pay academics to gloss their policy turds. And some good science might actually come out of it too.

But the only problem was that it wasn't working anymore. The experiments weren't replicating. And they weren't replicating because people were changing. Only nobody knew it. The change was slow, random, and totally personalized: it was different for every person, everyone had their own unique trail, undetectable at each incremental step, but undeniable at its length as a million years of species firmware gradually faded away, simply falling out of use, and ending up just a vestigial artifact of a prior and long distant world, like the coccyx, and the appendix, and wisdom teeth.

And this is what Hillary was seeing in the data that made no sense, and the brain scan voxels that were the wrong color in the right place and the right color in the wrong place. And even though she didn't realize it at the time, what she was seeing was that the world, and everybody in it, was gradually getting their cerebral clocks reset to the great cosmic flashing 12:00am from almost a million years ago.

Chapter Seven

Small World

Perhaps they were right, perhaps he had over-reacted, perhaps it wasn't the end of the world. Kaye insisted he do something to clear his mind, so Hertell left Paris with his two daughters and proceeded toward Rome where he could see Kaye and their son sitting on the Colosseum waiting for them.

It wasn't your traditional miniature golf course, it was bigger, over an acre in the middle of one of the largest Mustard Seed great halls. It was a stylized, almost cartoonish relief map of the world with continents, major mountain ranges, bodies of water, and countries denoted by their respective iconic structures or natural wonders.

It wasn't to scale or in any way geodetically correct since it wasn't arranged in any of the standard world map projections, Mercator, Robinson, etc. It was instead arranged as a wandering, serpentine, vaguely elliptical track, with picnic tables, a jungle gym, some swings, and a snack bar at the center. Disney Imagineers had been secretly involved in the original design and construction of Mustard Seed back in the '50s, so the configuration was reminiscent of the

Magic Kingdom with Americaland, Europeland, Africaland, etc. The 1st hole was Bakersfield, the 2nd Washington DC, the 3rd London, and so on, all the way around the world, and ultimately returning back to where it started in Bakersfield.

While regularly used for birthday parties and such, its primary purpose was educational, a traversable setting to teach world history, geography, and the like to the youth of Mustard Seed; however, it wasn't a school day, so Hertell and his crew were among many enjoying a fun but challenging journey around the world: tapping colored golf balls through the slowly turning blades of windmills on the Zuiderzee, between the pyramids at Giza, and over the great wall of China.

Toodlah was lining up his next putt as Hertell and the girls approached Rome. His son was nearly eight now and his actual name was Hertell Daggett III, but his younger sisters had struggled to pronounce "Hertell" so they approximated with "Toodle-uh". It was cute, and it stuck.

His daughters were nearly five now. It had been a difficult pregnancy for Kaye. She was already in her forties when she'd had Toodluh, and only a few years older when she'd had the twins. They were fraternal twins, Ginny and Dot, and both resembled their mother for the most part, Shirley Temple dimples, eyes the color of Junior Mints, only in Dot's case, it was their shape that differed.

Hertell had carried her from Paris, as he had from Bakersfield, DC, and London. She wasn't quite able to actually play, so he used her as his putter by hugging her in his arms and swinging her feet at the colored golf balls which made for a very erratic and boisterous game.

Toodlah was keeping score, "How many strokes on that hole?"

Hertell shrugged, "I think we can safely round it up to around 30." He thumped his fist on Dot's head, "Which is really weird because I'm using my lucky putter."

Toodlah nodded thoughtfully and updated the scorecard, "What about you Ginny?"

Ginny hopped on one foot, "One, two, three, four, five."

Hertell and his putter took a seat on the Colosseum next to Kaye, who was watching Toodlah analyzing his next shot. It was a demanding one since the leaning tower of Pisa stood between the tee and a bridge across the Adriatic connecting the heel of Italy to the rump of Greece.

Hertell took a long look at Kaye. She was still very much the girl he'd met as a teen, confident, angular, copper colored hair. Still in her prime but now with slight signs of visible wear, her eyes softened by a few more laughs, her brow contoured by a few more concerns, her nose broken sometime during a career on the surface as a Kern County deputy sheriff; nevertheless, still the girl he'd married and then abandoned, and then met again and married again.

He put his arm around her, "Thanks for thinking of this, it's really helping. Getting me grounded, getting me outta my headspace." She tilted her head to cradle his hand, "Yeah, people can forget stuff, it's okay, it's not the end of the world."

Time stood still for an instant as Hertell savored a happy moment. He had a theory, the theory-of-happy-moments, that a person only has a few truly happy moments in a lifetime, and that all the other happy moments they experience are just echoes of those few, precious, 'true' ones, and that one's ability to be happy at all was a function of how sensitive and attuned they were to the echoes of those rare, truly happy moments. He'd had a few earlier in his life and they were totally random and unexpected—walking across a parking lot, drinking water from a garden hose, making a sandwich on a Saturday afternoon. And now here was a new one, this instant: he was with his wife and kids and the world was not ending—or even if it was, it seemed to be of no consequence.

He marveled at the feelings that overtook him as he looked at them all. He remembered how the first time he fell in love, with Kaye, back when he was a teenager, how all the sappy love songs he heard on the radio, all of a sudden, almost instantaneously, made sense to him. He now understood them. They had mass, and meaning. The same thing had happened when Toodlah was born, only that time it was the whole rest of life that made sense, instantaneously. He now understood it too. He'd lived most of his life without them, but once they were born, he couldn't imagine his life without them.

He knew that scientists had rational explanations for those kinds of feelings: that they were merely a biological mechanism, an evolutionary expedient to improve genetic fitness, whatever that was, and ensure the successful preservation and propagation of the species. That "love" was a mere illusion, but that those who had the illusion were more likely to survive and pass the useful illusion on to future generations who would similarly thrive and pass it along. He had to admit that they may be right. He'd once been a scientist himself and was devoted to analyzing, theorizing, and explaining all manner of observable phenomena. He therefore understood their impulse to explain human feelings and interactions logically, rationally, statistically, as they would for plate tectonics or solar eclipses or snowflakes; to devote their precious time on Earth, their intellect, their energy, their lives to explain away the mystery, the miracle, the majesty of it all, and otherwise toss turds into the punchbowl of the human experience, and all the associated illusions.

He looked up at the painted sky. And that's what he loved about Mustard Seed. It was all such a magnificent illusion, the sky wasn't real, the horizon wasn't real. It was a set, it was a façade, it wasn't real, and made no illusion about being an illusion, it celebrated its *illusioness*, it rolled around and splashed in it, it skipped and gamboled in the illusion of it all. And everybody in Mustard Seed seemed pretty happy with it, or at least content. Nobody was demanding, or complaining, or even yearning to return to the world above.

They'd had a short but eventful experience on the surface of the Earth and thought it best to return to their sanctuary beneath it. They missed the sun and moon and sky and clouds, the real ones, and wind and dogs and such, but those were more than balanced by the harmony and safety that the illusion afforded, and nobody was trying to throw them in jail anymore, or failing that, kill them. They were in a good place, they were at home in comfortable exile and would emerge when the world was ready for them.

Kaye patted Hertell and his putter on the knees, "It's your turn."

Hertell picked up Dot and took a few practice strokes with his putter. They all hooted as the shot glanced off the Leaning Tower of Pisa and rolled into the Mediterranean Sea.

The rest of the game was spirited, and high scoring in Hertell's case, but was otherwise uneventful, and he was able to let concerns about the end of the world fade from his thoughts.

Chapter Eight

Lawn Day

D oug spent the better part of an hour excavating the garage looking for that... thing you mow lawns with. A thing he'd used to mow their lawn almost every Saturday of his adult life, at least up until the whole Mustard Seed thing, and going to jail and getting rich and buying a big house and everything. The garage was full of stuff from their prior life in the old house. It wasn't particularly well organized, but he finally found what he sought under the ping-pong table and hidden behind the croquet set and his daughter's Cozy Coupe. And he couldn't stop sobbing.

It's funny people's response to the passage of time, sometimes fear of what's ahead, sometimes regret for what's behind, but in Doug's case it was a wordless combination of overwhelming gratitude for the life he'd lived, the joys of his daughter's youth, and it all seemed to bubble up from deep within and express itself in jets of tears squirting from his eyes. He didn't use to be this emotional about things, but lately, maybe forgetting the names of stuff or something, seemed to bring everything closer to the surface for him.

He recovered, almost as quickly as he'd succumbed, blew his nose on a stiffened paint rag, and pulled the ancient McLane mower out of his cherished past. He couldn't remember the last time he'd mown the lawn, or any lawn for that matter, possibly in the old house when he was still under house arrest and before they moved to the big house overlooking the Li'l Pal. He was excited about mowing the lawn, he had a purpose, there was something that needed to be done, something he'd done almost every Saturday of his adult life after making pancakes for his daughter.

He slapped at the McLane with the paint rag to clear away the cobwebs and dust, then grabbed the handles and wheeled it to the mouth of the garage where he paused in the sunlight to savor the moment. It didn't last long because he could see the front lawn and why he'd stopped mowing in the first place.

Doug stood at the lawn's edge and watched a pair of Lawnbots nibbling at the grass. The lawn was immaculate and looked like a putting green, so there was no real point in his mowing the lawn. He watched them for a while and reflected on how quickly it had all happened, the rapid onset of all manner of bots that descended upon civilization.

While there were many dark warnings about bots and AI and self-replicating machines and algorithms and such taking over the world and making people irrelevant, or slaves or grinding them up for fertilizer, it actually wasn't like that at all. It was fairly benign in fact, and actually kind of convenient too, and it only took two, maybe three, years depending on how you were counting. Kind of like when the internet happened back in the '90s and smart phones back in the

2K-teens—something that wasn't there one day and nobody seemed to miss it, and then one day it was there and nobody could live without it.

The bots couldn't do things like hang drywall, or fix a car, or unplug a toilet, but they could do a lot of other useful stuff and for the most part they didn't draw attention to themselves, no more than a thermostat would or a garage door opener. They just kind of blended in. The Japanese were the only ones who made bots that looked like Hello Kitty with faces and eyes and smiles and so on, which tended to creep out Americans, but the Japanese seemed to be okay with it.

Doug laughed at a thought. His former financial adviser had urged him to invest in a hot new technology a few years before, but the whole humanoid-type sexbot bubble burst because of some feminist hackers who exploited a vulnerability in Chinese 9G network chips and took control of millions of cyber-vaginas, resulting in tens of millions of embarrassing visits to emergency rooms where the the Jaws of Life quickly became required equipment. The market never fully recovered after that bubble popped, and Doug was glad that he'd never invested in it. For the most part bots either looked like prehistoric animals or glorified versions of what they were replacing: Lawnbots looked kind of like a Trilobite, Geezerbots looked like a hi-tech walker and so on.

But the Geezerbot didn't care about the enfeebled geriatric they were keeping from falling and breaking a hip. They didn't know that the wobbly jumble of bone and hair and skin had wisdom and would be missed, had dreams, and hopes, and regrets, had affected lives, sometimes for the better and sometimes for the worse, had a history, and a

44

future, that while finite and foreshortened, nevertheless held the promise of one more dawn, or one more sunset, or one more cup of coffee and one more piece of pie.

One of the Lawnbots was evidently running low on power, so it automatically trundled over to its charging station. Doug watched the hungry Lawnbot suckle peacefully at its charging station while the other one continued to nibble along the bender board. He knew that Lawnbots didn't know or care what day it was, or how the lawn looked, or his daughter, or her pancakes, since people were irrelevant. He knew that they obeyed their own laws not ours – like the mountains and the wind and the ocean, they were simply indifferent to us. It was nothing personal. They wished us neither good nor ill, because they, unlike humans, didn't wish for anything, at all.

Doug muttered as he approached the Lawnbots, "Fuck'm, I don't care how good the lawn looks, those little bastards don't care, their little feelings won't be hurt if I shove'm into the woodchips and mow it all myself, because it's Saturday and it's my fucking lawn and it matters to me." He dragged both Lawnbots past the bender board at the edge of the yard and stacked one on top of the other, like a pair of mating tortoises he'd seen on YouTube. "Now go on you little bastards, have at it!"

He laughed at the mental image of a swarm of weed-whacker tadpoles maturing into a new generation of Lawnbots as he walked back to the garage and his cherished McLane lawn thing that you mow lawns with.

There was a problem though. He couldn't remember how to start it.

Chapter Nine

Inertial Guidance

W hat had started slowly and almost imperceptibly, had allowed Hertell to convince himself that what was actually happening was not actually happening.

It reminded Hertell of a landslide he'd once caused when he was a boy, the summer after his mom left—his dad insisted that she was dead, but Hertell knew that she just had moved to Sacramento. Hertell had followed a dirt road and spent the better part of a day in a remote corner of the Li'l Pal Pet Cemetery throwing rocks at the abandoned ground squirrel burrows dotting the face of a broad road cut. He walked the length of the road cut, testing his accuracy on each burrow, and with each rock he threw, a few grains of the road cut would trickle down its face. And then, right about dusk, when he was looking away to find some more rocks, he sensed something and turned just as the entire broad face of the road cut seemingly surrendered to its own weight, and the weight of all the earth that had already fallen away, and with what sounded like a dull sigh, simply collapsed in one fluid motion, and spilled down and across the road on which Hertell stood, astonished, with his hands full of rocks.

His dad accepted the news of the road cut landslide quite well, and took the opportunity to teach Hertell how to operate the D-6 caterpillar as they cleared the road leading out to Whisper Hill. "Them ground squirrels burrow all through these cuts and weaken'm so slides like this are real common. It wasn't your rocks that did it, it woulda happened anyway, but probly not for another couple hundred years though."

It was like that. Just a random trickle of things at first: what a compass was, who won the Civil War, how many ounces in a pound. But once enough memories were gone, there simply wasn't enough left to hold up the rest, so it all just fell away, carried by its own weight, and the weight of everything that wasn't there anymore.

The really weird part was that everything seemed so normal. People still walked and talked and laughed and did their jobs, went to school, played miniature golf, everything. And it astonished Hertell how essentially immaterial the accumulated knowledge of western civilization and science was to the conduct of daily life, as if manners and patterns of interaction were carried on by inertia or something. And this was a big concern for Hertell since he'd once been a fairly accomplished physicist, at least up to the point when he'd been shot in the head, and as a physicist he knew that inertia, if left on its own, generally led to a crater in the ground.

Back when he was still a physicist, he'd once dabbled in inertial navigation systems, basically boxes packed with gyros and accelerometers and computers and then put in airplanes and ships and submarines and ICBMs. The great thing about them was that they were completely self-contained and thus completely impervious to jamming and spoofing and radio interference and so forth. Given an initial starting reference point, typically a latitude, longitude, and a few other parameters, it could sense and measure its movements and then calculate where it was at any particular moment.

However, what it was really calculating was more where it *thought* it was, or at least where it *should* be, which wasn't necessarily where it *actually* was since tiny measurement errors led to position errors and emergent bias which would accumulate and then compound over time, so that unless periodic corrective inputs were applied, the airplane or submarine or ICBM or whatever would eventually end up in an entirely different place, such as a smoking or bubbling or glowing crater respectively, rather than where they thought they were.

Hertell knew himself to be something of a math whiz before the copper specks entered his life and that he'd once been sought to help with these corrective inputs using Kalman filters and Bayesian something or other, which evidently he was an expert in at the time. Though he still remembered the context and the words themselves, he no longer had any idea of their meaning or application. Nevertheless, he made the connection that inertia, whether physical or social, if left to its own devices, in isolation and uncorrected, would eventually lead to something really shitty.

Hertell concluded that social, cultural inertia, when not anchored to the civilization and knowledge that gave rise to it, and ultimately its purpose and direction, was free to follow wherever the spurious headings and misguided paths that its inherent errors and embedded biases would lead. In fact, he'd already begun to see it in various forms in the weeks since he'd first discovered the pole reversal. In one case of excessive politeness, three bowlers spent the better part of an hour at the door of the bowling alley arguing over who should go in first. Tempers grew short leading to a shoving match that Hertell and several others had to break up. There were other incidents, similarly curious and for the most part benign, but Hertell feared that it would only grow worse, more chaotic, and probably less benign.

Chapter Ten

A Pivotal Event

H ertell resolved to take it upon his shoulders to anchor the people of Mustard Seed to their historical and cultural heritage by reacquainting them with all the things they'd forgotten since the poles reversed, whenever that was. He'd already recognized that it was largely the knowledge acquired long before the reversal that was fading from their memories and that they didn't seem to have a problem learning and then remembering freshly taught information. But he wasn't sure where to begin the teaching process since there was no common baseline of ignorance to start from because everyone was forgetting things in their own way.

However, Hertell was familiar with this phenomenon since he'd experienced it himself after being shot in the head.

A bullet in the head can be a pivotal event in a person's life, and Hertell was no exception. He'd initially awakened and found himself in a hospital room. He observed his surroundings and the various monitoring devices which all seemed to indicate that all was well; nevertheless, it was disorienting and he had no idea where he was or how he got there. So, he asked his dad, who was sleeping in the chair next to the bed.

"Dad, hey, Dad, what's going on, why are you in the hospital?"

His dad groggily woke up, "What?"

"Why're you in the hospital?"

His dad cleared his throat and blinked a few times, "Well I'm mainly here to see you, 'cause you got shot in the head."

Hertell shook his head, it felt heavy, "I didn't get shot in the head, I'm sitting here talking to you."

"Yes, you did, and hell I oughta know, I shot you..." And then his dad broke down crying.

"Oh, okay." Hertell sat quietly watching the monitors as his dad regained his composure, and then after a thoughtful pause, "Why'd you do that?"

"Well, it was a accident a'course! I didn't shoot you on purpose!" He was obviously very sensitive and defensive on the topic, but then he softened a bit, "I was out the back of the house shootin' the Luger in the air, I forget exactly what for. Is today New Year's Day or something?"

"I don't know what day it is, I've been shot in the head."

"Doesn't matter what day it is, anyway, I was shooting the Luger in the air and a bullet come down and hit you in the top of the head and got stuck in there, but the doctors got it out okay, so you'll be fine. I mean what're the odds of that, bullet falling outta the sky, hitting you in the top of the head? Hell, I oughta go out and buy a lottery ticket now or something..." And then he broke down crying again.

"Oh, okay, well that makes sense then. Except for the lottery ticket thing, odds are still against you on that, statistically."

His dad wiped his nose on the hospital blanket, "But you're not dead and that's the main thing. But you're kinda fucked up though, and that's my fault and I take full responsibility, but you ain't dead. So, there's that."

A woman entered the room, a Kern County Deputy Sheriff in full regalia. Hertell looked at her, "Officer, is my dad in trouble for shooting me in the head? It was an accident."

The woman deputy took a moment to respond, "No, he's...."

His dad interrupted, "Officer? For hell's sake Hertell, don't you know who this is, it's your..." but he quickly fell silent as the deputy caught his eye and motioned to him.

She looked at Hertell, "Don't worry, he's not in trouble. It was an accident. Like you said." She gave Hertell a thumbs-up, "Glad to see you're okay." With that she left the room, her official business apparently concluded.

Hertell later learned that the deputy was actually his ex-wife, Kaye, who later became his wife again, but he just didn't recognize her under the circumstances for some reason that day in the hospital.

Eventually it was officially determined to have been an accident and they took away his dad's Luger and then put him on a list so that he couldn't get another gun. Which didn't bother his dad so much as the class they made him take on gun safety, so he'd know not to shoot guns up in the air again, which seemed completely stupid to him since he couldn't get another gun again anyway.

Hertell had to abandon his former life as a physicist of some renown and return to live in his father's house on the grounds of the Li'l Pal Heaven Pet Cemetery. There he would convalesce and eventually start a new life, his prior life for the most part surgically removed along with the bullet fragments, except for the elusive specks of copper.

His new life started with an exploration of the Li'l Pal Pet Cemetery, sometimes accompanied by his dad, but usually alone, following the dirt roads and paths connecting the property's assorted parcels and plots—Snuggle Bottom, Everlasting Slumber, Whisper Hill, the ground-squirrel-landslide-road-cut. He rattled through the sallow hills in a little Cushman cart wandering his childhood home, a world that was at once as familiar to him as it was now mysterious.

However, it wasn't in the hills that he reconstructed his own past, it was in an unremarkable storage shed out past the leach field, and it was there that he recovered not only his own history, but also the entire history of life on Earth.

It happened quite by accident. He was looking for his high school yearbooks and instead found a massive collection of old National Geographic Magazines going all the way from the 1920s up to the point where they got all political, talking about global cooling then global warming then climate change and that it's all our fault, so Hertell's dad had cancelled the subscription somewhere in the Bush administration, the second one.

And as Hertell read the old magazines, he actually began to experience, in varying degrees, the places and events they described, land divers of Pentecost Island, dung beetles in Madagascar, cactus in Mojave. It was as if he was actually there. He knew he wasn't actually in an arroyo looking at a prickly pear cactus, but was in reality sitting on a stack of tires in a storage shed reading a tattered magazine from 1953 about them. It was as if he could see and hear and smell and experience the past, and that somehow, he was able to be present both in the storage shed and also in a desert from a long-forgotten article in National Geographic. The same thing happened with the other books his dad had stored in the shed, the *Encyclopedia Britannica*, Durant's big book set on civilization, Gibbon's *Decline and Fall*, the *Sunset Illustrated* book of basic plumbing, etc.

Though the phenomenon was sporadic and uneven since days would go by without an incident, or he'd only get a faint scent of the volcano or the swamp, it was always there to some degree, and he presumed it was just the brain injury and merely his imagination. Or perhaps he was simply delusional and hallucinating it all. The doctors said it was probably an artifact of getting shot in the head, and the trauma of having portions of his brain removed, or possibly an electrolytic effect attributable to the copper slivers that were still floating around in there. However, they were confident that it was nothing to worry about unless it was affecting his appetite or interfering with his sleep, but cautioned him that if he started hearing voices telling him to do things, he should definitely ignore the voices and call the doctors again. And that he should also cut down on sodium.

Hertell eventually formulated his own theory, that the copper specks were connecting parts of his brain that weren't connected in other people, and that all brains we've ever had were still in there, each brain built on top of an older brain: the man-brain, the monkey-brain, the dog, the turtle, the lizard, the snake, all the way back to the beginning of time, back to when we were all just a bunch of amoebas floating around eating each other all day. The tiny copper specks were connecting him with every living thing that ever was, with filaments of species memory going back to the beginning of time, from clumps of amino acids in the primordial soup, to mats of blue-green algae in the warm Precambrian shallows, all the way up to us.

He clearly remembered the rubbery smell of trilobites, and the yodeling sound that dinosaurs made. And he gradually grew accustomed to it and ultimately it became his way of experiencing the world—as intuitive and effortless as balance or digestion.

But all this had happened long before the poles reversed, before he'd gone to live with the Mustard Seed civilization after their brief but eventful interlude on the surface, and well before he'd even discovered the Mustard Seed civilization buried beneath the parched dry hills of the Li'l Pal Heaven; nevertheless, he would use his unique experience and perspective to save the Mustard Seed civilization not only from its growing ignorance, but also its ignorance of its ignorance.

Chapter Eleven

Abercrombie Disease

"Why are you listening to that?"

Hillary was sitting in the driver's seat but wasn't actually driving since the car took care of all that, steering, collision avoidance, navigation, staying on the road, and so on. The only thing that the passengers had to do, after they indicated where they wanted to go, was manage things like climate control, and the windows and sunroof and the movie and music selection, though that could be delegated to the car as well.

Getting no response, she asked again, a little louder this time, "Why are you listening to that?"

The question drew Donnie from her thoughts, partially. She was jackknifed in the passenger seat with her feet on the dashboard, gazing up through the open sunroof at the sky and the clouds scrolling by far above. She wasn't thinking so much as obsessing, and then as if batting away a fly, "Listening to what?"

"That... well... shit you're listening to right now."

Donnie tilted her chin up toward the sunroof, "I'm listening to the wind." And then, as if tutoring a small child, "The wind is not shit."

Hillary looked up from her laptop and pointed at the dashboard, "No, not the wind, the shit on the Sonos, why are you listening to that?"

Finally surrendering to the distraction, Donnie glanced at the entertainment console which had a very compelling graphic for the song that was currently playing, surrounded by a variety of statistics about it, the number of shares, likes, hits, and ads and links and touch-bait. With her attention now diverted, Donnie visibly relaxed and began bobbing her head to the overproduced beat, "Oh yeah, this."

She was short and compact, but long-waisted and muscular like an Olympic wrestler or a gymnast, but without the eating disorder. Her hair was coarse and wavy, which she kept short and heavily gelled. She had Freida Kahlo eyebrows over a perfectly oval face, and the Mexicans she used to work with called her *Prieto*, partly because of her color and partly because of her carriage. Her DNA test said she was mostly Native American, so basically Mexican, which was genetically the same thing, plus a heaping helping of African, and whiff of Celtic for a garnish.

She flicked her hand at the console, "This is okay, kinda simple, kinda rhythmic," and then looked back up at the sunroof and the clouds. "Besides, I'm listening to the wind anyway."

Which was true. She was listening to the wind, but she was also thinking about the subtle changes in Hillary's behavior.

There was nothing specific, it was more of a general sense that something was changing, but she wasn't sure exactly what. She took a deep cleansing breath, "And the wind is not shit."

Hillary didn't look up from her laptop, "I didn't say the wind was shit, I said the music was. And the lyrics are totally misogynistic."

Donnie looked over at the console, "There's words?" She tilted her head and listened to the song for a moment, "Hmm, what'dya know, I never really paid attention." She arched her back and stretched, looking back up at the sky and clouds, "It doesn't sound misogynistic to me."

"What do you mean it doesn't sound misogynistic? He just called his girlfriend, baby-momma, or whatever, a bitch and a cunt and a whore and a hole, doesn't that seem kinda misogynistic to you?"

"Well...," Donnie closed her eyes and shrugged, "maybe she is."

Hillary was drop-jaw dumbstruck. There was silence, except for the wind and the music. She stared straight ahead for a moment, dazed and uncertain how to respond. "I...", she tapped her fingers lightly on the laptop. "I never..." she shook her head and struggled for a moment as if searching for the right words, "I, well..."

And then after a period of internal reflection, she finally shrugged her shoulders, "Well, you know, I never thought about it like that, so, yeah, maybe she is." And then Hillary laughed, which was characteristic of her since she didn't laugh at things immediately or instinctively. She'd always think a thing through before laughing about it, so her laughter was always slightly out of phase with the rest of the world, but on the whole more rational.

"Yeah, and he's a misogynist for pointing it out the way he did, in a song, so everybody's right, everybody gets a trophy. What if we just switch it to NPR, then it's just those people talking, and that way we don't have to think about it."

Hillary couldn't disagree, the music and resultant conversation had dissipated the last fumes of her concentration anyway, and besides she was stressed out and spent from trying to make sense of the brain scans that made no sense at all. She closed her laptop and then to no one in particular said, "Tune, DC assholes."

They rode in silence for a time, Hillary with her laptop and Donnie with her thoughts. Silence except for the wind and NPR, where someone was talking softly and sincerely about something of some importance to someone somewhere in the DC metroplex. And as they rode, the car dutifully followed the I-5 descending from Tejon Pass down the Grapevine, smoothly threading its way between all the rattling 18-wheelers jockeying and Jake-braking in the truck lanes on the long grade down to the valley floor with its endless fields and farms and abandoned little towns.

The sky through the sunroof was turning from a Smurf blue to a bleached and yellowed pastel, which was typical of the thick, particulate-laden air of the Southern San Joaquin Valley they were descending into. Donnie looked over at Hillary, who was looking out the window at the scenery such as it was, her hand resting on her laptop, her fingers tapping out a rhythm that apparently only she could hear.

Her hair was up, and held in place by a cheap "Hello Kitty" hair clip Donnie had given her on a Valentine's Day early on in their courtship. She hadn't seen the Hello Kitty clip in many years and wondered why Hillary had chosen to wear it that particular day. Her gaze wandered across Hillary's body as she sat looking out the window. She looked at the back of Hillary's neck, and the delicate turn of her shoulder, the soft promise of her girls, Donnie had always been a big fan.

Even though she couldn't see Hillary's face, she knew and cherished its every curve and contour, the arc of her upper lip and how it seemed to make her look sad, even when she was happy. But to Donnie it suggested a vaguely suppressed smile, something that she found to be strangely compelling. She'd often told Hillary that there was something about her aspect and demeanor that made her one of those rare women that seemingly without any effort at all, drive men to seek their approval. She'd pointed it out to suggest that she was aware, and therefore impervious to it -- in reality though she knew it definitely did work on her, though she never would have admitted it.

Hillary was curled up in the driver's seat with her feet dangling over the edge. She was wearing some argyle socks Donnie had given her the Christmas before.

Donnie thought about how much she loved the woman in the Argyle socks, the sound of her voice, her smell, how lucky she was to have met her and won her *approval*, and how she was now losing her slowly to that... that disease, she couldn't quite remember the name of it, but it was that disease that made you forget stuff. But whatever its name was, there was no official diagnosis anyway, yet. It was just a logical conclusion on her part based on an accumulation of incidents and interactions and words chosen and not chosen.

She knew that Hillary had face blindness, which had a fancy name that she couldn't remember, or pronounce even if she could, but she'd looked it up on Wiki and saw that even though it made it so that Hillary couldn't recognize faces, even her own for that matter, it was just a perception issue and wasn't related to any memory stuff. So if Hillary had that forgetting stuff disease, it wasn't because she couldn't recognize faces—although that had made their courtship somewhat unique and comical at times.

She knew that Hillary vaped for a few years back when they were first dating, when it was very fashionable to have personal weaknesses and the attendant addictions and tattoos and such, so she presumed that at some point in the future it would be discovered that vaping led to that premature forgetting-stuff-disease… "Abercrombie disease, that's it."

Hillary yawned, "What?"

Donnie looked up through sunroof, "Nothing. I just remembered something I heard somewhere."

They usually flew Donnie's old Cessna to Bakersfield to visit the in-laws, but there was solid overcast in Santa Barbara so they opted to drive instead. It took longer but it was a pretty drive, for the most part. It was also undemanding and allowed her to think, actually obsess, about a recent incident. There had been other, lesser incidents, but this one kind of crystallized the whole Abercrombie issue for Donnie, and she kept running through it, over and over again and again, trying to find some kind of alternative explanation for how Hillary could possibly forget something so central to her own history and identity.

It had happened at Trader Joe's some weeks before.

Donnie maneuvered the IoT-shopping cart around a Stockbot, basically a glorified shopping cart with arms that was replenishing the supply of frozen Gyoza. Donnie took a bag of Gyoza offered by the Stockbot in passing which started the whole chain of events. The Gyoza sent Donnie into a childhood reverie about her happy, halcyon days in the last twitching spasms of the 20th century.

"Mom drove us from Slab City all the way over to El Centro so she could stock up on frozen Gyoza, 'cause this was right before Y2K, and she had this like total TJ-frozen-Gyoza Jones, so we bought'm out, like a whole pallet of frozen Gyoza."

Hillary checked the nutritional information on the bag, "Awful lot of sodium..."

"And then me and Dad collected five or six old freezers that some assholes from Nyland had dumped out by Salvation Mountain, and got'm all working again, and hooked'm up to a buncha solar panels and a windmill rig and batteries and inverters and stuff that dad had set up for his shortwave radio station so anyway we had plenty of power and we put it all in the freezers and waited for Y2K and the world to end. Only it didn't, and we end up eating frozen Gyoza pretty much every day until we finally ran out..."

Donnie trailed off for a moment at the thought of her parents, both now dead, and the most kind and loving people she had ever known, and probably would ever know. Her parents were preppers living off the grid. They were childless and already quite old when they found Donnie in a dumpster behind a Walmart in El Centro during prom week. They didn't call the police or the fire department, but instead just wrapped her in a blanket and got some formula from the Walmart and took her back to their compound, a collection of salvaged trailers, doublewides, and RVs in Slab City, where they would love and cherish her for the rest of their lives. They named her *Dawn* because she was the dawn of a whole new life for them.

Hillary had moved down the aisle and was reading the nutritional information on a box of something, "And you still like'm?"

Donnie tossed the bag of Gyoza in the cart, "Well it's not so much that, it's mainly that these remind me of the '90s, a great time, great time to be a kid anyway, but they really had mom and dad freaked out, the Northridge earthquake, Ruby Ridge, Waco, Rodney King riots, that big volcano blew up, Piñatatubo or something like that, Bill and Hillary and Y2K ..."

"Hilary? From the Disney movies? What'd she have to do with Y2K?"

Donnie laughed, but there was something in Hillary's voice, something different. Her laugh faded a bit and drifted away. Hillary was serious.

Donnie tried to keep it light, "No, not that Hilary, I'm talking about Hillary Clinton, President Clinton's wife, I mean she did other stuff since, but at the time that's all she was, Clinton's wife." And then as if to confirm, "You were named after her, Hillary Clinton."

Hillary seemed confused, "I wasn't named after Clinton's wife. Besides his wife's name was Monica or something." She turned and moved down the aisle, "Do we need rice cakes?"

Donnie followed, and then shook her head, "No." But she wasn't really there anymore, her mind was now light years away searching for a reason, as she would again a thousand more times, as she was doing right now, gliding across the valley floor on the way to visit Hillary's parents for their anniversary in Bakersfield.

Donnie looked at Hillary again, staring vacantly at the fields and farms in the distance. Yes, she was losing her to Abercrombie disease, or whatever. She decided that she would savor every remaining lucid moment she had left with Hillary before the woman she loved was gone.

She rested her hand on Hillary's argyle clad foot, "Hey, I gotta lotta frequent flyer miles I gotta use, we should use'm up and go somewhere."

Hillary nodded but kept looking out the window at the dirt fields, "Okay, but let's go someplace weird, someplace you'd never think to go like Dayton or Lubbock or Tulsa, someplace you'd never go if you didn't have to, like for work or for a funeral or something."

Donnie had actually been thinking more like Tahiti or Patagonia or Iceland but recognized that she'd better act soon since Hillary's world was getting smaller and smaller. A wave of anticipatory grief washed over her, she could feel tears welling up behind her eyes. She cleared her throat and looked up at the sunroof and the formerly Smurf blue sky, "Yeah, Tulsa, sounds fun."

Chapter Twelve

Arrived!

Hillary's ears popped as they passed a Google semi on the way down the Grapevine to the valley floor. She'd tucked her legs up under herself and made herself comfortable for the long stretch up Highway 99 to her parents' house in Bakersfield. It wasn't the house she was raised in, but the new house, the big house her parents built on the Old Merle Haggard estate after her dad got famous from the whole Mustard Seed thing.

She had to think, and it was hard to focus since so many things were happening all at once. She'd been watching Donnie as they drove through Castaic and Gorman and Donnie was just sitting there staring blankly into space the whole time, listening to the most heinous excuse for music, just looped beats and people shouting about stuff they wanted or stuff they hated. It was unbearable, but it was not only unbearable, it turns out she wasn't even listening to it.

It was all part of a depressing pattern. Donnie was too young for Altman's disease, or whatever, but she had been a crop duster pilot in her early twenties before the Farmbots basically put an end to that livelihood, so it might be a long-term effect of pesticide neurotoxins she flew around with. She was also a foundling so there was no telling what kind of weak links were in her DNA chain if you yanked it hard enough. And Donnie had gotten a tattoo before they met, a vaguely Celtic pattern on her shoulder to cover a childhood scar. She presumed that eventually some study would reveal that tattoo inks cause premature Altman's disease. But it was the incident at Trader Joe's that had driven Hillary to take action.

She and Donnie were shopping and Donnie had been reminiscing about an incident from her childhood, actually a very charming and revealing story that Hillary had never heard before. She'd always been impressed with Donnie's life journey, she'd come from very humble, bordering on blighted, circumstances, and Hillary loved all of her funny stories about growing up in Slab City, a squalid, off-grid settlement overlooking the scummy shores of the Salton Sea. But then Donnie veered off on some tangent where she thought that Hillary was named after some tween actress from the '90s, and then tried to cover her mistake by insisting that she was named after some other person, when she knew full well that Hillary had been named after Sir Edmund Hillary, the first person to top Mount Everest—though actually Tenzing his Sherpa got there first, but at that time and in those days, it only counted when the white guy got there. The incident scared Hillary so much that she changed the subject, "Do we need rice cakes?"

She forgot what Donnie answered, but the incident was a significant one for Hillary, and she immediately got Donnie added to one of her experiment replication sample groups and ran a battery of MRI scans.

As part of her fake-science piñata project proposal, Hillary built and demonstrated a convolutional neural network classifier that she'd trained with a massive database of brain scans across a full range of pathologies from totally normal to horrendously abnormal. So, she was confident that as soon as she fed Donnie's scans into the classifier, she'd be able to quickly isolate and assess the level of the disease and hopefully find some way to stop it or at least slow it down.

Except that she couldn't because the brain scans revealed that Donnie's brain structure was totally normal. But perhaps it wasn't a structural thing at all, perhaps it was a dynamic or metabolic thing, so she repeated the process with a battery of fMRI scans. Same result, all normal. Thinking that maybe all the machine learning stuff wasn't as good as everyone insisted it was, she added a retired neurologist to her piñata project, ostensibly to cross-check and validate the machine learning stuff, but mainly to look at Donnie's scans the old-fashioned way, hoping that the human eye could see something the geeky neural net software couldn't.

Only the human eye couldn't either, and the nice doctor pronounced the MRIs totally normal and free of the usual plaques and tangles normally associated with that disease that makes you forget stuff, same for the fMRIs except for slightly elevated metabolic activity in the fusiform gyrus.

She and Donnie had often talked about having kids, and because of various nano and bio technologies, they still had another good 30 or 40 breeding years ahead of them so there was no hurry in that department. Nevertheless,

Hillary thought it best to wait until Donnie's condition could be diagnosed and hopefully some kind of treatment and prognosis offered. But whatever it was, Hillary knew she was losing the woman she loved.

She felt Donnie's hand on her foot. It was warm, and she wondered how many more years she would feel that warm loving hand.

They were scrolling across the valley floor now, and she looked out over the fields where the Farmbots were nodding down the rows of crops. They resembled dusty little armadillos slowly making their way down the rows of whatever those crops were, pulling weeds, and zapping bugs, checking for fungus or whatever it was they did. The Mexicans in their big hats and bandanas were long gone, as were all the cars, SUVs and vans that used to ring such fields. She remembered them from her youth growing up in Bakersfield, but she hadn't seen them in many years, not since her late teens anyway.

She wasn't resigned to Donnie succumbing to Altman's disease since she'd been raised on Lifetime TV and YA fiction where the true love, soul mate, whatever was always a vampire or a shape shifter or dying of something, so she naturally fell into that groove. She was determined to find a cure for whatever it was that Donnie had.

Donnie's voice drew her from her thoughts, "I've gotta lotta frequent flyer miles I wanna use up, so we should go on some trips."

They'd always talked about going to all the normal places with their kids, once they had them: Paris, Scotland, Greenland, and so on. And then after the kids were grown and gone, they'd start going to all the weird places, out of the way places that the kids would never want to go. But since the chances of having kids and a normal life seemed to be fading in her mind, she opted for the end game.

She reached down and rested her hand on Donnie's hand that was still stroking her foot, "Okay, as long as it's weird places like Dayton or Lubbock or Tulsa and places like that, someplace you'd never go if you didn't have to, like for work or for a funeral or something."

NPR was now talking with an earnest medical expert on the sudden spike in Alzheimer's disease, which seemed to be on the rise across all demographic groups.

"... and moreover, what's puzzling medical experts like myself, is that there aren't the usual plaques and tangles normally associated with Alzheimer's that we can easily see on MRIs..."

The NPR interviewer interrupted and summarized for the less discerning listeners in her audience, so that state college graduates and the like could follow the expert's reasoning, "So we've got the symptoms but no obvious or at least currently known cause..."

"That is correct, we don't know what's causing it, but many in the scientific community, like myself, believe that it may be traceable to climate change and increased levels of CO_2 in the atmosphere..."

The NPR interviewer dramatically concluded, "So climate change may be the cause of this new kind of environmental, or actually technically it's more of a global and even planetary case of Alzheimer's caused by climate change?"

"That is correct. It is possible, very very possible, and in fact highly probable. But more study is needed, and more funding in particular if scientists and medical experts like myself are to say with any certainty..."

Donnie shook her head in disbelief, "Oh now, this is some serious bullshit here. There's no fucking way that Alzheimer's is caused by climate change or CO2 or any of that bullshit."

Hillary didn't look up from her laptop, "Climate change is not horseshit, it's settled science, and what's Alzheimer's, another virus from China or something?"

"No, it's that thing where if you eat your food too fast or don't chew enough or somebody says something funny while you're eating, you end up inhaling the buffalo wing or slider or whatever and it gets stuck in your throat so you can't breathe and you're about to suffocate to death until somebody grabs you from behind and squeezes you 'til the food pops out."

"Oh..." Hillary blinked a few times, "...pops out the front or the back?"

"Well, the front, so you can, you know, breathe."

Hillary looked out the window at her old hometown, "Well that makes more sense then."

"Yeah, popping something out the back wouldn't help if you can't breathe, and besides it'd kill a person, you squeeze'm hard enough to make the buffalo wing pop out the back." Donnie cackled at the mental image of a buffalo wing flying out of a butt. Hillary thought about it a moment and then laughed herself.

The NPR host was wrapping up, "So our listeners should be careful not only to control their carbon emissions but also to thoroughly chew their food so that they don't require Alzheimer's to dislodge any large chunks of food they have stuck in their..."

"Well, no, actually, Alzheimer's Disease is the one where you forget stuff..."

"ARRIVED!" In a crisp Scottish accent, the car announced that Hillary and Donnie had reached their destination.

They were now parked in the driveway of her parents' new house. The front lawn looked like a putting green, presumably manicured to perfection by a pair of trilobite-shaped Lawnbots that for some reason were stacked on top of each other on the gravel strip bordering the driveway. But it was what they saw in the garage that had their attention.

Hillary's dad was standing in the garage in front of an ancient McLane lawnmower, the one he'd used every Saturday morning of her youth. He was pointing what appeared to be a TV remote control at the unresponsive machine, and she could see his thumb hammering at the buttons.

Hillary and Donnie sighed and then simultaneously diagnosed, "Altman's" ... "Abercrombie's."

Doug waved at them as they pulled up, "Hey kids! How was the drive?" He pointed at the lawnmower, "Hey, you know, I must be getting asthma or something, I can't remember how to start this dang thing."

Chapter Thirteen

Stacks

"**H**ere he is!"

Hertell looked up from his notes, "Shhh, come on Toodlah, you're in a library…"

Which was true enough, Hertell was working in the stacks in the massive library annex, a towering steel structure housing a comprehensive collection of books and microfiche worthy of a quality state college and preserving the essential knowledge of humankind, at least as it existed in 1963 when the original Mustard Seed was founded.

A voice called from far below, "What level?"

Toodlah, cleared his throat and called down, "We're up on eight, in the T-R section!"

While the main library reading room was on the town square with the compass rose and the bowling alley and the Zeiss Planetarium, the vast majority of the books were in one of the more remote stretches of the lava tube complex, in the library annex where Toodlah found his dad sitting on the floor surrounded by open photography books.

Hertell noticed that Toodlah was in his Boy Scout uniform, "Is the troop meeting out here today?"

Before Toodlah could answer, Stan the scoutmaster called up from below, "Didn't you hear us calling for you?"

Hertell was confused by the question, "When?"

Toodlah scowled and folded his arms, "Just now... and for the last hour or so, the whole time we've been here."

Stan was a portly man in his early fifties, flushed and breathing heavily from the climb to the top of the stacks and accompanied by a squad of pre-teen boys. He took off his scoutmaster hat and fanned himself with it, "Yeah, I was calling for you, Duncan was calling for you, Toodlah, and Quentin you were calling too weren't you?"

The boys nodded vigorously and confirmed that they'd been calling as well.

"Didn't you hear us?"

"No, I didn't hear anybody calling me." He could hear footsteps climbing the stairs zigzagging their way up through the core of the stacks, "I was just sitting here reading."

He'd been reading about a billion-year gap in the geological record: below it was nothing but sterile rock, and above it was an explosion of slithering, scuttling Cambrian life and eventually, us. He was leafing through photography books and pictures of the Grand Canyon to see if it could trigger his memories of that missing billion years, when he was interrupted.

"You've been missing for three days Hertell, everybody was worried about you, we thought you mighta fallen down somewhere or got lost in the logistics bays or in one of the old pressure buffers..."

Hertell laughed, "For hell's sake, I haven't been gone for three days..." Hertell paused momentarily, noting that that he was extremely hungry. "What's today?"

"What day do you think it is?"

"Monday, no, Tuesday, yeah Tuesday."

"No, it is not. It's... it's that day that comes after Wednesday."

Quentin raised his hand, "Thursday?"

"Yeah, that's it, Thursday, and you've definitely been gone three days, but luckily me and the boys are expert trackers and Toodlah spotted your shoe down by the drinking fountain, and then we found a pile of books on the first level, and then we kept finding other piles of books, all up and down the stacks, and we just tracked you up here, but we were calling out the whole time."

Hertell looked down at the mismatched socks on his feet, but at least now he knew the fate of one of his shoes, though he had no idea where he'd abandoned the other one.

Kaye and a few more Boy Scouts in uniform arrived, "It's okay Stan, I can take it from here. And you guys did a great job. Thank you."

"Yeah, Toodlah spotted a pile of books way down on level one and then it was just like in the Boy Scout Handbook..."

Toodlah nodded, his chin was quivering and his eyes were welling with tears as he spoke in a tumbling rush, "Yeah only it was big piles of books instead of little piles of animal scat, which is Boy Scout for poop and things like that. But I just followed'm just like they were poop and so I found you up here, in a big pile of... books."

Hertell looked at Kaye, and then rose and hugged his boy, "Mom and the girls musta been really worried about me, thanks for taking care of them like that, for tracking me down so they wouldn't worry anymore."

Toodlah shrugged and adjusted his Boy Scout cap, "Yeah, they were pretty scared because nobody knew where you were. But I knew you had to be somewhere, so I just followed the trail."

Hertell had indeed left a well-marked trail since he'd gone missing. The Library Annex was organized in accordance with the Library of Congress Classification scheme and started with the A and B category books, such as encyclopedias and philosophy books, on the first level, and then worked its way level by level up to the top level of the stacks where all of the T and U and V books dealing with technology and military science were shelved.

Hertell had built a snug little fort of neatly stacked philosophy and general history books on the first level where a footnote had sent him climbing up to the 5th level in search of more detail, which resulted in another fort of books where a reference sent him down to the 3rd level for some geological information – this generally random process was repeated on different levels for different subjects several times a day with occasional breaks for short naps and drinks of water from the drinking fountain on the first floor.

Stan, Toodlah, and the rest of the Boy Scout search party left to inform Mustard Seed that the missing Hertell had been found, but Kaye stayed. She sat on the floor while Hertell finished his second SPAM sandwich and leafed through the notes he'd been taking on a crinkled yellow legal pad.

"You know your handwriting has gotten a lot better since you were shot in the head." Hertell chewed and nodded in acknowledgement, "Yeah, I gotta concentrate a lot more now." He took another bite and then mumbled, "And thanks for bringing the samwiches."

Kaye flipped a page, "Well I knew that if we found you alive, you'd be hungry."

Hertell swallowed, "Yeah, definitely hungry."

"I'm taking this really well don't you think?"

Hertell continued chewing, "Taking what really well?"

"Oh, I dunno, the kids asking where you were for the first day, then the search parties not finding a trace of you up in the pressure buffers or any of the manifolds or any of the egress corridors."

Hertell put down his sandwich, "Why would you look there?"

Kaye fished a small note from her pocket, "Because you left a note, 'gone to save civilization, don't wait up.'"

"Lemme see." She handed Hertell the note. He looked at it carefully, "Yeah, that's me alright, and my handwriting has definitely improved, but I didn't mean that civilization, the one up on the surface, that one doesn't count anymore." He tapped a pile of books, "I meant this one... here, ours."

Hertell went on to explain to Kaye how he'd constructed an outline and syllabus of all human history and civilization, and that he had all kinds of ways he was going to teach it to everybody and make it fun and stuff, and that it was really interesting but really depressing too.

"History doesn't repeat itself, it doesn't even rhyme, it just kinda harmonizes I guess. Basically, we're, you know, fucked. It's the same shit over and over again, slavery, genocide,

76

just part of the routine, different costumes, and languages sometimes, but it's the same shit every time."

Kaye was finishing the remains of Hertell's SPAM sandwich, "So don't tell people about the shitty stuff then."

Hertell tried to put up a good fight, "Well you need the shitty stuff to put the good stuff in perspective, you know just for variety if nothing else. You can't have good stuff on top of good stuff, every day can't be Christmas otherwise Christmas is just another day, nothing special." But his heart wasn't in it.

"Don't tell'm that the shitty stuff ever happened, nobody'll miss it. I promise you that." She then fell silent and sat staring straight ahead thinking about a particular Christmas.

Kaye had been a Kern County Sheriff Deputy for a number of years on the surface and was quite familiar with people and shittiness, and sincerely wished that she could un-see many things she'd seen and would rather forget. But sometimes as much as she tried to, she couldn't. The call was for a restraining order violation at a '60s tract home on up on Christmas Tree Lane. An older woman, presumably a neighbor, was standing at the end of the driveway, hugging herself in the cold. She wordlessly pointed at the house as Kaye pulled up. The front door was open, and the living room was lit only by the TV. She could hear Yukon Cornelius singing "Silver and Gold". The grandfather and two boys were on the floor in front of the TV. It looked like he'd tried to protect them with his body. She didn't call for backup since another unit was already on the way. She drew her Glock 17 and moved toward the kitchen where the smoke alarm was shrieking. The table was set, the candles lit, grandma was over by the phone, the husband and wife were in front of the stove, the Remington 870 on the floor between them. And then she saw the highchair.

Yeah, she thought, *people don't need to know about the shitty stuff*. She pushed the sandwich away, "And if they do it just makes shitty stuff an option. This way they won't know it's even possible to do shitty stuff, it wouldn't be in the playbook because it never ever happened."

Hertell started to laugh but it quickly faded as her offhand comment soaked in, and a whole new story of humankind unfolded before his eyes. He fell silent as the crystalline beauty, the tectonic scale, and the cosmic grandeur of the concept first overtook, then engulfed, then swept him along, helpless as a twig in a stream toward a whole new world. It was a good idea. It was a fantastic idea.

"Yeah, well, you know, maybe you're right, maybe I'm just thinking about this too hard. The outline and the syllabus and everything, the perfect is the enemy of the good and all that. Maybe I'm just making it all harder than it needs to be, maybe I'm just over-thinking this." He paused and reflected a moment, nodding to himself, "Yeah, over-thinking this... And you know that's what got the wooly mammoths into so much trouble."

Kaye threw her head back and laughed, but it sounded strangely sad to Hertell, as if in a minor key. She then stopped, leaned forward and kissed Hertell. He was surprised at first but then reached out and took her hands. He felt a trembling in his bowels, so did Kaye. Then there was a low rumble, and then a jolt as the whole annex shuddered, swayed, and creaked. A few books fell off the shelf and thudded to the ground. And then there was silence.

Hertell looked over at the fallen books and then back at Kaye, "Some kiss."

Kaye wiped something from her eye, "I thought it was the SPAM I just ate, so an earthquake is a big relief."

They both listened quietly for a time, "That was probably an aftershock from that quake we had a couple of years ago."

While it was constructed to withstand sustained nuclear bombardment, earthquakes were a significant concern in Mustard Seed; nevertheless, it had managed to survive numerous quakes over the years with minor damage only from the Sylmar and Northridge quakes.

Kaye nodded, "Yeah, probably just an aftershock from that one."

They listened a bit longer just to be sure, and then Hertell helped Kaye to her feet and they set about dismantling his little book fort. And as they re-shelved the books, Hertell was completely lost in thought, feverishly contemplating his new mission to treat the people of Mustard Seed to a world and a history and a civilization of his own invention, a world that never quite existed and a history that never quite happened the way it really did. He would create a civilization forged by goodness and logic, and without any of the shitty stuff.

However, his quest to reinvent the history of humankind was interrupted by a sound, faint at first, then louder and undeniable.

"What is that?"

Hertell looked up at Kaye, "What?"

"Listen... that. It sounds like the wind?"

Hertell listened for a moment, then dropped the armful of books he was carrying and ran to the edge of the level.

He reached the railing and looked down toward the floor of the great chamber, "No, it's not the wind." The floor was shimmering and it was flowing and there were books bobbing on it like twigs in a stream. "It's water."

Chapter Fourteen

Lunch Notes

H illary was in the kitchen helping her mom make lunch, which she considered a cisgender normative cliché, but Donnie was out in the driveway helping her dad get that thing you use to mow lawns with working again, so it all balanced out. And besides, she loved hanging with her mom, and the tuna sandwiches and tomato soup lunch they were making was her specialty anyway.

Hillary had come of age during the woke ascendancy and had fully embraced and internalized it after her divorce. And even though it had since collapsed of its own weight a few years before and was now completely out of fashion, she would nevertheless often perform ad hoc and generally informal calculations to ensure compliance with the antiquated gender-emancipation orthodoxy. People had simply gotten tired of trying to figure out which pronoun to use and getting in trouble or fired for using the wrong one, and trying to avoid micro-aggressions, and nano-aggressions, and femto-aggressions. It all became so exhausting that they just started using 'dude' and simply stopped caring when some snowflake drama queen (or king) got their panties in a knot over some word used or not used because nobody was afraid of being sued into bankruptcy anymore since, for the price of a gourmet iced coffee, they could buy a LawyerBot app to automatically analyze case law, conjure damages, counter sue, and appeal ad infinitum. Since there were no billable legal hours for actual lawyers made of meat to collect, there was no way to monetize injustice, so the meat lawyers turned their attention to the deeper pockets of Big Tech, which had taken the place of Big Tobacco as a social toxin, and the whole grievance industrial complex just kind of faded into a punchline on open mic night and a few snarky podcasts.

Hillary was telling her mom about one of the perks of having her own lab and a posse of grad students. "So, I'm doing fMRIs on myself for this whole month, did one this morning before we left, because I wanted to see the effect of menstruation on neural physiology and cognitive capacity because Donnie insists that I'm more afraid of spiders when I'm on my period, to which I said bullshit, but actually I'm kind of curious, because I think she might be right... is that the lawn mower?"

She leaned over the sink and looked out the kitchen window toward the lawn, "I guess they got it started, but it sounds weird..."

Only it wasn't a lawn mower, it was a modest transverse shift along the San Andreas fault centered about 6 miles beneath the Salton Sea which moved LA a foot closer to San Francisco. It only took about 45 seconds for the p-wave to reach Bakersfield. The fault observatory up in Parkfield would later determine that it was an aftershock from the much bigger quake that rattled California several years before, but today, to an untrained ear, it sounded like a lawn mower, only louder and with a much deeper voice.

It was at that point that the whole kitchen did a mercifully brief twerking routine causing some tomato soup to slosh out of the pot and splatter onto the floor, accompanied by the sounds of some breaking glass in the next room. The sound was quickly overwhelmed by the shouts of Doug and Donnie as the back door flew open and was then immediately filled with them, comically wedged shoulder to shoulder, both trying to get through the door at the same time like an old Three Stooges gag, only with two stooges in this particular episode with both shouting in an overlapping blind panic, "Hillary!... Audrey!... Who's bleeding?... I love you!... First aid kit is under the sink!"

Donnie and Doug had been in the garage trying to figure out how to get the old McLane started. Donnie had unscrewed the gas cap and was dipping her finger inside to see if it was dry, "Classic lawn mower, where'd you find it?"

Doug snapped his fingers, "Lawn mower! Dang it, that's right!"

Donnie took a deep breath, savoring the smell of the old McLane, "What?"

"Found it behind the Cozy Coupe back there, it was from the old house on Gill, forgot we had it, 'til I found it again." His throat began to ache and he was afraid he was going to start crying again, so he pivoted, "I should check the batteries in this remote, they're probly dead and that's why it won't start." He busied himself taking the batteries out of the remote.

Donnie grabbed the handlebar and rocked the mower, listening for a sloshing sound. "Nah, the problem isn't dead batteries, there's no gas in this thing." She shined her flashlight into the tank, "It's totally dry."

Doug loved that about Donnie, she always carried a flashlight and a pocketknife, and she knew how to construct, dismantle, and repair almost anything mechanical or electrical. She'd once helped him install a tankless water heater and taught him how to sweat solder copper pipe. She was like the son he never had, only she was a girl. He loved a lot of other things about her too, but mainly that she totally adored his daughter and made her happy, as opposed to the asshole Hillary had been married to back when she was in Atlanta.

"And this thing is way old, so the remote won't work on this, even a universal one." Donnie examined the mower and waved her phone over it, "There's no IR sensor anywhere and it's not showing up on my Bluetooth app..." She stopped suddenly and cocked her head toward Doug and laughed, "Boy you must be really hungry, is that your stomach?"

Only it wasn't Doug's stomach. The thing you mow lawns with began an impromptu Irish dance along with the CozyCoupe and the rest of the garage in a Riverdance finale.

"Earthquake!" Donnie dropped her phone and had scarcely gone three steps toward the backdoor before she was overtaken by Doug who was shouting, "Audrey! Earthquake!" She caught up to him as he reached the door and threw it open, at which point they performed their Two Stooges entrance.

After that, it was a fairly uneventful lunch.

The lunch conversation was animated, varied and wide ranging as it always was with this cohort: the earthquake, the big one a few years before, Hillary's research and how it was going, or actually not going, how Donnie's Crop Duster game was still selling really well. But whatever the topic, the discussion kept circling back to how weird people were getting, not scary weird really, well not exactly, not yet anyway. They all pretty much skipped over the memory stuff, though it did come up when Donnie said how much bigger the house seemed without the confetti of sticky notes on everything. But the subject was quickly changed since Abercrombie's disease, Altman's disease or whatever was simply too sensitive a topic to contemplate, much less discuss.

Doug opened a bottle of Tabasco, "And then there'll be these swarms of people agreeing with each other about something or all doing the same kind of thing, and then just as fast they move on to something else. It's like in the ocean where all of a sudden there's a school of fish, and then poof they all scatter and then form a school again somewhere else. Did I tell you about how there's a bunch of people in Oildale that just kind of sit in the parking lot of the old Walmart? It closed a couple of years ago from the earthquake damage from the big one, but the parking lot is always at least half full of cars."

Donnie laughed, "And there's a buncha those exact same kinda people in Goleta, parked outside the old Target, like some kinda wildman on a mountain top in Fiji or whatever with an airplane made of bamboo waiting for a pallet of SPAM to be dropped on'm from the great shining bird…

Hey'd d'I tell ya me and Hillary are gonna go to Dayton as well as Tulsa, big Air Force museum there, I gotta lotta frequent flyer miles..."

Hillary wasn't paying attention, she was scribbling notes on a paper towel: *Cargo cult, random coalition formation, fusiform gyrus, PFC, inhibition centroid, endorestiform nucleus, sticky notes...*

A pattern was taking shape. It was hazy and amorphous, and she had no idea what it was yet, but whatever it was, she knew it probably wouldn't be good.

Chapter Fifteen

Flicker of Recognition

"We've got several options, none of them particularly good, well actually, one bad and one worse." Hertell was sitting in the cathedral with several dozen people, the President, the Cabinet, all branches of the Mustard Seed bonsai government plus an assortment of other interested parties.

Hertell had been in a complete state of denial at first since it wasn't a particularly bad quake, and the river running into the Library annex could be managed by the pump system installed when Mustard Seed 1.0 was first constructed back in the '50s for just such a contingency as flooding was a fairly common occurrence underground. The pumps were part of an elaborate and quite capable defensive purge system with the ability to flood certain chambers and passageways and had been fully tested when the surface world authorities tried to tunnel into Mustard Seed and arrest everybody a few years earlier—it successfully flushed a large cluster of SWAT team members out of the cornfields which they'd managed to reach after some determined drilling and blasting. After washing the SWAT team up and out of the Mustard Seed complex, the purge system quickly drained the flooded areas and restored them to their former state. Surely if the pumps could do that, they could easily deal with a probably temporary trickle of water from the earthquake.

Only they couldn't. And it became apparent to Hertell that the Library annex was a lost cause and that eventually they would all be either drowned or driven to the surface by the rising waters. Some of the lower logistics bays were already starting to flood and the pumps couldn't keep up.

"We can stay down here for another few weeks by my estimate and then we'll all drown in the dark when the Oceanoid bays flood."

He was met with disbelieving stares. Chuck, the Secretary of the Interior, spoke first, "Why can't we stay down here?" Others joined in, "We'll just pump the water out like we did when we washed all those SWAT army guys out of the cornfield... Yeah, that worked okay, even though they bombed us for doing that... And we drained the cornfield and all those upper chambers in only a day or two..."

Hertell let them continue until they were all satisfied that everything was going to be okay.

"Yeah, I agree, that worked, there's no debate on that, but it's a little bit different this time. We could turn off the water that time. We can't this time. The pumps can't keep up."

There was a thoughtful pause, then the lights flickered, triggering the emergency lighting, which got everyone's attention as the cathedral went from warm stained-glass brightness to a dull sullen crimson.

The lights flickered back on and then stabilized, which was followed by a few seconds of silence as the reality began to sink in. President Higgs finally spoke, "So if we can't stay down here, what do we do?"

Hertell wasn't expecting a question since he couldn't imagine that there could be any doubt about what was their one and only remaining option. Evidently reality wasn't sinking in enough to displace the collective denial and thought inertia, but Hertell presumed that it was probably at least partially due to people forgetting stuff like, "if you can't stay where you are, you have to go somewhere else". So he decided to remove all doubt about what needed to be done.

"We salvage what we can and go back up to the surface."

Which was met with uniform disapproval.

"They tried to kill us the last time we did that... dropped a bomb on us and everything!"

Which was true. After Hertell's initial discovery of Mustard Seed and their emergence into the surface world, there was an initial honeymoon period, but they eventually ran afoul of some Casino Indians who wanted the property for a new casino. Complications ensued, Federal authorities got involved, and it concluded with the bunker buster bomb and the collapse of the western pressure buffer which contributed to the difficulty of their current situation since it was the primary mechanism to purge water to the surface.

"Well they didn't try to kill us at first. They were really into us at first, remember how they cheered for you at the stock car races, and all the TV people that wanted to talk to you?

Even the President of the United States came down here and wanted to talk to you, remember?"

There was a scattering of nodding heads... "Oh yeah, that guy...the rolled-up shirt sleeves guy...what a creep..."

"Yeah, they didn't wanna kill us at first, it was only after I squirted those guys with a garden hose and got everybody so pissed off at us, that they decided to kill us and throw us in jail and stuff, and I take complete responsibility for that garden hose thing, I don't know what I was thinking..."

There was a chorus of reassurances that nobody blamed him for the SWAT teams and the bunker buster unpleasantness.

"But the main thing is that they're forgetting stuff up there just like we're forgetting stuff down here."

Several Cabinet members were dubious and somewhat indignant, "You keep insisting that we're forgetting things... I'm not forgetting anything... Neither am I... What are we forgetting?"

Hertell looked at the assembly and then pointed up to the massive crucifix towering above the altar at the far end of the cathedral, "Who's that guy nailed up on the cross?"

There was silence for a moment, and then the President spoke, "Everybody knows that."

Hertell tilted his head toward the President, "What's his name then?"

Which triggered an animated name-that-martyr exchange between the Secretary of Agriculture, the Vice President, the metal shop teacher and several others: "It starts with a 'J' ... Yeah, it definitely starts with a 'J'... Jack, Jason, Jamison... This close, tip of my tongue, gimme a sec..."

The President then stood, gestured toward the crucifix, and conclusively intoned, "John Fitzpatrick Kennedy."

The pronouncement was immediately followed with nodding murmured agreement, confident affirmations, and thoughtful conjectures: "Yeah that's right, Jack Kennedy, JFK... it starts with a 'J'... Wow, I thought they just shot him, they nailed him to a cross too... Yep, shot him in the head, then nailed him up on the cross... Boy, he musta really pissed some people off... Yeah, definitely pissed off a... lotta ... people..."

The Vice President and the others trailed off in response to the circle of astonished faces staring at them. The Secretary of Commerce shifted in his seat, and then dismissed the critical stares, "Well don't blame us if you forgot who that is, I mean, Jesus H. Christ everybody knows who that..."

He stopped suddenly as a flicker of recognition rose in his face and burst into a bright illuminating epiphany, "Oh yeah! That's him, that's the name of the guy on the cross, son of God and all that... Oh." He then dropped his head slightly, in tacit acknowledgment of his mistake, slumped back in his seat and exchanged sidelong, knowing glances with the other name-that-martyr contestants who all then begrudgingly admitted that they'd indeed mis-remembered the name of that guy on the cross.

Hertell threw the downcast contestants a lifeline, "But his name did start with a 'J', so you got that part right." Hertell could tell by the looks on everyone's faces that he'd made his point.

"The point is, they're forgetting stuff up there, just like we're forgetting stuff down here." He pointed to the crucifix,

"There's probably a lotta folks up there that've forgotten that guy's name too, and if we're lucky they'll have forgotten that they were ever even pissed off at us in the first place. Some of'm might have even forgotten that we ever even existed. And the ones that do remember probably think we're all dead anyway. I mean they dropped a bomb on us, so I presume that was their intention. At worst, we'll be just another bunch of confused people wandering around up there, forgetting that guy's name, among other things, and hopefully we will be one of those things they all forgot too."

Hertell stood up and faced the assembly, "So, we've got to choose between bad and worse. All those in favor of bad, say 'aye.'"

But before anyone could respond, the lights flickered again.

"Anybody for worse?"

Chapter Sixteen

The Croquet Set

It was fun but kind of weird too because she hadn't played croquet since she was a kid at the old house with her friends. The friends were all grown up now with husbands and kids and lives of their own, but here she was playing it again in Bakersfield at the new house with her mom and dad and her bull dyke soul mate.

Since she was a lesbian herself, and the whole every-word-hurts industrial complex had petered out, she was totally free to use the most ancient, offensive, and surprisingly satisfying slurs to stereotype Donnie. She was just so masculine, from her Danner boots, to her Levi 501s with the button fly with her wallet in the back pocket, to her hand tooled leather belt with a trophy buckle, to her Carhartt shirt, to her high and tight haircut with the frosted tips—only with tits and a vagina. It was the best of all possible worlds. After her divorce, Hillary avoided the lesbian ecosystem, since she felt it combined the worst aspects of both sexes, male promiscuity compounded by female manipulation, and she knew she'd be easy prey and just end up embittered carrion. But Donnie happened quite by accident so she'd avoided all that.

She watched Donnie line up a shot at the wicket out in the middle... "Wicket! That's right.!"

Donnie looked up, "Yes, yes it is. Very good." She gestured with the thing you hit croquet balls with, "And this is a Mallet, and next week we're learning foods." Doug laughed since he'd forgotten the name too. So did Hillary though it was for a different reason. Perhaps Donnie wasn't succumbing to Altman's disease, at least not as aggressively as she'd thought. Perhaps there would be time for both children and travel after all, before her beloved butch better half faded away.

It was Doug's turn, but as he approached the ball, Audrey laughed, "You playing on our team now?"

"Huh?" Doug looked down at the black ball at his feet, then up at Audrey, and then froze. He stared at her blankly for a moment, confused, as if seeing her for the first time.

Hillary instinctively reached for her phone to call 911 thinking that her father was having a stroke, but before she could fish it out of her pocket, Doug laughed brightly.

"Well ok, get technical, we're not the same person." He shrugged and approached the yellow ball, "But I look at you and it's like I'm seeing myself, I keep forgetting that you're a whole different person."

Doug took his shot, "I guess we're just old married people now."

Hillary watched as her mom took her turn. She wondered what it would be like, to look at somebody you love and just fade into them. Must be nice, though she'd be happy to just look at somebody, anybody and recognize them at all.

It was now her turn. Hillary hit her ball too hard and the grass was so flat and smooth that it rolled off the manicured lawn and off into the woodchips by the two stacked Lawnbots. The lawn at the old house was thicker and the ground more uneven, so the croquet skills she'd mastered as a child, simply didn't apply at the new house.

She didn't like the new house very much, but was glad her parents did. She was living in Atlanta when the whole Mustard Seed thing happened, and it had happened so quickly that it all transpired between her Christmas and 4th of July trips home to Bakersfield. Her husband hated Bakersfield and would typically stay in Atlanta with some lame excuse like he couldn't find a cat sitter. She had no direct exposure to the Mustard Seed incident or the people, just what she'd seen on YouTube along with almost everybody else in the world, and on the cable channels in the airport on her way home as the saga of Mustard Seed played out its final scene.

She'd just gotten to the old house when the whole siege part was in full flower. Her dad wasn't there but was at the Lil' Pal, inside the heavy security perimeter and down in the bunker trying to talk the crazy cult into surrendering. They didn't, they died, and life went on. And even though she'd been a mere spectator, she could see the impact it had, and still had on her father all these years later. Which is why she accompanied him at sunset to the cyclone fence and the National Cemetery.

She stood at the fence with her dad as he tuned his bagpipes beneath the big wooden cross. She knew that he'd gotten extensive counseling after the whole Mustard

Seed thing to cope with a toxic stew of self-contempt and remorse with a garnish of survivor guilt. Evidently, the piping at the cemetery was considered a good healthy way of coping, reconciling, coming to terms, or whatever fuzzy word they use for that kind of thing. But at least it was better than some of the more customary options, anti-depressants, scotch, etc. Nevertheless, she hoped he'd eventually stop the self-flagellation, so going from daily to weekly funeral piping was definitely a sign of progress.

She'd gotten into psychology because of her dad, though he was a how-do-you-feel-about-your-mother kind of psychologist and had gotten into the field rather circuitously after having been a geologist for a big oil company. He described his approach to psychology as "geology for what people do." Hillary had a more mechanical approach, in fact when she was a kid, everyone thought she'd end up some kind of engineer designing elevators to space and such. She and her dad, at her insistence, must have dismantled and reassembled the Briggs & Stratton on the McLane at least four times before she was six years old, and they built every visible model engine that Revell made, the 4 Cylinder OHC, the V-8, even a Wasp radial airplane engine.

From her earliest memory, she was fascinated with machines, not fairies or unicorns or princesses. Well, okay princesses sometimes but only certain ones like Merida with her bow and arrow and Moana because they were bad-asses and not really princesses anyway. In any case, her interest eventually shifted toward a 5-pound electro-chemical machine capable of anything: conjuring up an omniscient and all loving God, creating often beautiful, but more often crappy, music, feeling and expressing love and life-affirming compassion, and conceiving and then inflicting unimaginable cruelty.

This was a machine worth exploring, the machinery of what people do. She had no interest in the individual, or the generally self-induced problems of people fucked up beyond fixing. She acknowledged that it was a very unusual sentiment for a psychologist of any kind to have, but she knew her limitations and her talents as well. However, there was one individual in which she did have an interest and hoped that he wasn't fucked up beyond fixing. Her dad had been bearing this cross for over a decade now, and she was afraid that something in him would eventually snap.

Doug finished tuning his bagpipes, and then stood silent for a moment, "I'm thinking, I'm gonna stop doing this. Someday."

"That's good, that's progress, you can't beat yourself up about it forever."

Doug looked up at the razor wire, "Yes you can." And then started playing.

Chapter Seventeen

What Would Jesus Dream

The name-that-martyr-on-the-crucifix quiz had triggered something in Hertell that would lurk and randomly torment him as he tried to focus on planning and preparing for the evacuation of Mustard Seed. It was a biblical event in which Jesus was sleeping on some cushions in the back of a boat while the apostles, who seemed like a very sincere but excitable bunch, were freaking out about a storm that was tossing the boat around and were moaning and wailing about how they were all going to drown. All the while Jesus was taking a snooze on the cushions in the back of the doomed boat. The biblical incident prompted a number of practical questions in Hertell's mind: *what was Jesus dreaming about, what were the cushions made of, was Jesus lashed down in some way so he wouldn't roll off his cushions in the storm-tossed boat, did the boat have a name?*

Hertell had experienced something of a religious awakening some years before, and in the years since had studied the Bible and tried to make sense of its contents which generally resulted in a proliferation of practical questions such as the ones surrounding the nap and the boat and the jumpy apostles and the waters that would drown them. Nevertheless, Hertell pushed the random thoughts of drowning apostles and cushions aside and tried to focus on the problem at hand. Namely getting the population of Mustard Seed to the surface and escaping the waters that were about to engulf them.

It wouldn't be as easy as the last time the people of Mustard Seed emerged from the earth, the day after Hertell had discovered them living beneath the Li'l Pal. That one had been extensively planned and prepared for in advance and started with a sudden and massive opening of an entire hillside from which rose the whole Mustard Seed population.

It was a memorable affair, complete with a ritual procession and a singing choir in silver robes, and some helicopters at the very end. If that exit route was still available to Hertell, he could evacuate the entire Mustard Seed population in less than an hour, and probably salvage months of supplies in a matter of days, but that route wasn't available to them anymore. It had been damaged by the determined efforts of the surface authorities to arrest the cult, and finally sealed by the bunker buster bomb that concluded the rescue effort.

The original Mustard Seed planners had only anticipated one emergence of the colony, which was to be at the conclusion of their century beneath the earth, when they would return to the surface and restart civilization, probably somewhere in the late 2000s depending on radiation levels. They never planned on Mustard Seed being accidentally discovered several decades prematurely, making a grand entrance, and then pissing off the surface world so thoroughly that they'd all have to retreat back into the earth.

Consequently, there was no Plan B massive hillside, to open up this time, and all Hertell was left with was the original scram-n-scatter plan—basically an all-hands SHTF evacuation procedure utilizing nearly a hundred emergency egress routes, scattered across the entirety of Mustard Seed, in the most remote corners of the complex, with all of them leading to widely dispersed locations on the surface. Since they now only had the narrow escape routes and not the big hole in the mountain this time, it also meant that they wouldn't be able to take out much more than they could carry. But they did have lots of Oceanoid byproducts though, gold and so forth, so they'd be able to buy whatever they needed on the surface.

Hertell and Garner surveyed the egress maps arranged on the gymnasium floor. Garner was the last surviving founder, and one of the original logistical planners for Mustard Seed. He was in a wheelchair that Hertell was pushing. The maps were arranged in a misshapen trapezoid mosaic about 30 feet by 50 feet with some of the maps face down since they represented sectors that were already flooded or were otherwise inaccessible. Hertell stopped at the far edge of the mosaic, "And this one puts people out at the foot of

Mt. Adelaide, that's almost two miles from the nearest other one and about ten miles from the furthest one over by Shark Tooth. Why'd they put'm so far apart? It'll be hard for everybody to find each other."

Garner adjusted his nasal cannula, "It's because we thought it'd be nothing left up there but radioactive mutants waiting for us, and we figured that at least some of us would survive if we came out all kinds of different places, so some of us would end up being decoys for the mutants who'd get busy eating us and whatnot, while the rest of us got away. Only none of us knew who the decoys would be. That was the thinking anyway."

"Well, I don't think anybody's gonna try to eat us this time, so I'll just work up some rendezvous places for everyone to meet up after we get up there."

"I don't think I'm going to make this party Hertell."

"What and drown down here in the dark like a rodent?"

Garner jiggled his cannula, "Won't need to wait for the waters, all I gotta do is stop snorting on this thing for a while, and I'm across the river."

Hertell wheeled Garner out of the gym and reviewed his evacuation strategy as they rolled through the wide arched corridors, through the miniature golf course, past the cathedral, to the town square where it was almost sunset. He parked Garner next to the compass rose facing west to watch the sunset.

Garner cleared his throat, "Well, I think you got it covered pretty much, at least as far as getting outta here anyway. Hard to say what'll happen when you get up there."

Hertell sat on the bench next to Garner, "Yeah, but at least the sunsets are gonna be real, not like down here." He could see Garner nodding his head which was followed by a vague approximation of a laugh, "You little fucker."

Hertell laughed, "Even if I gotta carry you up there myself, you're going up there to see at least one more sunset, ya creaky old bastard."

Garner gestured toward the starry night above their heads, "You don't need to carry me kiddo, you're carrying enough freight already."

Chapter Eighteen

Fight or Flight

It wasn't good. In fact, it was bad. And probably very bad. Hillary had spent the rest of her parents' anniversary weekend trying to be present and make conversation and celebrate with them while being mercilessly gnawed by the vague and elusive pattern of human weirdness that was emerging. That and the recognition that her parents were getting older and starting to forget stuff like the name of the little wire things you hit croquet balls through.

She and Donnie left Bakersfield the next day and took the 166 to the West instead of the 5 to the South since it was closed because of the earthquake which evidently was more serious toward LA than it was up in Bakersfield. She spent the next few days and nights resetting some of the model parameters to localize on the inhibition centers in the prefrontal cortex and rerunning the fMRI data through the I2OHAB software.

It was a replication of a classic experiment from the mid '90s to localize and measure activity in the PFC for fight-or-flight response. The human lab rats, mainly undergrad students, were shown a random assortment of photos: faces of famous or at least recognizable people, monsters, movie stars, spiders, Santa Claus, etc., and since the subjects knew that the vampires, zombies, and snakes, and other scary things they were seeing were pictures and not a real threat, they didn't actually need to fight or flee. So, it was a great way to isolate and measure the inhibition centers; those parts of the brain that keep us from killing, copulating, eating, or running away from everything we see.

Only in Hillary's replication of the experiment with all her fancy math and 3D visualizations, the inhibition centers weren't lighting up at all. There didn't seem to be anything stopping people from what they were instinctively hard wired to do, kill first and ask questions later, if at all. Only everything still seemed pretty normal. Perhaps all that was missing was some triggering event, like an earthquake, to start the zombie apocalypse ball rolling.

A chicken was clucking, it was her dad's ringtone. "Hey pappy, what's up?" She listened for a moment, and then began to quietly cry.

Donnie was on the floor doing back exercises, she was wearing earbuds and listening to bagpipe music, but could tell something was wrong. She pulled out an earbud and propped herself up on her elbow, "What's up? Everything okay?"

Hillary had her hand over her eyes, she was rocking slightly, "Well that's great Dad, that must be a great relief for you."

Donnie could see the sadness wash over Hillary's face. And even though the phone wasn't on speaker, she could hear Doug shouting and laughing. She couldn't make out what he was saying, but by the sounds of things he was very happy and excited about something.

Hillary waved her off and then listened and shook her head, "What? No, I'm fine. I'm very happy for you. Yeah, yeah, everybody loves Spaghetti..." And then in a distant, soft, and almost childlike voice, "Okay, I love you too, bye bye."

Donnie took out the other earbud and then sat Indian-style looking up at Hillary's anguished face. Hillary set down her phone and looked for something to wipe her nose with, then finally gave up and wiped it on her sleeve. "I need to go to Bakersfield. Mom's gonna need me."

Chapter Nineteen

Boatie

Main Street USA was quiet and the moon was rising as Hertell sat at the compass rose with his clipboard reviewing all his plans and checklists. He'd put the kids to bed hours before after reading them a chapter from "Tik-Tok of Oz" complete with different voices for the characters. The last bowlers had left the Atomic Lanes for the night and Hertell was alone except for Travis, up on a ladder, changing the letters on the marquee across the square for the next feature, *Forbidden Planet*, even though nobody would be there to see it.

Garner was mostly right about carrying freight since Hertell was the only one who had taken active ownership of getting Mustard Seed out of Dodge. Everybody was great at doing what Hertell asked them to do, but nobody seemed to have their own ideas about what needed to be done. Which was nice since Hertell didn't need to be diplomatic about rejecting stupid ideas. It also meant that he wasn't able to exploit any good ideas that didn't come out of his own head.

But his own head was not only awash with logistical issues associated with getting everybody to the surface, but also the random flotsam that would pop up: those Jesus cushions were probably packed with horsehair, which was probably a fairly common commodity at the time and not kapok, which Hertell knew due to all his *National Geographic* reading to be from South America and therefore unavailable for the Son of God's nap cushions. So yeah, horsehair cushions, but then what if Jesus was allergic to horsehair, could the Son of God have allergies like regular people, and if so would his allergies have religious significance? But the random thoughts would quickly get swamped by the torrent of logistical and operational issues swirling around Hertell.

Such as the time element that was pressing on him. The egress routes were all well marked and well lit, but the lights were powered by the Oceanoid reactors and once those bays flooded everybody would be evacuating under battery power which was only good for a few hours at most. He'd already timed it all out, and with 80 or so egress routes, with an average length of 2 miles and with about a dozen people each, he could complete a full evacuation in about four to maybe six hours max. So even if the Oceanoid bays flooded and they lost power, they'd still be able to escape with battery-powered lighting before switching to candles and such.

But lighting was the lesser problem, the bigger problem was that the actual escape doors weren't actually doors at all, and not hatches in any sense of the word. They were essentially dirt plugs filling the last 30 or so feet of an egress route, all of which ended near existing drainages. When triggered, the scram-n-scatter system would clear out the dirt plugs with high pressure water thus allowing the people of Mustard Seed to seemingly emerge from naturally occurring, remote, protected and usually hidden arroyos, dry washes, and creek beds—nothing to see here mutants, move along.

A very ingenious system, the only problem was that the high-pressure water for clearing the dirt plugs required high-pressure water pumps, which required electricity from the Oceanoid reactors, so if the bays flooded before the dirt plugs were cleared, then the evacuees would be digging their way out by hand and probably in the dark after the first few hours. Hertell had already checked several of the egress routes and found them to be well lit and fairly easy to negotiate and largely downhill which was a big relief.

He also saw that at the far end of each route, just short of the dirt plug, there was always a locker containing a variety of supplies: shovels in case they had to dig out, pistols and rifles for shooting mutants, plus blankets, tents, food, water, and such. There was also a clipboard with a log of when the locker was last inspected and replenished, quite recently in the ones that Hertell saw. Hertell asked the Secretary of the Interior to assign crews to inspect the remaining egress routes to make sure they were serviceable and pre-position additional supplies they'd need on the surface, and also assess their degree of difficulty so that he could assign people to routes based on their physical ability.

He'd started with the original scram-n-scatter plan, basically some cracking and yellowed laminated flip charts, and constructed a plan which he was confident wouldn't be as chaotic and panic fueled as the original plan which had the population fleeing hordes of invading mutants. His evacuation would be orderly and calm, and ideally with a degree of excitement about returning to the surface, or with at least enough to outweigh the justified apprehension. They'd all leave with what they could carry, and if all went well, they might even be able to send some teams to bring some additional supplies to the surface before the waters overtook.

He made a note to add that to his post-rendezvous checklist and then rocked his head side to side until rewarded with a satisfying crack. He put down his clipboard, put his hands behind his head, leaned back on the park bench, and looked up at the stars overhead, silently advancing over the clouds he had so lovingly painted on the rock ceiling far above.

"Boatie McBoat Face" was the name on the little boat in the storm-tossed sea of Galilee. Jesus was stretching and yawning, just having risen from His nap. Hertell was examining the cushions that were still warm from the body of Jesus. It turns out they were actually filled with polyester foam, which greatly surprised Hertell since he knew polyester wouldn't be invented for nineteen more centuries.

He looked at Jesus as if to say, "WTF?" Jesus was totally cool with that and apparently, He was even better at non-verbal communication than He was with all the sermon-on-the-mount stuff, because He just looked at Hertell and kind of shrugged. But it was a Jesus shrug, which clearly communicated that, as the Son of God, He had some latitude with the whole space-time thing, thus the polyester foam filling, which was much more comfortable than horsehair, plus He was allergic to horsehair anyway, but there was no religious implication. And all that with a shrug. Truly the Son of God.

Hertell asked Jesus what he'd been dreaming about, but before Jesus could answer, the Apostles, who were being a total pain in the ass, were poking at Hertell telling him to ask Jesus to save them. Jesus was way ahead of them though, He pointed at Hertell and spoke, only it didn't sound anything like you'd expect, it sounded like a choir.

When peace like a river, attendeth my way,
When sorrows like sea billows roll

As planned, everyone was converging on the town square for final instructions from Hertell, who'd been sleeping on some cushions, and, as was the custom in Mustard Seed, a choir was singing to keep everyone calm.

Whatever my lot, thou hast taught me to say
It is well... it is well
With my soul... with my soul
It is well, it is well with my soul

Hertell sat up and rubbed his eyes. It was moving day.

Chapter Twenty

Moving Day

"Can everybody hear me okay?"

The entire population of Mustard Seed was gathered in the town square, with some spilling into the miniature golf course and a few of the larger corridors leading into it. It was mid-morning according to the Zeiss planetarium's mechanical sun. Hertell was still a little groggy from his Jesus-dream snooze, but he now stood on top of the compass rose addressing the assembly with a bullhorn.

There were gestures and sounds of general agreement from the assembled. They could hear him just fine, even at the furthest edge of the group since the acoustics were quite good in the massive domed chamber thanks to the original Mustard Seed designers who had installed the necessary baffles and acoustic materials to dampen the natural reverberations you'd expect in a massive cavern.

"This will be the last time I'll be able to talk to you all as a group down here..." The finality of what he heard himself saying caught him by surprise and his throat began to ache. He could tell by the faces on those nearby that the feeling was grimly shared. "At least until we all get together again up in the surface world, ok?" Just saying that made him feel slightly better, not good, just a bit elevated from where he was only a few heartbeats before when he acknowledged that he was leaving his world below, never to return.

Hertell had arranged a rather ingenious scheme for synchronizing the evacuation of Mustard Seed. They were organized into groups of a dozen or so and generally a mix of families, sexes, and ages so that the groups would travel at about the same speed and arrive at the surface at roughly the same time, though in geographically scattered places. Hertell had also identified several rendezvous points on the surface so the groups could all find each other when they got up there.

"You all know what crew you're in, and all the crew chiefs have their maps to the rendezvous checkpoints and the schedule." Hertell and Travis, the geography teacher, and several of his best students had prepared detailed maps for each one of the escape routes based on Hertell's knowledge of the landscape and the major landmarks that could be used for rendezvous points.

Hertell took a deep breath, and checked his clipboard, "Crew chiefs count off!"

Dannon's voice rang out from the edge of the crowd, "One ready!" She waved her map in the air for emphasis.

"Two ready!" and "Three ready!" followed in close succession from other corners of the crowd with the accompanying waving of maps.

The crew chiefs continued to count off as Hertell thought through the plan one last time.

All crews will collect their man-portable belongings and form up at their escape route step-off points within the next 90 minutes.

"Eleven ready!"... "Twelve ready!"

At the signal, all crews will simultaneously commence the estimated 4 hour walk through their respective escape routes.

"Eighteen ready!"... "Nineteen ready!"

At the 3 hour mark, the high-speed pumps will begin flushing out the dirt plugs to clear the last thirty feet of the escape routes.

"Twenty-nine ready!"... "Thirty ready!"

At the end of hour 4 or when the escape route is sufficiently cleared, the crews will collect required additional equipment from the emergency lockers and exit to the surface.

"Forty-four ready!"... "Forty-five ready!"

Upon reaching the surface, crew chiefs will confirm all present and accounted for and conduct an equipment check.

"Fifty-seven ready!"... "Fifty-eight ready!"

Each crew will then proceed to the initial rendezvous point in accordance with their assigned map and wait at the rendezvous point until joined by the ten other crews identified in their map.

"Sixty-five ready!"... "Sixty-six ready!"

The combined crews will bivouac at their assigned rendezvous points until the following morning.

"Seventy-three ready!"... "Seventy-four ready!"

The morning of Day 2 all combined crews will proceed to the Great Wooden Cross which should be visible from all initial rendezvous points.

"Seventy-nine ready!"... "Eighty ready!"

All in all, it was a pretty good plan, and Hertell was reasonably satisfied that it would work. There weren't mutants up there to eat them, and it was late April so the nights should be nice and warm, and he figured everyone would enjoy their first night on the surface under the real moon and real stars.

He checked his watch, more out of habit than anything else, "It's a Saturday up there today, and at the time of day we'll all be getting to the surface, it should be sunny and warm because, well, it's Bakersfield."

He looked down at Kaye, and the kids who stood beside the compass binnacle with a pod of other children, all of them beaming and seemingly very excited about the whole enterprise. Ginny held a butterfly net fashioned out of an old coat hanger and some scrim material, Dot with a tiny shopping cart heaped with her treasures, Toodlah wore a coonskin cap and carried a croquet mallet which confused Hertell. "Toodlah, what's with the…" Realizing he was still on the bullhorn, he released the trigger and lowered it, "What's the croquet mallet for?"

Toodlah tilted his head knowingly, and then in a stage whisper so as not to alarm the others, mouthed the words, "SWAT… teams… and… mutants," and then gestured with the mallet.

Hertell laughed and gave him a thumbs up, "Good idea."

He then looked over at Kaye. She wasn't beaming, she wasn't even looking at him. Her head was held high and her eyes were closed. He knew this pose. She was praying.

He raised the bullhorn and cleared his throat, "So let's do this then." He checked his clipboard and then looked out over the assembly, "Proceed to staging areas! Repeat, proceed to staging areas!"

Everybody seemed to be in agreement and were nodding their heads, but nobody was moving and it was completely silent.

Hertell checked the volume on the megaphone, and clicked trigger a couple of times to get the carrier tone and make sure it was working, "Testing, Testing…" Yes, it was working, so he tried again.

"No really, it's okay, you can go ahead and go to your staging area, this's gonna be great, we're going back to the surface world, nothing to worry about, it's gonna be a lotta fun, birds, trees, dogs, clouds, it's all up there waiting for us, so let's... let's go!"

Nothing, they were all just nodding and smiling at him expectantly, until someone in crew number 6 finally said what they were waiting for.

"Aren't you going to say a prayer or anything?"

Well, this was a nasty surprise. Hertell was fine saying grace at the dinner table since it was a small audience and he knew the script, but he'd never just made up a whole motivational prayer, extempore from his mother wit before. Though he'd often prayed silently for Toodlah and Kaye and Ginny and Dot, mainly just thanks for bringing them into his life and giving it meaning, He'd never been much of a pray-out-loud-prayer type person, and had always been a listener on those occasions when someone was motivated to pray aloud on some topic of interest.

He'd had a good friend on the surface who conjured up astounding out-loud-prayers for road kills that he and Hertell would bury at Li'l Pal, and Mister Frosty would think them up on the spot as they dug the tiny graves, and then he'd say them as Hertell lowered the plastic bags into the graves, and then he'd have a cigarette. But Hertell knew Mister Frosty to be totally committed to his faith and therefore able to pray with complete confidence and abandon, as if he really knew who he was praying to, and for what.

Hertell on the other hand was deeply conflicted in his faith, such as it was, and generally uncomfortable with the whole concept of praying out loud since it seemed to be an impertinent public request for a favor from some celestial favor bank, a bank where you never knew your balance, or what counted as a debit, or a credit. Thus, his reticence to conjure up a benediction prayer for the scram-n-scatter evacuation that the people of Mustard Seed were about to undertake, and the whole Jesus napping on the sinking boat thing was still nibbling at the edge of this thoughts. Perhaps he was overthinking things.

Luckily, someone else started praying. He couldn't see who it was, but it was actually pretty good.

> Merciful and Loving God, bless the souls here assembled as we leave our sanctuary in the warm embrace of the dim, silent earth and ascend to the light of Your world and the glories that await us on the surface, the sun and moon and clouds and wind and sky, the smell of rain and sour grass and hazelnut gourmet coffee and horse shit, depending on how fresh it is, and roadkill skunk depending on how close it is.

The guy had a creative flair, no doubt about it.

> Great and Everlasting Father, You know our inner torment, our fear of the world above, a world of greed and hate with devils filled, and SWAT teams and helicopters; our hope that the world above has forgotten that we ever were and won't try to throw us in jail again or drop a big assed bomb on us.

He noticed Kaye. She was staring at him. Her head was tilted slightly and she had a WTF look on her face, so she obviously didn't appreciate the non-traditional nature of the prayer. Then he noticed that Toodlah, Ginny, and Dot, in fact everybody he could see in the town square, were staring at him in much the same way.

O Blessed Redeemer, guide us through the treacherous narrows, give us strength to reach the radiant light of Your day and stand together again as one in the blessed shade of the old rugged cross.

Then he noticed that he was still holding the megaphone to his mouth for some reason, and he could feel that he was holding the trigger down. And then looked down at Kaye.

Kaye knew that when Dannon asked him to say the prayer, Hertell would be uncomfortable with it since he'd often told her that he was a rookie at the sport and that praying out loud made him feel like a phony at best and a hypocrite at worst. She, on the other hand, was raised a fire-breathing Pentecostal and was just about to volunteer to take the megaphone and give the prayer herself when Hertell began to blink rapidly as if getting ready for a Category 5 sneeze, but instead of sneezing, he raised the megaphone to his mouth and keyed the mic and spoke.

And all were amazed.

Especially Kaye who stared in stunned disbelief at Hertell, who was staring back at her with a look of confused panic on his face as he prayed out loud. He had no control over what he was saying, the words were just coming out of him, he was on a runaway train.

> Lord High King of Heaven, from the waters You
> lift us. We shall rise then, alive, from this grave,
> from the world that was, to the world that is, to
> the world that shall be, to a world without end.

And then as suddenly as they started, the words stopped. And Hertell now stood awkwardly on the compass rose with the megaphone still raised. He had no idea what to say next. There was a long pause. He finally keyed the mic, and casually asked, "Uh... Amen?"

And then with an explosive roar, the entire population of Mustard Seed, answered as one.

"AMEN!"

Chapter Twenty-One

The Police Dog Funeral

D oug stood in the shade of the big wooden cross for what would be the last time. He didn't know it though. He'd made the decision to only play the pipes at the edge of Mustard Seed National Cemetery on special days – the anniversary of its discovery, its destruction, St. Paddy's Day, Christmas, Good Friday, Groundhog Day, the usual. At least once a month, but not a regular schedule like he'd done when playing for each of the dead beneath the hills on the other side of the razor wire.

He wasn't wearing his kilt or any of the trappings that pipers usually wear when they play, just the Levi 501s, Carhartt shirt, and cowboy boots he'd worn the better part of the morning clearing some brush over on the west side of his property. He'd stopped at the house to pick up his pipes, but didn't bother to unload the tools and the chainsaw from the Cushman since it was getting late and he wanted to clear some weeds from the base of the big wooden cross, play the pipes, and get back to the house for an afternoon beer.

He stood beside the big wooden cross, tuned his bagpipes, and looked through the cyclone fence toward a massive crater, actually more of a trapezoidal gash in a hillside some distance away. The gash was what remained of Whisper Hill, the site of Mustard Seed's original emergence. It was also the point of impact for the GBU-57 that entombed them.

It was late April in what had been a wet year, so the gash was covered with wildflowers, mainly wild mustard, with some fiddleneck on the south facing slopes and some lupines in the more protected cracks and folds. He started playing.

His thoughts tended to wander when he played the pipes. They wandered back to the day he'd stood atop the former Whisper Hill, back when it was still an actual hill, to play the pipes for a police dog funeral. Before the hill became a flowery gash, he'd stood quietly on it waiting for his cue to play "Amazing Grace" and noticed that he was standing on what appeared to be a partially exposed slab. At first glance it looked like granite, but it wasn't the Mesozoic diorite typical of the area. It looked like rhyolite but it couldn't be that either. And it was this random geological curiosity that led him back to the Li'l Pal and Hertell some weeks later, into the saga of Mustard Seed, his contribution to its fate, and ultimately to where he now stood playing "Amazing Grace" as the shadows lengthened on the distant remains of Whisper Hill.

As he played, he wondered how many people there were like him, people who had not only been pretty much responsible for nearly a thousand deaths, but who also personally knew all of the dead. Not the bomber pilots in

WWII, they could have easily killed a thousand or so each over London or Tokyo or Dresden or Hiroshima, probably a lot more than a thousand in fact. But they didn't know the people in the bombsight below, they were just specks, living specks, human specks, specks with souls no doubt, but specks nevertheless. Not that creepy doctor in Philadelphia who put all the dead baby parts in jars in his fridge, he killed at least a thousand, probably more, a lot more, some of the moms too, though probably not on purpose. But the creepy doctor didn't know any of the dead babies, and they too were just specks, to him anyway. Maybe the Nazi concentration camp guys, they probably, over time knew, by sight at least and maybe by name in some cases, at least a thousand or so out of the million or so they gassed. But none of them ever seemed to feel bad about it the way he did, and they were all dead themselves by now anyway, and probably suffering in hell, as Doug was almost sure he would eventually.

But then again, perhaps he was just yielding to his Catholic self-contempt. Perhaps Hillary was right, that he can't beat himself up about it forever, that he should move on. Perhaps he was being overly dramatic about the whole thing. The world doesn't revolve around him, there were much larger forces at play in the destruction of Mustard Seed, and he was a minor and pretty much irrelevant cog in a massive machine. But it didn't feel that way to him. No, not many people can claim killing nearly a thousand people they personally knew, so Doug accepted that he was pretty unique in this regard.

Doug would often marvel at the human ability for time-travel. No big whirring time-machine required, or secret incantations or amulets, since it's something we do in our own heads a thousand times a day probably, and as involuntary and instinctive as breathing. As Doug was doing just now, playing the pipes and thinking of a police dog funeral and Mesozoic diorite and eternal damnation.

He finished the tune, and was about to start another one, but then he saw something and stopped abruptly, and as the pipes issued their final plaintive moans, he raised a hand to his face and softly said, to no one in particular, "Dear God help me."

Chapter Twenty-Two

Walking on the Moon

The klaxon sounded five times and everybody knew what it meant. Hertell and his crew set off as the final klaxon blast faded. Hertell checked his watch and addressed his crew. "Okay, off we go, into the wild blue yonder." Nobody really knew the words, but several started humming "Wild Blue Yonder" as they set off.

Kaye led the group, and Hertell rode drag at the very back. Lox and Babs and their girls were in trail behind Kaye along with Tim and Tina and their boys, followed by Karen and Josh, and Garner in his wheelchair. Toodlah and the twins were up front with Kaye, and Hertell could hear the wheel of Dot's toy shopping cart, full of her treasures, rhythmically squeaking as they walked through the dimly lit escape passage. She'd always had difficulty walking, and the shopping cart served as a child-sized walker, even though it wasn't one to her. To her it was just her shopping cart.

It wasn't a traditional refugee scene with traumatized people with pushcarts full of their worldly possessions, coughing and dragging luggage and crying children, to the frontier. It wasn't like that at all, since most of the stuff that people would need or wanted to take with them had already been pre-positioned near the ends of the escape routes, so they were not only traveling light, but they also seemed to be in no particular dread of stepping into the surface world.

Squeak, squeak, squeak, squeak, squeak. They were holding a good steady pace and Dot's shopping cart was almost like a metronome. But it was eventually drowned out by singing. The Dow girls had tired of humming "Wild Blue Yonder" and had replaced it with "Precious Memories," which actually worked really well as a marching tune.

Precious memories, unseen angels
Sent from somewhere to my soul

Squeak, squeak, squeak... Hertell smiled at the bizarre syncopation of the song and shopping cart metronome.

Everybody joined in, but not Hertell. He was thinking about what awaited them on the surface, and it seemed to him that he was the only one thinking about that. The rest were certainly heartbroken about leaving their underground world but were almost uniformly kind of excited about it. Consciously or subconsciously, they didn't see themselves as survivors, or victims, or refugees, but more as explorers on an expedition.

How they linger, ever near me

And the sacred past unfolds

Toodlah had taken the helm of Dot's shopping cart since she had tired, and was now walking hand in hand wtih Kaye and Babs who started swing walking her in time to the music—every few steps they'd hoist her into the air as if she were walking on the moon. Soon all the adults were doing the same with Ginny and Hazel and all the kids of the right size and age, with all shouting "Wheee" with each lunar jump.

Precious memories, how they linger... Wheee!
How they ever flood my soul... Wheee!

Squeak, squeak, squeak. By the look of it all you'd think they were all going to a big picnic or an Easter egg hunt, not fleeing a beloved world that was rising to engulf and drown them, not toward a world that had once tried to imprison them, and failing that, opted to bury them.

In the stillness, of the midnight... Wheee!
Precious sacred scenes unfold... Wheee!

Squeak, squeak, squeak. Then again, they didn't have Hertell's advantage of being shot in the head, and had therefore simply forgotten the more problematic aspects of the surface world. Yes, that must be it, they'd forgotten all the shitty stuff, and only remembered the good stuff.

He wondered how much the people on the surface were forgetting. Maybe they were forgetting why they wanted to throw Hertell in jail and why they wanted to kill everybody in Mustard Seed. Maybe forgetting stuff isn't such a bad thing after all, depending on what's being forgotten. And maybe forgetting stuff isn't like the ground squirrel holes in the Li'l Pal road cut above their heads, perhaps forgetting stuff won't cause the whole hillside to collapse like it did that day he was throwing rocks. Maybe forgetting stuff is more like homeopathy, something he'd read about in the *Encyclopedia Britannica* after he'd been shot in the head.

It seems that you simply take a drop of a poison, or whatever's killing you, and put it in an Olympic-size swimming pool, and then take a drop of that and put it in another Olympic-size swimming pool and then take a drop of that and put it in another pool and repeat that a hundred more times, a thousand more times, until the poison is effectively gone. Until you can't find a single molecule of the actual poison in the water anymore. But the theory is that the water remembers, because the poison that used to be there, in the water, has left empty spaces in it where it used to be, and the shapes of the empty spaces in the water kick our cells into gear, so they can protect us since we're mostly water anyway.

Hertell considered it to be laughable quackery, and it was, as far as the science of it. But he also considered that sometimes a thing that couldn't possibly work at the physical level in a cell, could work at a conceptual level in a brain. Perhaps all those empty spaces in the brain that were previously filled with shitty stuff, that was now forgotten, were actually like a vaccination to help keep people from doing shitty stuff again when presented with the opportunity.

An opportunity such as the reemergence of the Mustard Seed civilization.

Then there was a rumble and everyone stopped singing and then stopped walking.

"It's okay, it's just the scram pumps starting." He checked his watch, they were right on time. "They're clearing out the last thirty or so feet of the escape passage for us." He reached down and touched his fingers to a large pipe that ran along the right side of the tunnel. It was cold to the touch, and he could feel the water churning through it. "It's all good, but it's a lot noisier than I expected." Which was true since the only way he could be heard now was by shouting. Clearly the singing part of the trip was over.

The scram-n-scatter tunnels weren't the smooth and graceful chambers and passages formed by the ancient lava flows like the rest of Mustard Seed, but were instead drilled, blasted, and hewn by human hands, then lined with cement, giving them the appearance of oversized drainage culverts. The floors were fairly wide and even, and there were narrow tracks in them, evidently part of the construction process for removing debris as the tunnels were bored back in the '50s. Along the base of each wall and on either side of the tracks were large flood pipes for delivering the liberating water needed to clear out the last few feet of each tunnel and open the way to the surface.

Dot was too tired to swing walk now, and Hertell was carrying her. He knew they were getting closer to the end of the tunnel since the walls were marked with large placards and painted stripes signaling the remaining distance. They had just passed 3 stripes, so they had 300 yards to go. The whole plan was going like clockwork, they'd be on the surface within the hour, but by Hertell's estimation they should be starting to see some daylight by now.

He started moving to the front of the group, and as he passed Kaye, he brushed against the opposite flood pipe. It wasn't cold. He picked up his pace to get well ahead of Kaye and the rest, and then stopped and put his free hand on the flood pipe. He didn't feel a thing. He knocked on it with his knuckle and got a hollow ding in reply. It was empty. This was not good. Dot was asleep on his shoulder, so he moved ahead of the rest and had just passed the 100-yard stripes when the lights flickered and it suddenly got quiet. Quiet enough to hear the last few squeaks of the shopping cart in the distance as everybody slowly came to a shuffling stop.

Squeak, squeak... squeak.

The emergency lighting came on, turning the formerly warm yellow passage into a dim and deep crimson red. Since he'd gotten slightly ahead of the rest, he turned and walked back toward the group and as his eyes adjusted to the emergency lighting, he called out to them.

"It's okay, it just means the Oceanoid bays have flooded. We're fine, we're almost there, and we've got a few hours of emergency lights, and we'll be outside by the time they run out."

That's what he was saying anyway. Inside he was in a complete panic. They were within 300 feet of what should be a comfortably large opening to the surface world. They should be feeling a breeze of some kind depending on the outside air pressure differential, and some light too, however faint it might be. Now that his night vision was in effect, he should be able to discern daylight. If it was there. Perhaps they'd made a mistake about the date and time on the surface, perhaps it was night on surface Earth and that's why it was so relentlessly dark up ahead. Perhaps, there was a dog leg at the end of the tunnel that was blocking the daylight that must surely be out there waiting for them.

He could smell water now, and mud. This was a good sign, but when he reached the storage lockers and all the supplies that his teams had pre-positioned in the days before, he knew that there was no dog leg, there was no breeze, and there was no daylight ahead. Just the dull crimson red of the emergency lighting and his group, who now stood looking at a solid wall of earth where a bright opening to the outside should have been.

Chapter Twenty-Three

The Formerly Dry Wash

As its name would imply, a dry wash is generally dry. But even though the last good rain had been in early March, and it was now late April, there was water in the formerly dry and nameless wash for some reason. And while there were numerous dry washes in the Mt. Adelaide watershed, this particular dry wash was the only one that wasn't dry. It was a very long flat wash that snaked up toward rising terrain to the northeast, but the curious thing was that all of the wetness seemed to be coming from a single gully near its midpoint. The gully was of a chalky character, and very narrow, scarcely more than a pair of outstretched arms, but it was cut into a low bluff and very deep where it emptied into the wash, probably 20 feet and some change.

The water wasn't flowing anymore, it was just kind of sitting there, in confused little puddles in the pale chalky mud. Once so determined and purposeful, the torrents of water that had churned out of the gully sweeping soil and stalk before it, had stopped, and all that was left were the puddles and the pleasant drip drop drip sound as the water trickled down toward the formerly dry wash.

While they'd confronted a solid wall of earth when first reaching the end of their tunnel, it eventually yielded to the determined shovels of Hertell and his crew. The dirt turned to mud the deeper they dug until they finally reached several large irregular and soggy channels that had been cut by the scram water.

Hertell crawled into the largest one. He couldn't see anything but he could feel what he thought was a breeze. He scrambled back out of the channel, grabbed the nearest shovel and tossed it into the muddy hole, "I'm going ahead to see how far it is to outside."

A slightly confused hush fell over everyone in the chamber as the word "outside" sunk in. Some of them even whispered the word, "outside?" They were confused since, from their perspective they already were outside. They weren't in their houses, or the bowling alley, or malt shop, or the cathedral, or the gymnasium, they were "outside" in their world. And then they all slowly recognized that Hertell was talking about the other outside, the real one, that was only a few muddy yards away. Some repeated the word again, only different this time, "Outside."

Hertell crawled on his hands and knees and disappeared into the channel again, but he could still be heard, muffled and distant calling back to them, "Keep digging, make it bigger, big enough for everybody!"

The muddy channel got bigger the deeper he went, and there was still some light spilling in from where he'd left the rest of the group. Hertell could hear muffled voices and their shovels scraping away at the mud. The flood water had actually done a pretty good job of clearing the dirt plug before the pumps shut down. He could see sections of the exposed scram pipe and the regularly spaced perforations on its side, and it reminded him of the oscillating lawn sprinklers he'd run through in his youth, only bigger, and stationary. No gentle arcs of cool water swaying to and fro as frolicking children gamboled in the sun. Instead, just determined jets of water clawing a muddy path to the surface and survival.

Hertell could see light. Just a dull glow, scarcely perceptible up ahead, but definitely there. He couldn't tell how far away it was, but he knew the surface couldn't be more than 20 feet away as he slithered on his belly through the mud, scraping a bigger opening with the shovel as he went.

Hertell felt the fluttering of his copper specks and a flood of Devonian memories wash over him as he dug. He felt the vague but primal joy of a lungfish crawling in the fragrant, comforting mud of a murky prehistoric pond. It wasn't joy like a person would feel. It was more the lungfish version of it. Just like they had their own versions of anger, fear, confusion (which was most of the time since they were lungfish), and disgust (seldom if ever since they were lungfish). But unlike us, Hertell knew that they felt only the simplest, instantaneous spirits like fear and desire, but nothing as contemplative as hope or remorse or faith or despair since those required an appreciation of time and a memory of it. For them there was no time. There was no past to cherish or regret, no future to hope for or dread, there was just an immediate, actionable present, with the happy smell of water and safe smell of mud.

The channel was now big enough for Hertell to rise from his hands and knees, and he could now proceed in a low crouch through the water toward the light which was getting brighter, and he could now distinctly see it streaming in through several openings up ahead. The closer he got to the light, the more he had to crouch, and he was eventually forced back to his hands and knees as the chamber grew shallower, and then finally to army crawl the last few feet to reach the biggest opening where he could now clearly see daylight up ahead. And then he heard the most wondrous sound, a bird.

Chapter Twenty-Four

Crowning

It was almost like one of those birthing videos on YouTube, only there was no vagina involved. Not even close. No pink epithelial tissue stretching to its elastic limit, just the creased, dry, and gritty wall of a nameless gully. First there was an explosive burst of rusty water, spewing mud and rocks in great arcing jets from the issuing gully wall, chewing away at the opposing face, and then tumbling down the narrows toward the dry wash in the unseen distance. The water continued for a time until stopping suddenly, leaving only the mirthful sound of trickling water as it dribbled from an assortment of oddly shaped holes scattered across what remained of the gully wall.

One of the oddly shaped holes was obviously crowning because a head was slowly emerging from it, only it wasn't covered in caul but instead by grey mud. Hertell blinked a few times to clear some of the mud from his eyes and to get used to the bright light of day. And then in a great heaving gush, he squirted out and tumbled to the ground as what remained of the gully wall collapsed in a muffled spattering thud.

He would not be lovingly gathered up and swaddled, instead he would cough and crawl and claw his way out of a full ten cubic yards of mud that accompanied him out of Mother Earth. He struggled to his feet and let his eyes adjust to the daylight that he hadn't seen in over ten years. He looked up, but the gully was so narrow that all he could see was a narrow strip of bright blue sky. He had two immediate objectives, actually three. They weren't prioritized and had no particular order, so he decided to take care of the easiest, and most urgent one first.

He pawed at the button fly of his Levi 501s and proceeded to take perhaps the longest and most satisfying pee in human history. And as he peed, he pondered several random but nevertheless pertinent observations. He knew from his extensive reading, that the average human bladder typically had a max capacity of about 800 milliliters or a little short of a quart. He estimated, based on the flow and duration, that he was above average in bladder size. The second thought, that would return to him many times in the days to come, was how symbolic it was, that his first act upon returning to the surface world, was pissing on it. Specifically, on a small, inoffensive, speckled rock, hosing it clean of mud and leaving it glistening in the diffuse light of the gully.

Having finished objective one he initiated the next, specifically to see where they were. The scram-n-scatter maps were over half a century old, and he wanted to confirm that they could emerge undetected since he wasn't confident that they'd been entirely forgotten on the surface in the years since their burial.

He looked down the gully and saw that it was not only narrow and steep but also serpentine since he couldn't see where it led. It was also very muddy and slippery, and he knew it would be difficult to make his way back if he went that direction. He looked up the gully and saw that he was near its head and that a determined climb would put him at the top of the hillside into which the gully was cut.

It was very steep and loose and Hertell had to concentrate on his footing to keep from sliding back down, and while the scram-n-scatter water had pretty much scoured the gully of all vegetation below, the stretch above Hertell was dry and also dotted with clumps of flowers. There was a knot of purple lupines perched above a large rock, like a crown, and the sight of them made Hertell stop. He looked at them for a few blinks and then he started sobbing at the sight of this randomly living thing, unbidden, unheralded, unknown, just life emergent from the hostile, indifferent dirt. Wherever the wind or God or a passing bird decided to poop. Yet there it was, alone, rising untended from the earth. He couldn't help himself, he grabbed a handful, pulled them from the clinging dirt, and took them with him as he went up the gully.

He picked every flower he saw as he climbed, alternately sobbing and laughing the whole time, and he decided that once he got to the surface and figured out where they were, he was going to pick every wildflower he saw and make a massive bouquet for Kaye, something he hadn't been able to do for the last 10 years below. Something he wasn't sure he'd done more than one or two times in the whole time they'd been married. He knew he must have done it at least once the first time they were married since they were in their teens at the time, and at that age he was generally observant of all the customary romantic clichés like flowers and chocolate and such.

As he got older, he switched to other, more utilitarian symbols of love, like flashlights and Swiss Army knives and such. But then, as the marriage progressed, the flashlights gave way to hand made cards, then to Hallmark cards with handwritten missives, then to Hallmark cards with just a signature and date, and then to just Hallmark cards unadorned, and then to flat spoken acknowledgments, and then to nothing at all. He couldn't remember exactly how it ended, but he knew it was something he'd done. For some reason the copper specks in his head that allowed him to remember so many things, didn't let him remember what it was, but he knew that it had been enough, for Kaye. Though he never could understand why he would have done such a thing, whatever it was, to the only woman he had ever loved. Perhaps it was the Swiss Army knives and the flashlights that had set the wheels in motion. Perhaps he should have stuck to the customary romantic clichés of their youth, like chocolate, and flowers—like the armful of flowers he now held to his chest, the colorful and massive bouquet he'd gathered for Kaye.

He then noticed that he was now standing on a low bluff at the head of the gully. The bluff was covered in wildflowers, mainly wild mustard, and above him was... the sky. The brightest, biggest sky he'd ever seen, and it was pulling him into it – the same sensation a person would have at the edge of a cliff or at the top of a skyscraper, an unseen but unmistakable gravitational pull tugging you over the edge and into the abyss, only in Hertell's case it was an upward tug into the jolting sky.

And even though he knew it was the sky and that he couldn't possibly fall into it, he nevertheless instinctively and involuntarily crouched low and finally dropped the armload of flowers and fell to all fours on the ground, clutching tufts of brome grass to keep from being pulled from the earth, into the yawning sky. He laughed at himself, at his ridiculous but now understandable response, a response he'd seen over a decade before when the people of Mustard Seed saw the sky for the first time after fifty years beneath the earth. At that time, he'd tried to rationally explain to them, as he was to himself now, that there was absolutely no danger of falling into the sky. Only now he understood that instinct generally overpowers rational... anything.

After several furtive glances up into the sky, he finally let go of the brome grass and rose to one knee. There was a light breeze and he could see the faint rippling in the grass and wild mustard on the bluff. The irrational fear of falling had passed, and he was outside, the real outside, and it was beautiful. He finally stood up, collected his armload of wildflowers, and caked in drying mud, surveyed his surroundings.

He immediately realized that it must have been a much bigger earthquake on the surface than it was under the ground. He knew approximately where they were supposed to have emerged, but unless the scram-n-scatter maps were really inaccurate, the surface world had been noticeably rearranged. Instead of being a mile directly south of his position, the old wooden cross was now to the west, and the hill it was on, was significantly taller than before. It was also closer.

From where he stood, he could also see, to his great relief, that they'd emerged on a barren hillside far from any visible structures or roads. In spite of the rearranged surface, he finally got his bearings and could see that the gully emptied into a broad dry wash only a few hundred yards from where he stood. They could follow the dry wash all the way down to the rendezvous point.

Kaye's distant voice from the gully, "Hertell! Where the fuck are you!"

Hertell collected his flowers and began his descent of the gully to get the rest out. "Coming dear! I got something for you!"

The scram water had widened the gully bottom to a negotiable size, so they'd have room to carry out some of their supplies and equipment. Hertell decided to get the falling-into-sky business out of the way which turned out exactly as he'd expected. The further they went down the gully, the wider it became, and with each step, and each widening glimpse of the looming sky, they all crouched lower and lower to the ground, and by the time they reached the broad flat wash, pretty much everybody was on all fours, crawling, and laughing about crawling.

They were muddy, but they were all outside, the real outside.

Chapter Twenty-Five

Don't Fence Me In

D oug stood motionless, staring through the cyclone fence at the dead that were rising from the earth. They were silent. They were ashen and grey. They were the color of death. And they were coming for him. All the people he'd killed all those years ago were now rising from their graves. They were coming to take him away.

He softly prayed to himself thinking it might help, but the shock of what he was seeing greatly limited his prayer conjuring ability, and he was reduced to a confusing but prayerful vamp.

"Dear God, Jesus, Jehovah, whatever, the Lord is my... uh... my protecting... uh... sheep dog type thing, who leadeth me to... no, through... through the... the... but not only that, forgive me for... for what I... or for how I... okay for fucking up and getting all these people killed..." He trailed off since the dead were getting closer.

Doug had gone full Catholic while he was in jail. More Catholic than when he was a kid, more than his parents, and even more that some of his aunts who were about as Catholic as you could be as a civilian. He went to Mass every Sunday at a throwback parish that still did the whole drill in spooky Latin. Did the sacraments, the vigils, all of it. But evidently it didn't help. The avenging spirits had come for him.

At the front of the ghostly formation was a man carrying a small child, they looked like chalk and he could almost see through them. The spirit waved his hand as he approached the cyclone fence and called out, "Hey Doug! 'Zat you?"

Doug didn't answer. Ghosts usually sound scary, at least that was the traditional expectation, with scary echoey 'oooOOOOoooOOO' sounds and such, so Doug was totally unprepared for a rather chipper and seemingly benign ghost, one that knew his name even.

And now that they were getting closer, Doug could see that even though they were of a uniform chalky character, that their eyes looked fairly normal, not like the hollow eyes of the dead as depicted in popular fiction or the glowing eyes from CGI in the movies.

"Figured it had to be you playing the bagpipes out here at the cross."

Doug didn't respond. He was staring at the small child the ghost was carrying. She was clutching a small bouquet of wildflowers and appeared to be a ghost with special needs, which puzzled Doug since he'd always assumed such physical afflictions were taken care of in some way in the afterlife. Evidently not. Doug had a tendency to pursue random thoughts down endless rabbit holes, even under extreme circumstances such as those he confronted with the ghosts, and he'd just begun contemplating the afterlife full of scarred burn victims, and hollowed out cancer patients, and shredded combatants, and all those babies he prayed for every Sunday at Mass, all those babies that would never even get the chance to breathe much less get a chance to sin, or be forgiven for it, but then the ghost spoke again.

"What's with the fence?"

The ghosts had stopped at the fence which surprised Doug since he'd presumed they'd just walk right through it, as you'd expect with ghosts, and then whisk him away to hell or wherever. Only they didn't. They stopped on the other side of the fence. So maybe going full Catholic actually did help. Maybe these particular ghosts had to obey the laws of physics just like regular people.

Doug finally managed to speak, "Hertell?"

"Yeah." Hertell grabbed a handful of fence and shook it, looking up at the razor wire at the top, "But what's with the fence? We never had a fence around the Li'l Pal."

"Hertell, you're dead, all of you are dead. You're all ghosts. They killed all of you almost..." He stopped for a moment, mentally calculating, "No, over ten years ago now."

Hertell put the child ghost down, "They did huh? I guess that's why they stopped digging around trying to root us out."

"Yeah, the president dropped a big bomb on you and killed you all."

"Well, I guess he took his job pretty seriously then, but no we never got the memo that we were all dead. I just figured they got busy with other stuff and forgot about us."

At that point, given the nature of the conversation, Doug concluded that the ghosts weren't going to take him to hell or wherever ghosts take people, and that there weren't actually any ghosts at all, but that he was just experiencing a guilt-induced psychotic episode. Which was a great relief since he could just get some counseling and some more meds for that. Or perhaps he'd been playing the pipes too hard. He was breaking in a new chanter reed after all, so he might have popped a blood vessel somewhere which was making him hallucinate and carry on an otherwise pleasant conversation with a person he knew to be dead.

The hallucination then sneezed loudly, "All this mud is making me sneeze." Hertell rubbed his face and scalp releasing a cloud of ghostly dust. He looked through the fence at the wildflower covered hillsides, "Or it might be the wild mustard. Maybe I'm allergic to it, like I am to horsehair."

The rest of the ghostly legion had now reached the fence, including an ancient ghost wearing a nasal cannula and sitting in a wheelchair. They all stared through the fence at Doug who still stood, stunned, with his bagpipes in the shade of the old wooden cross.

Hertell looked up at the wooden cross, "How'd this get here? It used to be on top of Little Sunrise next to the 178, did the earthquake move it here?" He looked north toward Whisper Hill and fell silent.

Doug slowly realized that he wasn't chatting casually with ghosts or having a hallucinatory psychotic episode. And while either of those scenarios offered a much more plausible explanation for what he was experiencing, the reality was sinking in that the Mustard Seed civilization had somehow survived a direct hit with a bunker buster bomb, and had gone on to live stubbornly and contentedly beneath the earth ever since.

Doug finally responded, "No, I bought it and moved it here when they fenced Li'l Pal and made a cemetery out of it.

Hertell was confused, "But Li'l Pal already was a cemetery."

"They made it a people cemetery, a National Cemetery, for all you dead people down in Mustard Seed."

"Well, that was thoughtful of'm." Hertell looked up at the razor wire, "Do we have to stay in here?"

The cross made quick work of the cyclone fence. Hertell moved all the former ghosts to a safe distance from the logging operation as Doug made three cuts with his chainsaw at the base of the cross. Then, with a determined nudge from the Cushman, the old rugged cross fell, bending the fence toward the ground, twisting about 30 feet of it down on either side of the cross, and snapping the flanking line posts in the process. The cross didn't fully flatten the fence, but was still slightly suspended by the twisted chain-link. It bobbed slightly up and down, as if fighting to raise itself again, or doing shallow crunches to strengthen its core.

Hertell climbed up onto the nodding crossbar, providing the additional weight to successfully flatten the fence, and then motioned Doug to bring the Cushman forward.

"Right up here Doug, right up to the top, up to where they had Jesus's hands nailed down!"

Somehow it just didn't seem right to be standing where the symbolic body of Christ would have been nailed, so Hertell shifted a few feet to the very end of the crossbar, to make room for the imagined arms of the suffering Savior. No crown of thorns this time, just a tangle of razor wire matted down beneath the massive wooden beam on which Hertell now stood.

The Cushman maneuvered into position next to Hertell, to provide the definitive ballast, and Hertell called for Kaye and the rest to proceed.

"Okay, come on over, watch your step and watch out for the razor wire."

Doug joined him on the 12-foot wooden beam, and as they helped the former ghosts up onto the cross, over the unseen arms of Jesus, and out of the cemetery, the group began singing.

This is my father's world
And to my listening ears
All nature sings, and round me rings
The music of the spheres

Chapter Twenty-Six

They Live

"They're alive! I thought they were all dead all this time, but they're as alive as you and me!"

Hertell was riding in the Cushman with Doug who was on his phone excitedly telling his daughter about the resurrection of Mustard Seed. They were bouncing down the dirt road back to Doug's house to get his Jeep and Silverado, so the former ghosts wouldn't have to walk so far, and to tell Audrey about the miraculous discovery so she could start getting the house ready for over a dozen special guests.

"I thought they were ghosts at first!" Doug was laughing for joy, shouting excitedly into the phone, and occasionally choking up and wiping his nose and tears from his eyes.

Hertell wasn't laughing or choking up. He was thinking. If the pumps failed for his route, then they probably failed for some of the other scram-n-scatter routes as well. He probably wasn't the only one that had to dig out through the mud of a partly cleared plug. Perhaps some of the plugs weren't even partly cleared, perhaps those groups were trapped and unable to dig out.

He kept the implications of that thought at bay. He managed to convince himself that everybody probably made it out, or were in the process of digging their way out, or were happily lounging on sunny hillsides, looking up at the sky, resting on beds of wildflowers, and laughing about falling into the sky as Hertell's group had done only a few hours before.

"And then one of'm starts talking to me! And sonofabitch, it's Hertell!"

Hertell decided that the first thing to do after getting his group to Doug's house was to find all the other escape routes and make sure everybody got out. He couldn't wait for them all to converge on the old rugged cross because they'd just chopped that down to get over the fence.

"I assumed it was a guilt-induced auditory and visual hallucination since I know you thought I was primed for a psychotic break, but then I see him standing across from me at the big wooden cross, and he's real, they're all real!"

Hertell thought that maybe cutting down the cross wasn't such a good idea after all since it was the main rendezvous landmark for all the groups to converge on tomorrow, the second day of the escape. But that thought hadn't occurred to him when they were chopping it down, so maybe he was starting to forget things like everybody else.

"They weren't hallucinations, they weren't ghosts, they were just dusty from crawling up out of the ground... you still there?"

No, the first order of business would be to go to all the escape exit points and confirm that all of Mustard Seed had made it out safely to the surface world, and if necessary, help dig them out.

"So, they're all gonna spend the night with us, we've got plenty of room in the house, plus the guest cottage and the Airstream out in the driveway."

The only problem was that Hertell wasn't sure exactly where everybody would emerge. The original scram-n-scatter maps were all underwater down in the flooded gymnasium where he'd left them, in the now submerged, and former, Mustard Seed. He had a general sense of where they would all come up since he'd painstakingly drawn up and distributed rendezvous maps to each crew chief so they could find their way to the old rugged cross, but he only had a map for his own group.

"And there's still almost a thousand of'm we gotta round up tomorrow and find a place for them too, so I'm thinking I'll get a buncha FEMA trailers for now and then we can just make a big modular home park out past the leach field, and call it Mustard Seed 2.0..."

But with the earthquake, and the big wooden cross on a different hilltop, and the cross being chopped down and everything, the maps would pretty much be useless anyway.

"Wait a minute, we better not, they might try to throw'm in jail again or kill'm or whatever like the last time, so don't tell anybody about this, you can tell Donnie, but don't tell anybody else though. We gotta keep this secret, so we can call it Tuscan Sun or Vista del Nalgas or something like that."

Hertell had taken the easternmost escape route, and it was the only one that emptied within the Li'l Pal proper. The rest of the scatter points were sprinkled to the west toward

Sharktooth Hill. All of them hidden in the gullies and draws and arroyos that drained into the Kern River to the south. He decided that he'd need to do a wide area search which would be hard to accomplish with the Cushman cart they were riding in. Even with Doug's other cars, it still wouldn't be enough to cover the other 79 scatter points in a day, much less help dig people out. He started estimating how many days it would take to cover the 20 square mile area with a Cushman, a Jeep, and a truck.

"So, we're just getting to the house now, to let mom know about our dinner guests."

Doug started laughing and crying again, but then shook himself out of it. "Spaghetti, we'll make a big ol' messa spaghetti for'm, what do you think?"

Hertell was momentarily drawn from his thoughts, "What? Yeah, spaghetti sounds good."

Chapter Twenty-Seven

Prosopagnosia

P *ros·o·pag·no·sia*—präsəpag'nōZH(ē)ə

a neurological condition characterized by the inability to recognize the faces of familiar people, even oneself.

Hillary had adapted to it intuitively as a child and typically used hair style, voice, gait, physical mannerisms, and such to distinguish between people, and she was pretty good at it. So good that people quickly forgot that she didn't recognize their faces, but a haircut or a shave was the equivalent of rearranging the furniture in a blind person's house.

All in all, it made for a very interesting courtship. Donnie called Hillary the C-word on their first date.

They'd initially met at a party in which they were both inexorably drawn, not to each other, but to a massive seawater fish tank populated with colorful chum, drifting among some dramatically arranged rocks, which were covered in pulsating stalks of protoplasm in various striking hues and accentuated by the black light that would randomly add to the moment.

It was a big party, and Hillary didn't really know anybody since she was new to UCSB. She didn't drink since it made her cheeks red, and she'd recently given up vaping since it was such a cliché, so busying herself with the fish tank was the obvious choice since it gave her a way to be present without being social.

While the party swirled around them, Hillary shared a repurposed picnic bench with another woman. The bench was positioned as kind of a viewing gallery for the fish tank for just such contemplation. They sat in silence for a long time watching the fish drift and occasionally dart for no apparent reason amid the squat sea anemones fluttering and waving their stubby tentacles in the unseen currents, hoping to sting, paralyze, and consume some unsuspecting or otherwise clueless speck of sea life.

Hillary sensed the presence beside her, and she could feel her warmth. It was benign, safe even. Better than safe somehow. Almost protective. But it wasn't the warmth that captivated her, it was the scent of the person who sat only inches away on the old, hard picnic bench. It was an intoxicating potion of puppies, pine needles, and fresh brewed coffee. More of a sense than an actual smell, and hard to describe, but still close to it. She couldn't tell for sure but it seemed like the longer they sat, the closer they were to each other.

Intoxicated by the presence beside her, Hillary drifted off in thought, observing that the sea anemones covering the rocks vaguely resembled a crowd of sad little misshapen choads, behatted with those knobbly dayglo condoms popular at bachelorette parties of yesteryear. For some reason she thought of her ex-husband and his meticulous manscaping as if it were some form of topiary art. She laughed at the mental image and then without realizing it, heard herself say, "A thousand tiny fingers urging her to let go."

She was surprised at her vocalization but was immediately rewarded with the most glorious and gratifying staccato laugh from the woman beside her. If the voice matched the laugh, she would be helpless. The woman beside her spoke after letting her laughter subside.

"I was thinking about soap holders, but you topped me." And then she cackled again.

Hillary finally looked over at her bench mate, introduced herself, and extended her hand. "Hillary, as in Sir Edmund, not Clinton."

Her bench mate gave her a firm handshake, "Donnie, as in Dawn of a new life, not Osmond."

They spent the rest of the party edging closer and closer to each other a breath at a time whilst engaged in a spirited and wide-ranging conversation that caromed from boisterous, to intimate to seditious to conspiratorial to bawdy.

Normally, for such a burgeoning relationship, there would be a montage of the two predestined soulmates washing a car and squirting each other with a garden hose, and modeling ugly sweaters at a garage sale, laughing at a joke at a candle lit dinner, all the while with Van Morrison singing "Crazy Love" in the background. But not this time.

It all unfolded on that old, cracked picnic bench. They revealed their inner selves as the night progressed, oblivious to the laughter and hookups and dramas and social maneuverings. It was as simple as that. And when they finally kissed, Hillary pounded a stake through the heart of her convenient escape clause, that she was bisexual, and accepted the fact that she was, no shit, a lesbo. Or at least she was now. And in a way it was a big relief, and besides she'd always been a big fan of Georgia O'Keeffe, and now she knew why.

She breathed in the scent of Donnie, as in Dawn of a new life, and after the kiss, looked into the face, a face she would never ever be able to recognize, into the face of the woman she decided she would spend the rest of her life with. And then said, "Let's set precedents."

Donnie was stunned, challenged, flattered, and otherwise completely smitten.

"Roger that," was all she could say.

Sex followed and would best be described in some other forum. Suffice it to say that both parties enjoyed themselves immensely and agreed to meet again for an official first date without the fish tank as their focus of attention.

The problem was that Hillary had mentioned, during their fish tank conversation, that she liked the hair style of the goalie for the Washington Spirit professional women's soccer team, so Donnie had immediately gone out and had herself shorn and frosted to match the goalie's coiffe.

However, this had the unfortunate side effect of making her totally unrecognizable to Hillary. She'd mentioned this to Donnie on the picnic bench the night before, but it was quickly dwarfed by the landscape of their subsequent conversation, and disappeared entirely in the sex that followed. Consequently, when Donnie approached Hillary at the restaurant and stood, expectantly before her with her new hairdo and an armful of flowers, Hillary just looked up at her as if at a stranger and registered a completely blank face.

It was the overpowering smell of the flowers that got her attention, Hillary looked up from her book at the dark-skinned flower vendor, then smiled weakly, and said, "Oh thank you, but actually I'm not interested." And then returned to her book.

Which was met by several tear-restraining blinks, followed by, "What a cunt!"

The couples at the adjoining tables visibly stiffened, and one of them got out their phone to capture the anticipated cat fight which would be great on one of those "Instant Karma" streams.

The voice she recognized, the face not at all, but it was the hair that really threw her off; nevertheless, she now knew who this flower vendor was. She immediately rose to her feet, and with both hands cupped the face she would never recognize, topped by the goalie hair, and then kissed the soft lips of the woman she'd fallen in love with only 24 hours before.

Explanations followed, they were accepted, and the two were inseparable from that point on, and the video of their kiss went viral for a few days too. Doug played the bagpipes at their wedding, and now here they were, several years, and several hair styles later, at 4,500 feet flying to Bakersfield.

The I5 was still closed because of the earthquake and the 166 was jammed with all the cars and trucks that would otherwise be on the I5, so Donnie was flying her Cessna since the weather was good, and Hillary was in a big hurry to get to BFL to help her mom with Doug who'd evidently gone off the asphalt and down a delusional embankment.

Hillary was looking out the window at the farms and fields below, her thoughts thrashing between her dad's deteriorating condition, what to do about it, the impending zombie-apocalypse predicted by her neurological model, and why everybody still seemed to be acting kind of normal even though their inhibition centroids were essentially offline.

Hillary knew for a fact that her inhibition centroid was working just fine since she'd wanted to scream several times during the flight, not out of fear or anything, just frustration. She thought that perhaps because of her prosopagnosia that there was some linkage between the fusiform gyrus and the inhibition centroid. She was just designing an experiment to test this new hypothesis, when Donnie handed her a stick of gum to chew for the descent into BFL, "Here, start chomping so you don't get an earache."

And as she reached over to accept the gum, she glanced into Donnie's smiling face, and then froze.

Donnie was confused by the response. Hillary was staring at her, unblinking, with a look of stunned disbelief. "What? I thought you liked Juicy Fruit?"

Hillary didn't respond, she just kept staring, as if totally confused.

Donnie fished around in her flight bag, "I might have some peppermint in my flight bag, but it'll be kinda old and stiff."

Hillary finally blinked and then spoke, "No. Juicy Fruit is fine." She took the stick of gum, but didn't take her eyes off Donnie, "Thanks."

"What? You okay?"

Hillary smiled and nodded and then looked straight ahead out the window, "Yeah." Her hands were shaking as she unwrapped the gum, but Donnie was now busy with knobs and switches and flying the airplane and didn't notice.

Hillary finally put the gum in her mouth. She was totally exhilarated and equally confused by what she had seen, something impossible, maybe even a miracle. She could recognize Pokémon's face, and Hello Kitty's face, and Sponge Bob's face, but not her mother's or her father's, or even her own. But today for some reason, she recognized Donnie's face.

Chapter Twenty-Eight

It Starts with an "M"

"**I**t's a Muh... it's a Mmm... it starts with an 'M'... it's one of those things that can't happen, but then it does anyway... like when Jesus walked on water and turned it into wine... a millennial, that's it, it's a millennial, a millennial!"

The landing at Meadows Field was uneventful, but the arrival at Doug and Audrey's was quite the opposite. The rental car turned through the gate and followed the drive up to the main house. Hillary was in the passenger seat with her eyes closed, trying to prepare herself for what was to come. Donnie was in the driver's seat, "What the fuck?"

Hillary opened her eyes to see a group of adults and children playing in the sprinklers on the lawn, while her dad hosed down a man at the head of a short line of dirty homeless people, one of them in a wheelchair. The man shook himself like a dog and then trotted onto the lawn to join the others playing in the sprinklers. Doug waved at Hillary and Donnie as they came to a stop but continued his hosing duties.

It was at this point that Audrey appeared at Hillary's window with a wooden spoon, shouting about millennials, so perhaps both of her parents had gone psychotic.

They were then joined by Doug and his garden hose, "Hey you're just in time for the spaghetti!" He gestured with his garden hose, "I got'm all cleaned up pretty much so we can take'm into the house when they dry off, but there's a bunch more out there we gotta go find!"

The Cessna made a low pass over the Mustard Seed National Cemetery. Donnie was flying and Hertell was looking out the window at the dry hills below, trying to get his bearings. He was also trying to visualize from memory, the mosaic of scram-n-scatter maps that now floated peacefully in the lightless, flooded gymnasium far beneath the brown hillsides he was now flying over. It was proving to be difficult, not because of his memory though. It was fairly easy to dredge up the mental image of the old maps, the difficulty arose from the fact that the surface world had changed so much in the years since the maps were originally drawn. Where there was once nothing but barren, trackless Sierra foothills with only an occasional dirt road or powerline for reference, there was now a spidery network of roads, and a patchwork of fields, and vineyards, and golf courses, gated communities, and gentleman horse ranches, there was even an artificial lake for high-decibel boat drag races.

"We can hear you, but we can't see you." It was Doug, he was somewhere below in the Silverado followed by Hillary in a van they'd rented right after they finished their spaghetti dinner the night before. Donnie had her cell phone paired with the Nav/Com stack, so they could talk to Doug and Hillary through their aviation headsets and not have to shout over the engine noise.

"Lemme climb higher on the return leg, so you'll have a better chance of seeing us." Which was true since she was loafing along at minimum speed at about 500 feet above the ground, and at that altitude they wouldn't see her unless she was right on top of them. She'd been a crop duster pilot, so she preferred flying low and slow anyway. "We're over the cemetery now and once we find Hertell's gully we'll work our way back to you, we'll let you know if we see anything."

The availability of an airplane had come to light during the spaghetti dinner. Audrey and Doug had pulled the ping-pong table from the garage along with some folding tables and chairs and served a massive spaghetti dinner on the driveway as Hertell's group was air drying. Hertell was eating in silence and obsessing about how to find all the other groups over a 20 square mile area with only a Silverado, a Jeep, and a Cushman, when the airplane was mentioned. That changed everything.

Donnie completed the preflight with a flashlight before dawn, something she was used to since she'd often had to make predawn crop duster flights to spray the nocturnal bugs, usually grubs and such, that chew through the night and sleep in for the day. She missed crop dusting, except for the shitty hours. And the other pilots, were generally okay, and most of them she actually liked. Funny thing about pilots, at least all the ones she knew, they didn't care how rich you were or famous or connected or degreed, all that mattered was how good a pilot you were, it was the only thing they all seemed to respect. They all respected her flying, and she was uniformly regarded as a good stick.

She'd started out as a fueler over at DesertAire on the eastern shore of the Salton Sea, just below Bombay Beach, mainly for rich doctors and dentists from LA who were there to get their floatplane endorsements. One of the floatplane instructors was also a crop duster pilot and got Donnie started as a flagger for Garriott's Crop Dusting down in Brawley. She traded labor for flight instruction, learned the trade from the ground up, was hired the day she reached 200 hours and passed her commercial check ride. She flew up and down the Imperial Valley and over south of Yuma spraying watermelon, sugar beets, carrots and lettuce and alfalfa until the whole crop duster business went extinct because of the Farmbots. They could look at a leaf or a bug, diagnose the problem, pick the right chemical and spray one leaf or one plant instead of a whole field.

She'd taken some black duct tape and formed the word "MUSTARD" on the underside of one wing, and "S E E D" on the underside of the other wing, and
"F O L L O W M E" across the top of the wings.

They took off at dawn and followed the 178 directly to Doug's house as the sun broke the horizon, but since they were flying due east, the sun was shining directly in their faces, so they'd have a better chance of spotting the other groups on the return leg when the sun would be behind them. They spotted the fallen cross first, then followed the dry wash to Hertell's gully which was about a mile east of the cross and still darkened from the previous day's muddy emergence. Now Hertell knew where they were.

"Donnie, from here we just go west and stay north of the river, everybody's going to be coming out from the gullies and washes that drain into it from the north."

Hertell had selected the easternmost scram-n-scatter route for his group since it would put him near the old wooden cross and allow him to reach the landmark first and be waiting for the rest of the groups as they made their way to it, on the second day of the emergence. Only it was now day two, and the cross was resting on a bed of razor wire and chain-link fence. It was also in an entirely different place, over a mile from where Hertell had marked its position on all the other 79 scram-n-scatter maps, and in an entirely different direction. The scram-n-scatter maps would be useless, and the other groups would be wandering, lost, looking in the wrong direction for a cross that wasn't even there anymore.

Donnie leveled off, reduced power, lowered the flaps a notch, opened her window for a better view down, and began the methodical, low, slow, back and forth pattern she'd flown all those years as a crop duster pilot. Hertell was surprised that you could fly with the window open, it was noisier but otherwise pleasant, so he opened his as well. He looked down at the brown earth below and wondered how many might still be trapped beneath it.

As it turns out, he needn't have worried about that at all. The escape route he'd picked was not only the easternmost escape route, it was also at the highest elevation in the entire network of escape routes. Consequently, when the Oceanoid bays flooded and the scram pumps failed, it largely only affected Hertell's group. The scram water continued to naturally flow downstream for the next 12 hours, where it slowly and meticulously cleared the remaining escape routes. And while Hertell was eating spaghetti and agonizing over their fate, the other 79 groups enjoyed pleasant candlelight dinners and slept comfortably through the night as the last few feet of confining earth was washed away leaving their escape passages glistening and wide open to the glorious outside world shortly before dawn.

The rest of the Mustard Seed population would emerge into the sunlight, clean and crisp and looking for an old wooden cross.

Chapter Twenty-Nine

Follow Me

"Okay we can see you now."

Doug and Hillary were standing next to the Silverado, shading their eyes from the morning sun, squinting at the shiny speck circling in the distance, and shouting into the cell phone, "We're on Rancheria where it crosses the river, we're at the bridge, and it looks like you're off a little east of us." Hillary corrected, "No, they're more northeast." The speck then turned and descended rapidly, disappearing from view behind a string of hills topped with freshly minted McMansions.

Hillary froze, "Donnie!" There was no answer. "Donnie, you promised not to crash without me!"

"No, we're here, we're fine." It was Hertell. "We're just... we just saw something..." There was garbled conversation in the background and it was hard to make out what they were saying over the engine noise. "And we went down for a closer look, and she's a really good pilot too."

Donnie finally joined the conversation, "We're just seeing something really weird."

After a long pause, Hertell finally spoke, "Okay, just drive north on Rancheria, we're a couple a miles up from where you are. You can't miss us."

Rancheria was a lightly traveled back road, used mainly by a handful of ranchers, and an occasional bird watcher, but it was still very early in the morning so it was basically untraveled, and unremarkable in every conceivable way, except for what Hertell and Donnie were seeing.

By all appearances, the surface world had experienced a spiritual reawakening in the years since the Mustard Seed civilization sought shelter, for the second time, beneath the earth. At least that was the supposition by Dannon and her group who stood beneath a large wooden cross. In fact, the place was abloom with tall wooden crosses, so many that they weren't sure which one to choose.

They'd emerged at sunrise since it had taken most of the night for the ebbing waters to clear the escape plug once the pumps went silent. They quickly but comically got over the fear of falling into the sky and, as the sun rose, proceeded down a sandy wash which ended at a culvert under a two-lane road. Dannon and her group looked up and down the road, and as far as they could see, in both directions, there were tall wooden crosses.

Sanford and Dannon examined the scram-n-scatter map, "Well, these aren't... on the map, but I figure we must be in the right neighborhood since... there's so many of'm."

It was at that point that they heard an airplane.

"Look, there's another one," Donnie turned the plane, "Right there, right around that bend by that other telephone pole." She pointed out Hertell's window, "Just follow the rivet line on the bottom of the wing, I've got it pointed right at them." Hertell's eyes dutifully followed the dotted line of rivets that ran the length of the wing down to the wing tip which was pointing directly at an awkward cluster of people.

Sanford and Dannon and the rest of the group looked up as the airplane flew barely 100 feet over their heads. They could see the words "MUSTARD SEED" on the wings. The airplane did a steep climbing, and as it turned, they could see the top of the wings, where it said, "F O L L O W M E."

It then circled back, flew over them again, and followed the road south, rocking its wings as if to say, "This way."

Sanford and Dannon waved at the plane as it passed, "Well it looks like Hertell... sent somebody to show us the way." The group started walking down Rancheria and watched as the airplane circled something in the distance.

Donnie was flying at 100 feet and minimum speed with the stall horn blaring, she lined up on the next group, less than a mile away, gathered beneath another telephone pole and flew over them, then throttled up, did her crop duster wingover so they could see the "FOLLOW ME," and then lined up on the road again to show them the way. Hertell tried to wave out the window at them, but the wind blast made it look more like a muscle spasm.

They repeated the process three more times as they'd sighted a total of four groups spread out along the road, usually separated by a hill or two, or a turn, but always gathered around a telephone pole. By the time they reached the last one, Doug and Hillary had arrived. Doug was taking on passengers and Hillary was driving ahead to meet up with the next group.

Since cellular technology had completely replaced the old, twisted pair, wired phone system, and the Oceanoid technology had replaced the entire power grid, the public utilities, in a last gasp to stave off bankruptcy, had salvaged all of the copper they had hanging from the biggest power transmission lines to the smallest sagging telephone poles. Leaving miles and miles of abandoned wooden crosses on the back roads and lanes of flyover country. So, the confusion of the Mustard Seed groups that day on Rancheria road was understandable, they'd all grown up underground where there was no need for telephone poles, or even telephones.

When the old wooden cross-telephone pole confusion was later explained to Hertell, he could not stop laughing about it, but that wouldn't happen for many more hours. Right now, they were returning to the river to follow it in search of the other wandering tribes of Mustard Seed. Donnie climbed to 1000 feet so they could take in a larger view and as they turned to the west, they saw something unusual in the distance.

Chapter Thirty

Street Faire

The Highway 178 express bypass had started out as part of the California Highspeed Rail Project at the turn of the century, to give California residents a more convenient, comfortable, and planet-saving public transportation option for losing their rent money at the sparkling new Yomash Indian Casinos crowding the shores of Lake Isabella. The casinos were made possible by a guilt and reparations-induced land grant from the US government in exchange for the tribe's claim to the property which now served as the Mustard Seed National Cemetery. The high-speed rail would cut straight east through the abandoned oil fields north of the river and along the foothills and then follow the Rancheria drainage north all the way to the casinos.

The roadbed was cut, graded, leveled, and then abandoned when the rail project was cancelled, and the governor and over a dozen dedicated public servants from the state assembly and senate went to jail. Undeterred, the industrious casino lobby got a bond measure passed and turned the abandoned high-speed railroad into a regular asphalt road. Specifically, a 6-lane freeway straight into acres of digital slots, climate-controlled Texas Hold'em, all-you-can-eat-buffets, covered parking with RV hookups, amphitheaters abloom with Beyoncé and Jay-Z retrospectives, and a water park for the kids.

Donnie and Hertell turned toward the west with the sun at their back, and were approaching what appeared to be a massive freeway. Only this freeway seemed to be in the midst of an early morning street faire or block party of some kind. Admittedly a very strange one because, in addition to people, it was sprinkled with casino tour buses, CalTrans trucks and workers in orange vests, Highway Patrol SUVs, and an assortment of cars blocking all southbound lanes. They could see that some sections of the freeway had collapsed into massive sinkholes, while other sections were riven with deep fissures.

Hertell looked down and noted a section of freeway that was blocked by a pile of muddy debris fanning out from a large hole at the center of a deep roadcut. He immediately thought of his Li'l Pal roadcut, and the rock and squirrel induced roadblock of his youth. No squirrels this time, just a large group of people on their hands and knees near the yawning hole in the roadcut.

"What the hell are they doing?" Donnie banked into a tight orbit, "Did everybody lose their contact lenses all at once or something?"

Hertell looked out the window and shook his head, "No, it's just Twila and her group getting used to the sky." It was at that point that Hertell clonked his head on the ceiling of the plane as Donnie executed a steep and terrifying, but mercifully

169

short, dive and then leveled out a few wingspans above the ground.

She'd developed a skill as a crop duster pilot and it basically amounted to: if you think you see a power line or an irrigation standpipe or anything else that could kill you, it's best to presume that it's real and act immediately and definitively. She'd once singlehandedly harvested a large swath of spinach this way diving to avoid a nearly invisible power line in the middle of a field outside Brawley. However, in this case it wasn't a power line or a standpipe but rather a Channel 29 News copter that was now passing over them, blissfully unaware of the near miss.

Donnie pulled up into a climbing turn to get back to a safe altitude and well above the helicopter now hovering over the unusual street faire below. Hertell was rubbing the top of his head, though the padded headset absorbed most of his interaction with the ceiling. Donnie punched in the air-to-air frequency, and keyed the mic, "Helicopter vicinity Rancheria Road, do you copy?" No response. She tried the fixed wing frequency with the same result.

The Channel 29 News copter was one of the last actual flying news helicopters, since most had been replaced by drones with gyro-stabilized HD cameras and teenagers flying them from their phones. But this was too big an event for drones and teenagers since it was clear that numerous communities north of the river were beset by broken water mains and heretofore unknown artesian wells, which for some reason seemed to attract people in casual attire of the early '60s.

"This is action news copter 29 with continuing coverage of the Bakersfield flooding emergency, and we've come directly from the Rio Bravo Country Club which has flood damage on several fairways and stranded a large group of early morning golfers. Authorities aren't sure at this point what's causing the flooding, but they believe it's most likely related to climate... uh... climate... that thing that happens when things don't stay what they were before. And what we're looking at now is flood damage to the Highway 178 Express which appears to be totally blocked by debris, so if you're heading up to the casinos, you'll want to take an alternate route to the shrimp and lobster smorgasbord, and the Snoop Dog Hoedown is fantastic so you don't want to miss that show."

Hertell and Donnie continued to circle and guide Doug and Hillary to round up, wrangle, and corral the new batch of confused and disoriented Mustard Seed refugees, but it was a losing battle because it seems that Bakersfield had grown quite a bit in their absence. So rather than emerging undetected in remote locations like Hertell's gully on Rancheria Road, Hertell found Mustard Seed clusters emerging right in the middle of things: a freeway in this case, but also a golf course, a luxury subdivision, a business park, a soccer complex, a mobile home court, a vineyard, and a Trader Joe's parking lot.

And while they found a few handfuls of Mustard Seed pods sprouting in these scattered locations, Hertell would soon learn that the bulk of Mustard Seed emerged in a single place a short distance to the west.

"And we're now getting reports that there's major flood damage on the CRAVE campus including the stadium and the performing arts center and the Rapture IMAX. We're coming up on it now, and if you haven't experienced the Rapture IMAX, you owe it to yourself, even if you're not a devout, you know... uh... it's a c-word... no not the one you're thinking... back to you Burleigh."

Chapter Thirty-One

Sunrise Service

O rbin woke up before dawn and reached out for his wife. He patted around on her side of the bed feeling for her, or just her warmth lingering in the blankets, but it was cool. "Hey, where'd you wander off to?" He finally fluttered his eyes open and then, as his hand stroked the cool sheets, he remembered, *Oh, that's right, she's dead.* He stared at the ceiling for a time as his head cleared, speculating on what the sleeping arrangements would be when he finally joined her in Heaven.

She'd died some years before, after he'd founded the Christ Resurrected Ascendant Victory Everlasting Church, but old habits and muscle memory linger, and no matter what he tried, he'd always wake up and feel for her. He tried sleeping on a couch, and a twin bed, and even a hammock once, but it didn't make any difference. Every time he emerged from REM sleep, he'd reach out for her no matter where he was. He eventually surrendered to it and returned to his side of their bed where he found himself the morning of what would be a most eventful Easter Sunrise Service.

Orbin was a large man, with a bullet-shaped head shaved to obscure his male pattern baldness. He had a sweet soft voice and tired eyes. He had taken a very sharp religious turn after the destruction of Mustard Seed, and in an act of atonement for his contribution to its demise, founded the CRAVE church. He was a good friend of both Hertell and the people of Mustard Seed from their first emergence. He'd helped Hertell introduce the newly discovered civilization to the modern world and knew most of them to some degree. He was a good friend up until he showed up in his Kern County Sheriff uniform that day over ten years before. He'd called in every favor he had in the favor bank to be the one sent, in the hope that, since he was a friend of Hertell and the people of Mustard Seed, there wouldn't be complications.

Nevertheless, complications ensued and resulted in the founding of Orbin's church. He was driven partly by self-contempt, survivor-guilt, perpetrator-guilt, bystander-guilt, a whole Crayola box of guilt hues, but mostly by a vision that came to him in a dream.

He was on a small boat with Jesus, who was sleeping on some cushions in the back. The apostles were there too and were discussing the weather because they were in the middle of a big storm, and the boat was getting tossed around. Jesus kept sleeping comfortably though, until He sneezed and woke Himself up, and then started patting around on His robe looking for a Kleenex. The apostles were still distracted by the weather and didn't notice. Jesus was just about to wipe His nose on His sleeve, but Orbin offered a Kleenex so Jesus could blow His nose, and when He did it sounded like all those trumpets they always talk about in the Bible. Then Jesus shook His head and spoke to Orbin, "Dang horsehair." He wound up and blew His nose again, and then as the trumpets resounded, threw the Kleenex into the water with a little bit of a swishy flourish "Thanks, and ya know you really worked for the wrong side on the Mustard Seed thing, you need to do something to make up for that. And if you do, I tell you truly, that you will be blessed in Heaven and sit at my side on Judgement Day."

Even though he was a regular churchgoer, Orbin had never once had a dream with Jesus in it, much less one in which His wishes and the consequences were so specific. So Orbin felt it best to not ignore such a gift and founded a small church on the corner of Golden State Avenue and "V" street in Bakersfield. And similar to Doug's experience with the blog, podcast, binge-worthy series, and Broadway Musical, Orbin's church seemed to tap into something in the global zeitgeist, and it succeeded beyond his wildest dreams.

It started out modestly in an old wrestling arena, the "Dome" as it was called locally. The Dome had started life as a cattle auction pen with an awning and some bleachers in the years before WWII. It went upscale when an enterprising professional wrestler, and occasional Hollywood stunt double, turned it into the central valley architectural marvel of its time during the war—serving and satisfying wrestling fans for several decades, long before WWE smackdowns and steroids and folding chairs. It went through several subsequent transformations, a concert venue, a Mexican Pentecostal Church, which closed when the minister died from a rattlesnake bite, but it sat vacant in its later years until resurrected by Orbin and his church.

Orbin's church rapidly outgrew the Dome, so regular Sunday services were moved to the Bakersfield Civic Auditorium, a massive affair that resembled the Seattle Space Needle, only without the needle parts. Just the gigantic flying saucer part, squatting on Truxtun Avenue looking as if it had flown directly from the set of *The Day the Earth Stood Still*. However, this flying saucer could accommodate nearly 10,000 people and reached that number almost every Sunday to hear Orbin make sweet and softly spoken sermons on a variety of topics.

His sermons always began the same way. He would stand staring silently at his feet, and when the choir stopped, and the crowd was silent, he would look up at them and smile and say, "Let's try to be logical about all this, for the Lord is not in the wind, and the Lord is not in the fire. The Lord is in a still small voice." He would always end with a prayer for the gone, but not forgotten, lost civilization of Mustard Seed, "Who once walked among us, and will someday again, hand in hand, on God's celestial shore. Amen."

Orbin had grown up going to Sunrise Services that were held every Easter at the foot of the massive old wooden cross that once crowned a barren hilltop at the western edge of the Li'l Pal Heaven overlooking Highway 178. He was quite young at the time, and it seemed to him that there were thousands of people in attendance, in addition to his grandmother and an assortment of cousins. They would park on the side of the 178, get out of the warm car and walk to the foot of Calvary and then join the multitudes to sing "The Old Rugged Cross" as the sun broke the horizon.

At the time, and at his young age, Orbin didn't realize that it wasn't the actual cross that Jesus was crucified on. Eventually an older and helpful cousin corrected Orbin's misconception, and confirmed that Jesus wasn't killed on it, or even in Bakersfield, but actually a good distance away, out in the desert somewhere, way out past Mojave and closer to Boron.

But they stopped going to the old rugged cross after Gramma Spencer died, and Orbin and his cousins thereafter slept in on Easter mornings. The Sunrise Services tapered off slowly over the years, and the old rugged cross was reduced to a mere roadside curiosity to any drivers looking east from Highway 178. It was eventually removed since it fell within the boundaries of the Mustard Seed National Cemetery where such religious totems were not allowed. There hadn't been a formal Sunrise Service in the greater Bakersfield area since the second Clinton administration, not until Orbin revived the practice.

The CRAVE Easter Sunrise Service grew quickly from the Dome's parking lot with worshipers spilling onto the Farmer John's Pancake House parking lot (which dramatically increased post-service pancake sales). The Pancake House eagerly anticipated the next Easter, but the CRAVE church had outgrown the neighborhood and the next Sunrise Service was conducted in Memorial Stadium on the Bakersfield Junior College campus. It was a great location since it ran east-west, enabling the rising sun to emerge over the end zone where a crane was positioned and fully extended with an old rugged cross crowning the very top.

The local ACLU protested as did the BC Student Atheist Club; however, an anonymous donor from Silicon Valley had made a generous eight-figure donation to the Junior College, so the governing board decided to permit the event in order to promote diversity and be inclusive, and they promised that any other religious group, or even anti-religious group, could use Memorial Stadium for Easter Sunrise Services too if they wanted.

Almost 20,000 people filled the stands because a rumor had swept the interwebs that a miracle was to occur, even though nobody was sure what the miracle would be or why news of it had spread so virally, but evidently forgetting things seemed to be making people more open to such possibilities. People seemed to be looking for something, something you couldn't buy online or get on your phone or from a bot or from the Government, and Orbin and his church seemed to be addressing this underserved and ever-expanding market. The Memorial Stadium parking lot had license plates from Arizona, Nevada, and even Utah because they were all expecting a miracle.

And Orbin delivered one. As the choir sang, and the crowd looked east, past the goalpost and the crane and the cross, toward the brightening sky, the sun broke the horizon.

Lives again our glorious King! Alleluia!
Where, O death, is now thy sting? Alleluia!

The crowd squinted, some put on sunglasses, but most held up their iPhones.

Once He died our souls to save, Alleluia!
Where thy victory, O grave? Alleluia!

The sun crawled up the goalposts and then up the crane toward the crowning wooden cross perched at its tip.

Soar we now where Christ hath led, Alleluia!
Foll'wing our exalted Head, Alleluia!

And then the sun came to a complete stop. And hung there motionless, directly behind the massive wooden cross, a radiant, blinding halo of light framing and engulfing it. And all who saw it were amazed.

Made like Him, like Him we rise, Alleluia!
Ours the cross, the grave, the skies, Alleluia!

And as the choir, and now the stands, trailed off the last "Alleluia," there was a big fucking earthquake.

The whole stadium seemed to slosh back and forth, but the sun, the crane and the crowning cross were motionless through the entire 17 seconds of the magnitude 7.3 event as if gyro-stabilized. And it was all captured by over 8,000 shaking, jerking iPhones and streaming the world over in seconds, accompanied by voices of a stadium full of people. Only they weren't screaming in fear as tradition, and human nature would dictate, but instead it was as if all 20,000 voices had naturally and instinctively converged on some cosmic, or more probably, miracle-inspired chord.

It was indeed a miracle, albeit a local one, and only observable by the people who happened to be in Bakersfield that day, sitting in Memorial Stadium, at sunrise, looking in the right direction, and at just the right angle. To the rest of California, it was no miracle at all, just stuff flying off shelves, freeways collapsing, and people freaking out, the usual. But to the people in Memorial Stadium that day it was definitely a miracle.

The miracle was of course immediately and reflexively denounced by a number of organizations as an obvious and laughable YouTube hoax, easily faked with Premiere or Final Cut Pro or almost any opensource video editing software. Though they did have to concede that it was identically faked from multiple angles in over 8,000 separate videos that were sweeping the globe.

In keeping with the tenets of the Christ Resurrected Ascendant Victory Everlasting Church, it was later determined that there was a rational explanation for the miracle since the crane actually was gyro-stabilized and that there was an inversion layer that morning that may have created the illusion that the sun had come to a stop behind the cross. However, it didn't really matter to the people in the stands that day, or the people viewing the video streams in the days and weeks after.

It was like one of those movies where the hero is captured by a tribe of primitives in some jungle, only he knows there's going to be an eclipse, and tells them that he commands the sun and they should do what he says, and then when the eclipse happens, they all think he's a god. It was kind of like that, only nobody in Memorial Stadium or on the web thought that Orbin was a god, since there was a rational explanation for the miracle. They just figured he was on to something, and they should come along for the ride.

And Orbin continued to deliver logical miracles every year that followed. Nothing as big as temporarily stopping the sun just when an earthquake happened, but still a string of noticeable rational miracles. He never planned them, they just happened, and compounded his following month on month and year on year, from the Dome, to the flying saucer on Truxtun, to Memorial Stadium, to the sprawling CRAVE campus and theme park.

Where Orbin now sat on the edge of his bed in the CRAVE Prayer Tower, wondering what miracle was mischievously lurking in the wings that morning, waiting patiently for the sun to rise.

Chapter Thirty-Two

Performance Art

C RAVE wasn't a mere megachurch with a university side car. It was more of an apocalyptic theme park with over 5000 acres of attractions nestled among the folds and slopes of the lumpy hills north of the Kern River. It included reproductions of Golgotha, Gethsemane, Via Dolorosa, various seven headed beasts, flaming chariots and the like, and the Rapture with souls streaming up to Heaven. The augmented reality glasses they gave to visitors made it almost like a really good video game, only with Jesus and the Anti-Christ, who vaguely resembled Jeff Bezos. It was all great fun and evidently quite compelling since Hertell would later learn that Orbin's ministry had gathered hundreds of millions of people in its worldwide net since its inception, many of them because of a "Mustard Seed" Duck-n-Cover app that had a dedicated and passionate worldwide following—bigger even than World of Warcraft.

The Performing Arts Center had been built into a low bluff to eco-blend with the local landscape. Kind of like one of those sod houses on the prairie scratched into the leeward side of a hill to shield the hard-scrabble homesteaders from the scourging winds. Only this one was much bigger and designed by a Frank Gehry acolyte so it looked more like a gargantuan glass and copper fish struggling out of the hillside. Some people felt it looked more like a boat. Others thought it was more like a boat-fish hybrid, while many thought it resembled a large misshapen loaf of artisanal bread or perhaps a swollen baguette. All of which were acceptable since boats and fish and bread figured prominently in the New Testament, and everyone appreciated the architectural nod to the glory of God and the suffering and sacrifice of His only begotten Son. And it looked really cool too.

The Performing Arts Center was regularly used for Sunday services, in addition to assorted popular specialty acts from Las Vegas and Branson on other days of the week. However, since it was Easter Sunday and the Sunrise Service was traditionally held in Rapture Stadium to accommodate the massive crowds, the center was empty. Empty except for the mud and debris which filled the orchestra pit and the first dozen rows of VIP seating near the front. There was a gaping hole in the north wall and a wide boulevard of muddy tracks that led toward the lobby. The motion alarms summoned security who arrived to find an assortment of people, in casual attire of the early '60s, gathered in the lobby, crouching near the windows, looking up, and somewhat apprehensively, into the moonlit sky.

Security had been quickly overwhelmed in the predawn hours with clamoring alarms from across the campus and adjoining theme park and worship complex as geysers, gushers, and flash floods riddled the length and breadth of the enterprise. And all of it was captured by motion tracking surveillance cameras and drones that would soon be streaming the video across the interwebs for all the world to see. The night staff at the operations center dozed through most of it, but were finally roused to a groggy state to witness the event unfolding on a hundred monitors as over 700 people emerged from the earth with the rising sun.

Orbin missed all of this excitement since his Prayer Tower was a windowless spire and completely off the grid. There was water and electricity of course, and a small bathroom, and a minibar in case he got hungry while praying, but he never did. It wasn't a monastic statement or anything since he had spacious living quarters on campus and generally ate with the students in one of the many dining commons. And as its name would suggest, he only prayed in the Prayer Tower, and the only time he slept in it was the night before Easter.

There was no internet, or WiFi, not even a TV or a radio, just the bed he once shared with his wife of 46 years, the bed she had died in only hours shy of that first Easter Miracle of the Halted Sun & Earthquake in Memorial Stadium five Easters past. It was as good a passing as one could hope to have, and she died peacefully in her sleep a few minutes after midnight as Orbin held her hand and told her how to recognize various relatives of his once she got to Heaven.

"Gramma Spencer was a chain smoker. Don't know if they allow smoking up there, but if you see a woman looks like

Lucille Ball smoking a cigarette, that's probly her. She'll probly know who you are, but just in case, just tell her that you're Butchie's wife. Uncle Beau looked like that guy in *Forbidden Planet*, only he had a laugh sounded just like a machine gun, actually more like how Popeye laughs, and he wasn't trying to be funny or anything, it's just how he laughed..." Her hand was cold, and he knew she was gone, but he couldn't stop talking. "He'll be pretty easy to spot if they're laughing about anything up there, I figure they gotta laugh sometimes, you can't sit around all day praying, you'd never get anything done, and heck, you gotta get stuff done, even in Heaven."

He went on like that for the rest of that night, then leaned over and kissed her hand one last time, "And Denise, when you get up there, tell'm we could use a miracle down here, nothing fancy, just noticeable, something to show people we're not just a buncha dumbass toothless snake-shakers. Something to show that we're... onto something." He got up, crossed her hands over her chest, and then got dressed, called the funeral home, and went to Memorial Stadium where his wife had evidently managed to arrange the miracle-of-the-halted-sun-and-earthquake, all the way from Heaven, fresh upon her arrival there.

While some might find it creepy, even ghoulish to sleep in your beloved's death bed, Orbin felt that taking it to the dump or trying to sell it on Craigslist would dishonor both her memory and the resultant miracle. He didn't consider it a shrine or anything, but felt that somehow it played a hand in the miracle, and he wasn't going to mess with that. And besides that, it was a really good bed and they'd spent many happy nights on it. So, when Prayer Tower construction was completed, he moved it in and slept in it every Easter since. And every Easter it delivered, as it would this day. He made their bed, showered and shaved, put on his golden robe, and took the elevator down to the pre-dawn campus.

He'd intended to walk to the Nicodemus Dining Commons for a cup of coffee since it had a 24/7 Starbucks for the students, and then proceed to Rapture Stadium well before sunrise to be ready for the choir and the opening prayer. In route he noticed a cluster of people standing in the headlights of an SUV interacting with several of the security staff in front the Performing Arts Center. He presumed they were some out-of-towners that missed all of the flashlight-wielding parking attendants directing traffic to event parking, and wandered onto campus and got lost. He approached the security team, who seemed to be engaged in an animated discussion with the group's leader.

"Hey troops, I can take it from here, I'm heading up to Rapture anyway, and we can get'm a cup of coffee too if they want..."

The security chief was greatly relieved to see Orbin in his golden robe, "Pastor Orbin, it looks like these 'Up With People' singers got locked in the PAC somehow, and they made a bigger mess than 'Blue Man Group' and got the lobby all muddy and tracked up, and you can see for yourself all the mud in there..."

The lobby was brightly lit, and true enough there were muddy tracks crisscrossing the golden lobby carpet.

"We unlocked it and told'm to come on out, and they wouldn't at first, saying they were gonna fall into the sky, and I don't know what they're on, but this ain't Burning Man here, that's over in the... the... where all the cactus is and Satan tempted Jesus."

The group stood quietly and politely squinting in the headlights, over a dozen of them and all looking at the man in the golden robe, who seemed to be a figure of authority.

"But we finally convinced'm they weren't gonna fall into the sky and got'm to come on out, and not one of'm have any kind of ID at all, not a driver's license between'm, and I don't know how they got here without one of'm driving. They just keep saying they're from Mustard Seed and that they just come up from outa the ground... Pastor Orbin? Pastor Orbin?"

Orbin wasn't really listening, instead he was staring at a man in the group, a tall black man in his forties. He knew this man, and then he recognized another man, and then a woman. He didn't recognize any of the kids but everybody over the age of about 30 he knew. "Travis?"

The man in his forties stared at Orbin for a few blinks, followed by a flicker of recognition, "Deputy Obi?"

Orbin pointed into the crowd, "Davey, Gwendy, Lloyd, Johnny Ray, Shelly, all of you, come on, follow me, this way."

Chapter Thirty-Three

Jumbotron

"This is action news copter 29 with continuing coverage of the Bakersfield flooding emergency, and we're now over the CRAVE campus, and there's extensive damage here as you can see…"

The accompanying imagery showed an assortment of muddy sinkholes, excavations, and debris flows scattered across the grounds, but strangely, not a single person was in sight.

"We're now approaching Rupture… no that's not right. We're coming up on the big stadium where the Apostles play, and they had a great season this year… and it appears that due to the flooding that everyone has been evacuated to the stadium that we're circling right now and as you can see the stands are completely full."

Rapture Stadium was built with the same east-west orientation as Memorial Stadium to maximize the Easter Sunrise Miracle Service viewing experience. It was well past football season, so the goalposts had been removed providing an unobstructed view of a massive cross towering above the Jumbotron screen at the east end of the field, and beyond it, the rising sun.

"And there appears to be another very large group of refugees approaching the evacuation area from the east." The 29 News Copter camera zoomed in on the large crowd approaching the Jumbotron led by a man in a golden robe. The frame was suddenly filled with the spiderlike image of a video drone and then went blank, followed by SMPTE color bars.

The 29 News Copter then reported in a much higher octave, "We seem to have hit something, we think a drone and we see several others in the area, and it looks like we've lost the ball camera, but it's quite a sight here with all the humanity and all the people but they all appear to be okay, so back to you Burleigh!"

Orbin hadn't stopped for coffee at the Nicodemus 24/7 Starbucks, but had instead led his small Mustard Seed flock from the PAC through the main campus toward Rapture stadium, collecting more Mustard Seed pods from all over the campus as he went. Drones were buzzing overhead helping the security teams locate and then shepherd the confused flocks toward Orbin's ever expanding procession, their radios alive with chatter:

"We've got a large group here at the trap and skeet range... Fourteen here at the Hidden Treasure Food Court... Horseshoe pit reports fifteen, no sixteen..."

Between radio calls directing security where to join the formation, Orbin was told the same basic story over and over again with each new group, by people he knew to be dead, Gwendy and Lloyd, Kathy and Craig and Mae and

Will. Only they weren't dead, they were very much alive and quite talkative and didn't seem to begrudge the fact that he'd played a hand in their death. Quite the opposite, they seemed genuinely glad to see someone they knew, first thing upon their reemergence onto the surface world:

"We've been down there this whole time... But the earthquake started water flooding in... That beard looks really good on you Obi... We're meeting the rest up here at a big wooden cross..."

They were unanimous in their agreement that they hadn't expected such a warm reception, and in fact had expected quite the opposite based on experience from their last visit to the surface. And as the sun emerged to the east and they made their way across campus, past the bell towers and the fountains and the dormitories, it was all starting to make sense to Orbin, and it all seemed very logical.

A helicopter swooped overhead angling toward Rapture Stadium, which Orbin could see in the distance. The stadium was now aglow in the morning sun. Normally, Orbin would have been delivering his sermon as the sun rose behind the Jumbotron cross, but rounding up the Mustard Seed resurrected had blown the original Easter Sunrise Service schedule. So Orbin had used his walkie-talkie to advise the stage manager of the delay, and that it was going to be worth the wait. The choir kept a vamp of hymns going as the sun rose higher in the sky, and the concessions and food trucks out in the event parking lot did a brisk business.

The last three flocks joined the procession as they approached the east end of the stadium. The helicopter was gone, but Orbin could now see that the stands were full and the choir was at full throttle. His procession was over 700 strong now, and he led them under the Jumbotron and the towering cross and into the end zone as the choir finished their hymn and the stands went silent.

Orbin led the procession down the length of the football field and then mounted the massive raised, golden pulpit, tapped the mic, and waited for the reverberating echo to fade. "So, let's be logical about this, for the Lord is not in the wind. And the Lord is not in the fire. The Lord is in a still, small, voice."

Only this voice sounded more like an airplane. It narrowly missed the Jumbotron and the towering cross; however, it didn't miss the formation of drones that were capturing the event for the worldwide audience watching on the web. Plastic and tangled bits of shredded electronic components showered the end zone, as the airplane's engine faltered, and then stopped.

Chapter Thirty-Four

Rapture Stadium

D onnie was clearly in violation of Title 14 of the Code
of Federal Regulations, Section 91.119 of the General
Operating and Flight Rules which states:

> No person may operate an aircraft over any
> congested area of a city, town, or settlement, or
> over any open-air assembly of persons, at an
> altitude less than 1,000 feet above the highest
> obstacle within a horizontal radius of 2,000 feet
> of the aircraft.

She was now well below 500 feet, losing what little altitude
she had left, directly into an open-air stadium brimming with
persons, and the only place to land was straight ahead on
the AstroTurf. The engine had stopped and her gliding, silent
airplane was festooned with an assortment of aerial drone
parts snared on the wing struts and tangled on the landing
gear. The highest, and only, obstacle was what appeared to
be a Super Bowl Halftime stage at the far end of the field,

surrounded by a large crowd, and topped by a man in a golden robe, flanked by choirs, a brass ensemble, a tympani section, a harp, a Hammond B3 organ, potted palm trees, and evidently, because it was Bakersfield, a guy in a cowboy hat with a pedal steel guitar.

Hertell had been keeping a mental tally of all the groups they'd spotted so far that morning, with each group comprised of happy people he knew and loved waving up at him. But this place was different. They had just finished circling a massive building that vaguely resembled a fish and Hertell wasn't seeing any of the Mustard Seed diaspora. He wasn't seeing any people at all, the whole area seemed to be abandoned. All he was seeing was an assortment of muddy excavations and debris fields scattered across acres of buildings and food courts and bike paths and swimming pools and greenspaces and dormitories.

He also knew that he was at the western edge of the scram-n-scatter maps, and as he saw and tallied each of the muddy scars, he had a growing sense of dread. Perhaps only the water itself had managed to escape to the surface, and the people he knew were still below, pale, and lifeless, and silent, suspended in the flooded blackness.

"Can you pretend like this is a cotton field and do the back and forth crop-duster thing? I can't keep track of where we are and what we've seen." Donnie didn't have a chance to respond since the conversation was truncated with a loud bang. "Sonuvabitch!" She was looking out her side window at a jumble of black plastic that was now hugging the wing strut, trailing wires, rattling, and slapping at the air, "Snagged a drone!"

She'd often encountered runaway mylar balloons as well as some agricultural drones during her crop-duster days, before that career went the way of the buggy whip, and she therefore knew how to deal with the nuisance. She started waggling the wings and walking the rudders to shake the tangled mess loose. But to no avail, the former drone was firmly wedged against the wing root, plus the rocking and yawing was making Hertell sick. He was about to let Donnie know about his condition when he noticed something looming into view.

Hertell tapped her on the shoulder and pointed straight ahead, "Are we gonna hit that?" Donnie looked up just in time to bank and avoid a massive cross which brought Rapture Stadium, and a gaggle of drones into full view. The Cessna's propeller shredded several drones but lost a piece of propeller blade in the process setting off an attention-getting vibration that shook the headsets and sunglasses off both Donnie and Hertell.

Because she had a passenger, Donnie didn't feel she had the luxury of panic; pilots are funny that way. She calmly pulled the mixture, shut off the fuel to kill the engine, dropped the flaps the rest of the way, and then in a very comforting shout, over the blaring stall warning horn, told Hertell, "It's okay, I've done this before."

Which was partly true, since all pilots have to simulate engine-out emergency landings every couple of years, and she'd also made numerous bladder-emergency off-airport landings on sod farms near El Centro, plus several real engine-out emergency landings. However, this would be her first time executing an emergency landing, stylishly accessorized with drone parts, on a football field with a crowd looking on. She picked a landing spot, side-slipped to lose her remaining altitude and touched down just past the 20-yard line.

The last few seconds of the flight seemed like so many days to Hertell. He looked out his window at the wing and the lazily undulating black plastic and wires trailing from the strut, and the wide-eyed people in the distant stands who were pointing at him. He looked forward and saw all of the Mustard Seed people he'd imagined to be dead in the watery darkness beneath the hills, now very much alive and determined to stay that way by scattering: Mike and Will, Ginger and Wayne, Johnny and Karen, Paulie and John, Kurt and Phil. He was just tallying the total headcount when he was distracted by a jolt.

The 205 skidded sideways and shuddered to a stop in the end zone, a little shy of the Super Bowl Halftime stage and the large group of people who were now approaching. Donnie's hands were still shaking from the fading adrenaline as she fished around for her cell phone, "See, told ya it'd be okay, gotta call before Hillary freaks out, you okay?"

Hertell opened his door and immediately puked on the tire. He unstrapped, carefully stumbled over the spaghetti he'd had for breakfast earlier that morning, and kneeled on the prickly plastic AstroTurf to let his nausea dissipate. And as his head cleared, he was approached by a man in a golden robe. Hertell wiped his mouth on his sleeve and looked up at him.

"Orbin?"

Hertell hadn't seen Orbin since the day he'd appeared in his Kern County Deputy Sheriff Uniform, accompanied by a pair of patrol SUVs and a line of prisoner transport buses to take Hertell and the good people of Mustard Seed into custody for a variety of offenses. But today Orbin wasn't wearing his Kern County Sheriff Uniform, he was wearing a flowing golden robe, and he stood motionless staring at Hertell. Orbin then spoke softly, in a disbelieving whisper.

"Jesus H. Christ"

Hertell looked up at the stands and the Jumbotron and then back at Orbin, "Looks like we caught you in the middle of something..."

Orbin raised one arm toward the heavens and turned to face the 20,000 faithful in the surrounding stands, all of them on their feet. He then raised his other arm into the air, and the stands sang out, all in one voice. But Hertell didn't recognize the tune.

Chapter Thirty-Five

Get Technical

Hertell offered no resistance when Orbin led him through the smiling, back-patting, and genuinely exhilarated Mustard Seed throngs as he made his way toward the stage all within a few minutes, though it seemed much longer to Hertell:

"Glad you made it out Hertell... We never saw that big cross on the map you made for us... Orbin brought us to this other big cross up at the top there... Quite a welcome, we coulda come up here a long time ago!"

Orbin had immediately recognized the significance of the morning's events. The pieces had fallen into a perfect crystalline order as he led the resurrected dead of Mustard Seed to Rapture Stadium, and now, as he stood on stage with Hertell, it was all so undeniably logical. He pointed at the people in casual attire of the early '60s surrounding the stage and then looked up into the stands.

"Behold the Mustard Seed dead, almost... no, over ten years in their common... uh... common... that place in the ground where you put dead people."

The harpist volunteered, "Grave?"

"Yes, exactly, grave! Behold the Mustard Seed dead, ten years buried, lifeless in their common grave, who now are arisen and standing among us!"

Hertell was surprised at the comment, "What? Well no, actually, we weren't..."

Orbin was on a roll and didn't catch the clarification, "Lifted from their graves by the cleansing holy waters that washed the corrupting earth away, to join fellow believers here above, including us, at the foot of the great cross, atop the Rapture Jumbotron."

The Jumbotron screen had a flattering close up of Hertell and Orbin with the chyron crawl along the bottom of the screen reading, "Breaking... Easter Miracle... Rapture...It's Here...Breaking..."

Orbin raised both arms to the stands above, who responded in what seemed like one voice. Hertell found the sound strangely beautiful, but also kind of troubling. He used the opportunity, to offer his clarification again, "Actually, Orbin, we weren't actually dead, at all."

Orbin lowered his hands and the stands went silent, "Please say that again, so everybody can hear it. Right here into the mic."

Hertell leaned into the mic, "I said that actually..." He leaned a little too close to the mic as he was immediately drowned out by deafening feedback. "Maybe not so close." Hertell backed off a bit, "I said that actually we weren't, you know, dead, we've been alive this whole time, we've been living down there since that whole dust up with the county."

Orbin lifted a massive bible from the pulpit, opened it, and held it up to the stands, "Ezekiel 25 or 6-2-4" and then as if reading, "I tell you truly, we weren't, you know, dead, we've been alive this whole time..."

Hertell was confused by the comment, "It says that? Really?"

Orbin turned to Hertell, "But see to us..." he gestured toward the stands, "You actually were dead, we thought you all to be dead down there. It was official and everything, you were legally all dead. You were so dead they even built a whole national cemetery over you. Say Alleluia!"

The choir responded with reflexive but sincere, head-bobbing murmurs of "Alleluia." If the stands responded, Hertell couldn't hear it over the humming of the drones which had returned to capture and stream the Easter miracle.

"So even though you weren't technically dead, you were logically dead to us, you see? And that's the beauty of this. It's logical, it's rational, it's undeniable. A prophesy has come to pass before our very eyes, and a promise has been fulfilled!"

He turned and addressed the towering stands, "Because we all know that the living Christ taught us with parables, and parables aren't technical, literal, they're symbolic, like this here, to reveal the larger and more... truthful truth." He gestured toward the people of Mustard Seed gathered below, "Behold! The risen dead of the Rapture, right here in Rapture Stadium."

He then turned and pointed at Hertell "Behold! The second coming of Christ the Blessed Redeemer!"

Hertell noticed that Orbin was pointing at him, so he turned and looked over his shoulder to see if the Blessed Redeemer was actually lurking back by one of the big potted palm trees. No obvious Jesus, just the choir and a brass ensemble, a guy in a cowboy hat, an organist, and a harpist, all of them smiling at him.

"Behold, Jesus Christ Himself, hath returned to the earth!" Orbin raised both arms into the air and the stands did that one voice thing again.

Hertell laughed, "Orbin, it's me it's Hertell, I'm not..." He then caught himself, and considered that perhaps Orbin had somehow forgotten his name in the short time since the plane crash, since that was certainly possible with the pole reversal and everybody forgetting stuff. He tapped Orbin on the shoulder to get his attention, "Orbin, Orbin..."

Orbin lowered his arms and the stands went quiet.

"Sorry for the confusion Orbin, and I know, because of the magnetic pole reversal that people are forgetting things, so you probably just forgot, but my name is Hertell, not Jesus Christ. Remember? Hertell?"

Orbin opened the massive bible again, flipped to a random page, and held it up to the stands, "Isaiah 65:17" and then as if reading, "See, I will create new heavens and a new Earth. The former things will not be remembered, nor will they come to mind!"

Orbin did the arms in the air thing again and the stands responded with the one voice thing.

Hertell blinked a few times, and considered that perhaps because people were forgetting stuff, including bible stuff, that they might in general be more open to any random statement, when said with confidence and authority, and properly referenced, as being valid. He nodded slightly and then shrugged, "Uh, okay."

Orbin smiled warmly and looked at Hertell, but spoke into the mic, "The Son of God can call himself anything he wants, and if he wants us to call him *Hertell*, that's good enough for us!"

"Okay, but I'm not Jesus, Orbin. I wanna make sure we're real clear on that, and all you people up there too, in the bleachers. I was never dead, technically like Orbin said, and it's true I did come up out of the ground, but I was never dead, and didn't rise from it, and didn't descend from Heaven in a lightning bolt with angels or anything like they talk about in the Bible. And yeah, I came out of the sky, but it was in that airplane down there with Donnie, and she's no angel."

He pointed down at Donnie who was sitting on top of the old Cessna. She seemed to be enjoying the spectacle and waved up at the stands and shouted, "Definitely no angel!"

"See, so this is all perfectly explainable, highly unusual, there's no denying that, and kinda weird too, but you can't make up stuff any weirder than it really is. And this is really weird, I admit, but it's not a, you know, miracle."

Orbin laughed and looked up into the stands, "Do we think that God can't do explainable miracles? That the only arrows in His holy quiver are angels flapping around in the air, and lightning bolts, seven headed beasts and all that?"

The choir and the stands responded in a deafening, "NO!"

"Do we think God could pull off something as simple as what we see here, a perfectly explainable, but highly unusual and weird and improbable miracle, without having to resort to cheesy gimmicks like burning bushes and flying chariots and shit like that?"

The choir and the stands responded again in a deafening, "YES!" Donnie even joined in from atop the Cessna, "Fuck yeah!"

Orbin turned to Hertell and put his hand on his shoulder, and then started very softly, accompanied by preacher chords on the Hammond B3.

"The hand of God is all over this Hertell, and I'll keep calling you Hertell if that's what you want. He had you find all those people all those years ago living underground. He had me betray you and try to put you all in jail. He dropped that bomb on you and buried you out there in the National Cemetery. He kept you alive beneath it, all of you. He flooded you out, so you had to come back up here. He put you in that plane. He made the plane crash right here in Rapture stadium, of all places. Imagine that. What are the odds? All the pieces are here, and they all add up, you just don't realize the significance of all this yet, and who you really are. The 'H' in 'Jesus H Christ' probly stands for 'Hertell' only nobody knew that except God. But we do now. And if God can send His Son down to us, the first time in a crappy little skid mark town in the Holy Lands with a knocked-up teenage girl and her clueless carpenter boyfriend, then I think it's safe to say He can do it with a hick from Bakersfield named Hertell in a shitty little airplane that says, 'Follow Me' on the wing."

Hertell heard Donnie's staccato laugh from below, and immediately knew why Orbin had such a large and devoted following since his was definitely not your average homily. However, he didn't know quite how to respond as he was unprepared for Orbin's line of reasoning, since admittedly if there was a God, and He was omni-everything, then He could do pretty much anything He wanted, including the Rapture and second coming of Christ in a Cessna as so described. There was also no denying that Orbin's style, while definitely unconventional, was nevertheless strangely persuasive in its own way.

Hertell decided that there was no point in arguing the matter in public, and that he'd be able to disabuse Orbin of his misconception in subsequent discussions without the 20,000 onlookers and the distracting one voice thing they kept doing. He shrugged and looked at Orbin.

"Well, okay Orbin. Your assertions are well reasoned and articulately expressed, and it's a free country, and you guys can all believe whatever you want. But to minimize confusion, I'd prefer if you'd just call me Hertell."

He thought for a moment, and then pointed to the Mustard Seed cluster surrounding the stage, "And maybe help me take care of the people here that just came up out of the ground."

Orbin turned to face the stands, "Can we help Hertell, the Son of man, care for the risen dead?"

The choir and the stands responded again in a thundering, "YES!" The Jumbotron even had a big zooming, "YES" that exploded into a starburst cascade of sparkling crosses.

Chapter Thirty-Six

Tiny Bubbles

I t all happened so fast that it immediately became a broadly accepted fact: a reassuring one to some, a troubling one to others, and a laughable one to the rest. At least at first.

An M-word of biblical proportions had occurred: the dead had risen from the grave, exactly 777 of them, a biblically significant number for those so inclined, and Jesus had descended from the heavens—even though He wasn't named Jesus this time, and didn't make His entrance on a white horse with a bunch of angels riding drag, but instead in a Cessna 205 on the Rapture Stadium football field. However, when the assorted earthquakes, locust plagues, COVID-666 outbreaks, and other sundry events were factored in, the basics of the millennial prophesy were fulfilled, and the coin toss for the End Times had just been officially flipped.

The event had instantaneously streamed from almost 20,000 phones and several hundred security cameras and drones, directly into the ravenous gaping maw of the content ecosystem, as it was happening. Within an hour, thousands of content aggregators had processed the raw imagery, audio, and associated text, and generated the basic narrative storyline. Thus, providing fodder to AI algorithms where it was colored, flavored, textured and extruded to maximize appeal to various monetized target markets, and the 24/7 news cycle.

The AI shaped and spun the story for every conceivable social, cultural, and political bubble that could be identified or otherwise conjured from the tracks and scat piles of a trillion clicks and taps and swipes left-and-right, so that each bubble could have its every fear fueled, every bias confirmed, and every conceit justified.

The classical bubbles of yore had long since gone out of fashion: left, right, progressive, moderate, religious but not spiritual, spiritual but not religious, etc. The bubbles didn't even have names anymore, they were just clusters of mathematical tensors in n-dimensional space along with some metadata with linear equation sidecars.

The people in the bubbles didn't even know that they were in a bubble, but the math knew what they needed to see, read, watch, and hear, and it obliged. The bubbles were quite reassuring since everything within them seemed to be reasonable and rational, where beliefs were shared, and common truths were held to be self-evident and therefore undeniable except to those too stupid, or too stubborn, or too evil to share.

And while the facts of the Mustard Seed emergence were solid—they had indeed risen from the earth and were not, in fact, dead—the collective perceived truth was so infinitely malleable and ductile that it could be heated, hammered, and stretched into any shape any bubble required.

Chapter Thirty-Seven

End Times Kick Off

I n Hertell's case, the bubble included not only the 20,000 or so in Rapture Stadium, but also upwards of 200 million worldwide in the first 24 hours, and north of two billion in the following weeks as news of the M-word propagated across all Christendom. No hammering or shaping was required for this particular bubble since it was a long-anticipated miracle, which they were totally open to, and very invested in. Some progressive Moslems even got into it, presuming that Hertell was the 12th Imam fresh out of the cave.

Hertell didn't know about the bubbles, but simply assumed that organized religion had undergone something of a change in the intervening years, and that the threshold for miracles had been significantly lowered.

Orbin was concluding the event with a long rambling blessing about walking hand in hand on God's celestial shore, and then asked Hertell if he had any final words to offer.

Hertell was drawn from his thoughts, "What?"

Orbin swept his arm toward the towering stands, "How shall we consecrate the miracle of this blessed day?"

Hertell looked up into the bright sky, and for a moment felt like he was going to sneeze, but it passed. He rubbed his nose, "Well, looks like it's shaping up to be a really nice afternoon, so you might just go and have a barbecue or something." He was struck by a thought, "Are watermelons ripe yet?"

Donnie called out from the Cessna, "Not for another month, unless you get the ones from Mexico."

Hertell nodded, "Well if there isn't American watermelon, then I guess Mexican watermelon could be fine, it wouldn't be a barbecue without watermelon." He loved watermelon, and he didn't realize how much he missed it until it became a possibility.

Orbin addressed the stands, "You heard the Son of God! He tells you truly, go forth, have a barbecue! And don't forget the watermelon, even if it's Mexican!" He then signaled the choir, brass ensemble, organ, harp, and steel guitar to start the exit music vamp.

Hail in the time appointed, His reign on Earth begun!

He then immediately started thumbing through his massive bible, as the Jumbotron lit up with flying graphics of hotdogs, hamburgers, and watermelons, and a big spinning "BBQ" that filled the massive screen.

He comes to break oppression, to set the captive free,
To take away transgression, and rule in equity.

Orbin caught up with Hertell as he was leaving the stage and held open his bible, "I found it right here in Numbers 11, watermelon, verse 5 and 6 where the Jews are bitching about not getting to eat watermelon like they used to when they were slaves in Egypt, but it doesn't say anything at all about Mexico..." He was struck by a thought, "Hey, you wanna use my Prayer Tower to chill out, it's got a minibar in case you get hungry, but no WiFi or anything like that to distract you from praying and checking in with God and such."

He comes with succor speedy, to those who suffer wrong.
To help the poor and needy, and bid the weak be strong;

Hertell rubbed his cheek and thought, "No I'll just go back to the airplane down there, I've got a snack in it, but thanks, I'm good."

To give them songs for sighing, their darkness turn to light,
whose souls, condemned and dying, are precious in his sight.

He sat in the plane listening to the choir and harp and steel guitar, and watched the people in the stands slowly stir. It was all strangely comforting, and it was at that point that he noticed he couldn't focus his eyes. He was staring into the stands, but he couldn't make out the actual people anymore, they looked more like pixels or little particles, specks, each with slightly different colors and textures that seemed to be jostling randomly and slowly moving. He knew that the blurry specks were actually people with thoughts and desires and souls, if there was such a thing, but all he could see were the blurry particles.

In his darker moments Hertell surrendered to the bleak recognition that people are simply particles: dead matter that for a mere flicker in cosmogenic time are randomly arranged in such a way that we are alive, and conscious, and aware of our existence, and the existence of the universe, and aware of how totally accidental and immaterial we are to it. And that once we die it's all gone, and we are mere dead matter again, our consciousness blinks out, along with all of our hopes and dreams and desires, and we cease to exist, and in a way it's as if we never did exist, or the universe either for that matter.

He didn't want to be a cynic because that was just too easy. He tried to believe all the Jesus stuff that Kaye and all those other people believed. He even managed to convince himself to believe some of it on occasion while fully aware that it was all irrational and childlike and simplistic, but that in biblical times they had to keep it simple since there was no knowledge of the scientific method or DNA or quantum mechanics and that the only way to explain things to people back then was with lambs and fish and mustard seeds and what not.

What a fellowship, what a joy divine,
Leaning on the everlasting arms;
What a blessedness, what a peace is mine,
Leaning on the everlasting arms.

But try as he might to be one of those contented believers, he nevertheless had the lurking suspicion, the dread, that it was all total bullshit – no heaven no hell no good no evil no salvation and no excuse. That in reality it all ends with us and that it's all basically pointless.

Leaning, leaning,
Safe and secure from all alarms;
Leaning, leaning,
Leaning on the everlasting arms.

The universe doesn't give a shit if we're here or not, or if we're aware of it, or marvel at it, or know how it works with big bangs and black holes and dark matter and all the math.

What have I to dread, what have I to fear,
Leaning on the everlasting arms;
I have blessed peace with my Lord so near,
Leaning on the everlasting arms.

Nevertheless, the music was nice, and the words often beautiful and reassuring, and people seemed happier for all of it. So maybe it wasn't total bullshit.

Leaning, leaning,
Safe and secure from all alarms;
Leaning, leaning,
Leaning on the everlasting arms.

And then he sneezed. His vision cleared, and the particles became people again.

It took several hours, but the people left the stands in a very excited and buoyant state, no doubt greatly relieved that the

End Times were not to be observed with prayer and fasting or self-flagellation or hair shirts, but rather with a barbecue, complemented by some Mexican watermelon. As such, it wasn't a very demanding miracle and generally one people were happy to accommodate. They completely bought out the T-shirt, baseball cap, and koozie vendors in the parking lot since everybody wanted a souvenir from the End Times kick off.

Chapter Thirty-Eight

"H" is for "Hertell"

T he miracle was long over and the stands empty when Hillary and Kaye found Hertell and Donnie at the Cessna. Hertell apologized again for throwing up on the tire, and they all left in the Silverado. The 178 Express Bypass was closed, so it was a circuitous but otherwise pleasant drive from Rapture Stadium back to Doug's estate. Hertell was lost in his own thoughts, and Kaye could not stop laughing.

"The H is for Hertell?" She was laughing so hard she gave herself the hiccups, "You gotta be fuck(hic)ing kidding me!"

Hertell shook his head, "Orbin's convinced, and there's no talking him out of it, same for all his people, thousands of'm, don't even know how many of'm were up there."

Donnie was driving, "An imperial fuck ton, the whole place was crammed fulla people and they kept doing this weird song thing that was kinda cool but kinda creepy too."

"Nineteen thousand six hundred and seventy-seven in the stands, it looks like 15 million streaming, and it's trending up..." Hillary was in the back seat thumbing her phone.

The conversation continued and ranged over such topics as how Donnie would get the Cessna out of Rapture stadium, how Hillary gathered the Mustard Seed evacuees from the various golf courses, parking lots, and freeways, and delivered them to her parents' house for spaghetti, croquet, and an Easter egg hunt among other diversions.

Kaye was trying to get rid of her hiccups while pointing out various scriptural inconsistencies concerning Hertell in the role of God's Son and the second coming of the Christ, "But techni(hic)ally, you're seven years ahead of schedule Hertell... I mean Blessed Redeemer."

Hertell listened and would occasionally nod and vocalize an acknowledgement, but he was mainly thinking about Orbin and his "miracle." It was a very compelling story, and even though their interpretation of events was preposterously and demonstrably false, Hertell had to acknowledge that it was obviously internally consistent in Orbin's head, and presumably the 20,000 other heads in Rapture Stadium. Obviously, like organized religion, logic had also undergone something of a transformation in the years since Hertell and the rest had abandoned the surface. Most likely it was another subtle effect of the magnetic pole reversal and people forgetting stuff which made them much more open to various permutations, shades, and approximations of logic.

Which was probably why nothing he said to Orbin and the 20,000 in Rapture Stadium could convince them otherwise. For every rational explanation Hertell made, Orbin offered a compelling alternative interpretation and counter argument, insisting that the miracle was entirely rational and logical.

It wasn't like the classical logic of the Greeks since nobody remembered that anyway even before the poles switched, or who the Greeks were for that matter, except perhaps for college kids in sororities or math classes. No rigid and unforgiving P's or Q's to wrestle with, but a more agile and evolved version of logic in keeping with the times.

He instinctively sensed that Occam's Razor would definitely slice in favor of a biblical miracle since it was a much simpler and therefore more plausible explanation—in contrast to the alternative which required the simultaneous and serendipitous appearance of nearly a thousand people, long buried and presumed dead, to emerge from the earth on Easter Sunday, and converge on Rapture Stadium just as an airplane landed on it.

"Because the present age, that goes from back when Jesus was cruci(hic)fied and rose from the grave all the way up through now, ends with the Rapture and all the dead rising up from the ground and going up to Heaven. So, if all of us coming up out of the ground is supposed to be the Rapture with a capital 'R', then we're all supposed to be in Heaven right now, not in Bakersfield..." She started laughing again.

"Tell Orbin then Kaye, you don't need to convince me."

However, Hertell knew from his time in the history shed that the concept of End Times appeared in every cultural and religious tradition, and that people intuitively, and subconsciously project their own flawed and finite lives onto that of the whole human experiment. And since everything eventually ends anyway, songs, movies, civilizations, meals, suns, us, why not humankind? What makes it so special to think it can dodge that bullet? He considered the assortment of existential-threat-end-of-the-world folk tales like climate change, K-T class asteroids, viruses from the jungle or Chinese bio labs, and so forth, that had been dazzling us for so many decades, to be the contemporary equivalent. Consequently, the whole concept of End Times was a familiar one, with everybody kind of looking forward to them in one way or another – the same way people want to see UFOs land or a professional wrestler or a game show host get elected President, just to see what happens.

"And we're supposed to spend the next seven years up there in Heaven sitting around God's throne with the 24 seated elders and the four beasts and a bunch of other stuff I don't re(hic)member, while everybody down here on Earth is going through the Tri... uh the Tribal... Triglyceride...you know... the thing..."

Donnie snapped her fingers, "Trilobite."

"Yeah, the Trilobite and the big Anti(hic)christ thing. And then finally at the end of seven years you come back, on a horse I think, or maybe it was a donkey, doesn't matter, you get back and do the whole Armageddon thing and destroy all the nations in a world war. You got that on your to-do (hic) list?"

Hertell shook his head, "I smell cigarettes." He sniffed the air and looked around the cab, "Anybody else smell'm?"

Hillary was still thumbing her phone, "No, but you're at nineteen million now, and you've got no-skip ads on YouTube."

Kaye was undaunted, "There's a buncha (hic) other stuff I forget, but just at the top level, the timing is all off, this doesn't meet the specs of the Book of Revelation at all. Orbin's got it totally wrong, it's not the End Times and you're not Jesus H. Christ..." Then she started laughing again.

"I know, but it's still very stressful because they're all looking at me and waiting for the other shoe to drop on the End Times. Nobody else smells cigarettes?"

Hillary looked up from her phone and sniffed the air, "No, and nothing against you, Hertell, I mean my dad says you're the best guy he's ever known and everything, but how fucked up must the world be, for it to think you're Jesus Christ."

"It's not so much me, I don't think, it's more the circumstances."

Donnie nodded in agreement, "Yeah and on the list of problems to have, you could do a lot worse than being mistaken for Jesus Christ, I mean..." She hesitated and although she wasn't raised in a particularly religious home, she knew the basics of the storyline, "Though... I guess it didn't work out so well for Him that last time."

Kaye had stopped laughing, but she still had the hiccups, "That's not in the playbook this time, Jesus wins this one, for like a thousand years, and then there's lakes of fire after that and a bunch of other stuff, but Jesus comes out okay and the oceans dry up and everybody gets a fig tree I think, no maybe it was different kind of tree, I forget the name, but you can make guacamole out of it."

There was a spirited discussion of the best guacamole recipes, but the conversation took an unanticipated turn when Hertell, who'd been otherwise slumped disconsolately in the passenger seat, slowly leaned forward, placed both hands on the dashboard as if to steady himself, and then said softly, "Garner just died."

Chapter Thirty-Nine

To-Do List

T here was a fire engine and an ambulance at the house when they arrived in the Silverado.

The day had passed pleasantly enough, with Doug and Hillary rounding up the scattered flocks sprinkled across golf courses, parking lots, and freeways, delivering fresh vanloads of the risen dead to Doug's estate.

The procession went on for most of the day, each new batch of arrivals greeted and directed to the bathroom or kitchen or library or game room, or sewing room, or music room or wherever their urges, appetites, or interests took them. But most stayed outside and lounged on couches, chairs, benches, stools, and any other stick of furniture that could be dragged out of the house or garage and positioned somewhere under the actual sky. Not painted rock, however artfully rendered, but a real sky with a few wispy clouds and an occasional bird or airplane. Most of the furniture was arrayed around the perimeter of the massive lawn where a spirited croquet tournament was under way.

Audrey and Kaye had made a Costco run the previous night, after renting the van, and had filled it with supplies for the multitudes they anticipated arriving the next day. It was the usual stuff you'd expect, plus Easter candy since it was on sale and plentiful. The only special request they got was from Garner, for a pack of Camel cigarettes, the old-fashioned kind, short and stubby. The kind you'd see drooping from Bogart's mouth in an old movie, but they had to stop at three different minimarts before they finally found some at Wimpy's Liquor on Chester, the only place that actually still sold them.

Audrey was a Basque from Reno and woke up every Easter until her mid-teens to find a beribboned Easter basket spilling over with green paper grass, jelly beans, Hershey Kisses, Brach's marshmallow eggs, and a towering chocolate bunny as the center piece. After Mass there were epic Easter egg hunts with locust plagues of cousins scourging backyards and front yards and side yards in search of marshmallow Peeps, and multi-colored, vinegar-scented hard-boiled eggs. She'd done the same for Hillary in her youth and carried on the tradition for the thirty or so Mustard Seed kids that had accumulated throughout the morning. She'd put a crew of moms and dads to work that morning boiling, coloring, and secreting the eggs and Easter candy across the extensive grounds.

By noon the Easter egg hunt was over, the candy inhaled, the Cozy Coupe resurrected, and the croquet tournament announced. There was a large assembly in the driveway surrounding the ping pong table, and some smaller groups down by the casting pond, the patio, the Gazebo, and the chicken yard, but Garner had decided to spend his day at the croquet tournament.

With some help from Dannon, who'd arrived with the second batch earlier that morning, he'd positioned himself midfield opposite the peg with the afternoon sun on his back. Sandy helped him from his wheelchair and settled him into a big Adirondack chair, and then went to join the game. Some of the kids were passing out multicolored hard-boiled eggs to the spectators. Garner accepted one, the first one he'd held in over 70 years, and then cracked and rolled it on the broad flat arm of the Adirondack.

From where Garner sat eating the hard-boiled egg, he could see in the distance, the faint line of cyclone fence on the hillsides of the Mustard Seed National Cemetery, where he'd been buried for so many years. It was maybe a mile away, and he could see the gap in the fence where they'd cut down the big wooden cross to bridge their escape from the cemetery scarcely 24 hours before. He'd watched the sunset with everybody else that first afternoon, the real sun, so his to-do list was officially complete. He'd only been hanging on to make sure everybody got out okay anyway. The sunset at day's end was the cherry on top, and he was comfortable with the idea that it would be the last he would ever see.

He pulled the pack of Camels out of his shirt pocket and then removed his nasal cannula and dropped it to the ground. He looked at the fragile little bundle in his hand, gave it a gentle squeeze, and marveled at the grip it once had on so many people. He was never much of a smoker, it was more of a ritual than a habit, and it was easy for him to quit once Mustard Seed ran out of cigarettes back in 1966 or so. Nevertheless, they were a happy memory of his youth on the surface many decades before.

He pulled the red tab to jettison the cellophane wrapper, tore off the three bits of silvery paper revealing the tight formation of cigarettes huddled below. He tapped the pack against his knuckle a few times to get the formation to advance, pulled one of the slim soldiers out of formation and put it in his mouth. He fumbled with the book of matches since he hadn't struck a match in over 70 years, but he finally got the soldier lit. He took a shallow drag, actually more of a puff, since he remembered his mistake from almost 80 years in the past of taking too big a drag and the convulsive, eye-bulging coughs it could induce. It was mainly for effect and resulted in a lazy halo of blue-grey smoke that gathered about his head and shoulders.

He didn't take another puff, but instead rested his hand on the broad face of the Adirondack and let his cigarette burn, almost like a stick of sacred incense. He took a deep breath and savored the smell. It smelled like being eighteen years old again with nothing but the future and freedom and promise on the horizon.

He watched the game for a while and then dozed off for a bit. It was a dreamless, non-committal doze. He was mainly listening with his eyes closed. He could hear everything, the wind in the trees, the sound the leaves made when they brushed against each other, Dot's shopping squeaking past, the Cozy Coupe horn tooting off in the distance somewhere. This was good. This was a good way to spend the afternoon, and the rest of his life, sitting outside, the real one, under a real sky.

He felt something warm in his hand. He opened his eyes and saw that Dot was standing beside him watching the game. Her hand was in his palm.

He looked at her tiny hand in his palm and closed his fingers over hers. Her hand was warm. Not hot, just warm, like a stone after a day in the sun.

He smiled to himself, "Well, ya know Dot, I think this is it. I think I'm ready to go now."

Dot turned to him and looked directly into his eyes, and then after a long pause, she nodded and said softly, "Bye bye."

Garner blinked a few times in disbelief. He then smiled, closed his eyes, and, finally, laughed one last time.

Dot stood with her hand in Garner's for the rest of the tournament, watching the game until Lox came to help Garner into his wheelchair. He leaned down to her and whispered, "Is he asleep?"

Dot shook her head, and sadly reported, "Bye bye."

Chapter Forty

Lights of Las Vegas

I t was the second time Doug had played the bagpipes in honor of Garner's passing. Today he was playing the pipes on a low hilltop overlooking the CRAVE Cemetery at the western edge of the Revelation theme park.

Like the campus and theme park, the cemetery itself was very new and well-manicured. While there were trees and fountains and benches and such, it only had two graves. One from several years back for Orbin's wife, Denise, which came complete with a massive statue of a grieving angel. The second, and freshest grave, was for Garner. No statue for him, just a plaque with his name, his birth year, and his death years, both of them. The first was for his bunker buster bomb death with the rest of Mustard Seed over ten years past, and the second was for his peaceful death the day after his resurrection while watching a croquet tournament in the afternoon sun.

Hertell had tried to use the occasion of Garner's death to disabuse Orbin of his belief that the emergence of Mustard Seed was, in fact, the Rapture: since, how could Garner die or stay dead if he'd already been Raptured or whatever. And if

Hertell was Jesus Christ, why didn't He just raise Garner from the dead like He did all those other times in the Bible?

However, Orbin insisted that there was a lot of wiggle room in the Bible and that more miracles weren't necessary anyway. Besides which, Garner was north of 90 years old and Orbin observed that miracles wouldn't be wasted on things you'd normally expect to happen anyway and especially on people who'd had such a good long run. So, it went out on social media that there would be a memorial service for Garner at the CRAVE cemetery officiated by Jesus Christ Himself, with the caveat that there would be no miracles this time.

The caveat worked and while north of 22 million virtually attended on the web, just in case there was a surprise miracle, Garner's memorial service was physically attended mostly by Mustard Seed folks since they actually knew him.

The service was over and the mourners were chatting and slowly ebbing away, mainly the adults since all of the kids had been taken to the Redeeming Blood Water Park adjoining Rapture Stadium.

It was a short service which Doug had concluded by playing "Amazing Grace." He stayed on his hilltop and watched as Audrey, Kaye, and Donnie chatted with each other by the funeral sprays and Hertell, Dot and Orbin and some others sat in the shade of the canopy beside the flag draped casket. Hillary was standing some distance away from the clumps of people below, near the grieving angel. She'd always been something of a mystery to Doug, in a good way though.

He was surprised and even flattered that she'd gone into psychology. He knew she wasn't much of a people person, so he figured it was a good choice for her to go into the research side of things and hook people up to jumper cables and whatever to explore what she described as "the mechanics of what people do." He wondered what she was thinking as she wandered over to the grieving angel statue and leaned on it.

Hillary was starting to hyperventilate, so she moved toward the stone angel to steady herself. She'd been looking at faces at the memorial service. Mainly the faces of the people she'd picked up from the various muddy craters and slopes and hillsides the week before. She'd transported over a hundred people that day to her parents' house and learned some of their names in the days that followed.

She'd resisted saying anything the day she'd recognized Donnie's face as they flew into Bakersfield, thinking that it may have been merely a transient, stress-induced delusion and not a neurological miracle. Besides which, it was completely overshadowed by the chaotic front yard scene that afternoon, and by the thundering hooves of the Mustard Seed stampede, and her role as head wrangler the following day. Nevertheless, the question of whether it was a delusion, phenomenon, miracle, whatever, demanded an answer.

While she'd recognized the faces of her mother and father the same day she recognized Donnie's, she'd written it off as based on subtle and otherwise subconscious morphological or auditory clues because they were all so familiar. She knew their gait, their posture, their mannerisms, the way they coughed and sneezed and yawned. She formulated a secret experiment to see if she could recognize total strangers, such as the people of Mustard Seed, that she'd met, conversed with, and transported to her parents' house. People she'd never, ever recognize again under normal circumstances.

But as she leaned against the statue, the realization kept sweeping over her that she was recognizing people's faces, and she couldn't catch her breath. They all looked... familiar. It was a feeling she'd never really experienced before, like seeing the ocean for the first time, or the sky. She'd lived her whole life seeing people only partially, and had never felt the joy of seeing a familiar face in a crowd.

And yet, there was Orbin and Hertell and Kaye and Dannon, like the yogurt. There was Sandy, her husband, they finished each other's sentences, and there was Lox and Babs, and Johnny and Karen, and Travis and Alicia, and it just kept going.

She knew what it was. Kind of. She'd had her grad students run the entire archive of fMRI imagery through the I2OHAB software with a series of new parameters. She was on a great correlation hunt, and her students were the game beaters, thrashing the underbrush until the elusive correlation took wing for Hillary the huntress. Only instead of clubs or flags or horns, they were using a series of parameters to fluff up the voxels in different parts of the archived brain imagery.

Sure enough, the PFC inhibition centroids were still basically offline, just as they had been in her fight-or-flight replication experiment, the one that predicted the zombie apocalypse, the one she presumed was still waiting in the wings for its cue to come onstage. However, the new parameters were flushing a new target into view. While the inhibition centroid was metabolically dormant, the fusiform gyrus was lit up like Las Vegas on New Year's Eve.

On a hunch, she ran her scary-spider-menstruation imagery with the same new parameters. She didn't have a whole month's worth of imagery since she'd stopped when the whole Mustard Seed thing happened the week before. Nevertheless, even on her laptop, she could see that her inhibition centroid was active, so she was different from the people in the archive imagery in that regard, but her fusiform gyrus, while not lit up like Las Vegas, was definitely illuminated on the order of a small casino off the strip.

It started as a dull glow, and incrementally grew brighter with each passing week, and it was brightest on the last image, the one she'd done the day she and Donnie flew to Bakersfield for her dad's presumed psychotic event. The day she'd recognized a human face for the first time in her life.

And now she was recognizing more faces as she leaned against the grieving angel. She didn't remember all their names, but she knew that she was recognizing their faces. Not just the features, the nose, mouth, eyebrows, but the whole face, the whole person almost.

Her breathing was starting to slow down and she didn't feel as lightheaded anymore. And as her thoughts cleared, she began to wonder if this thing, this Las Vegas fusiform gyrus thing, was making it so she could now recognize faces, something she could never do before, what effect could it be having on everybody else?

She was mentally constructing a new experiment to consider the time domain and determine the chronology of the Las Vegas fusiform gyrus phenomenon, but she was drawn from her thoughts by a helicopter landing on the cemetery lawn.

Chapter Forty-One

Notice to Appear

Most of the mourners had drifted off, Dot had fallen asleep on Hertell's shoulder, and a few others remained chatting around the gravesite when the helicopter landed. It landed a safe distance away, but still a little too close to the canopy tent adjoining the grave, so the propwash rolled the canopy over on its side and ultimately onto its back, like a giant beetle kicking its spindly aluminum legs in the air, which Dot thought was really funny.

The helicopter issued a young woman and a camera crew who approached Hertell and presented him with some papers.

"Hertell Daggett AKA Jesus Christ of Nazareth?"

Since he'd recently returned from the dead, and his prior address had been bulldozed and made into a National Cemetery, Hertell had no legal, formal, actionable presence on the surface of the earth: no street or office address, no email or cell phone, no Twitter handle or LinkedIn page. All he had was his mere existence. Consequently, when the subpoena was issued, no one knew precisely where to send it.

Hertell looked up from the subpoena, "I... is this referring to me?"

The woman stood with her hands on her hips and struck a pose of high dudgeon for the camera crew, "Yes, that is correct, it is referring to you."

It was an impressive document, with lots of parentheses and various blocks of text in **BOLD CAPS**, informing Hertell that he was in a big steaming pile of trouble and that they'd like to talk to him about it. Hertell presumed it to be related to the squirting of two Kern County employees with a garden hose some years prior, which escalated to SWAT teams, and assorted complications. However, the subpoena didn't mention any of that. So, Hertell assumed that because of the poles switching, all the offended parties had forgotten that historical affair, and that his offense this time was a fresh one.

Apparently Hertell's comments about Mexican watermelons, when combined with his high profile due to the widely held belief in certain circles that he was Jesus Christ returned to Earth, had prompted a rather extreme response from a spectrum of concerned, aggrieved, and otherwise outraged constituencies. It wasn't so much that he'd been outed as Jesus Christ, but rather it was his position on Mexican watermelon that had triggered the cascade of serious concerns, accusations and condemnations leading up to the subpoena to appear before the Congressional Joint Committee on Sensitivity, Hate, Inclusion, and Tolerance:

WHEREAS, HERTELL DAGGETT (YOU) AKA JESUS CHRIST (YOU) HAVE PUBLICLY AND OUTRAGEOUSLY OTHERED NOT ONLY MEXICAN WATERMELON AND THEREFORE MEXICO AND ALL MEXICANS AND ALL OTHER PEOPLE OF COLOR BY EXTENSION, YOU/YOU HAVE DONE IT ON THE BASIS OF AN EXCLUSIONARY AND OFFENSIVE RELIGIOUS PREJUDICE.

WHEREAS, THE COMMITTEE RECOGNIZES THAT WHILE THERE ARE MANY HISTORICALLY INDULGED PRECEDENTS FOR RELIGIOUS, CULTURAL, SPIRITUAL, AND OTHERWISE PRIMITIVE SUPERSTITIONS CONDEMNING VARIOUS FOODS BELIEVED TO BE UNCLEAN, HARMFUL, OR OTHERWISE EVIL (E.G., PORK, LOBSTER, SODIUM); YOU, THE ALLEGED SON OF GOD HAVE CONDEMNED THE REFERENCED FOOD ON THE BASIS OF ITS ETHNIC SOURCE, AND THE COMMITTEE HAS DETERMINED AND MOREOVER CONSIDER IT TO BE A VILE, DIVISIVE, DETESTABLE, AND DISGUSTING SENTIMENT, HOWEVER DIVINELY INSPIRED, HOLY, OR RELIGIOUSLY MOTIVATED.

WHEREAS AND MOREOVER, BY SPECIFICALLY EMPHASIZING THE WORD "WATERMELON" YOU/YOU HAVE INTENTIONALLY AND INSIDIOUSLY EMPLOYED AND OTHERWISE WIELDED AN OBVIOUS AND OFFENSIVE RACIAL SLUR OF THE MOST ODIOUS KIND WHICH ALSO SERVES AS AN INFLAMMATORY DOG-WHISTLE TO AROUSE AND INCITE LATENT, SYSTEMIC, SUBCONSCIOUS, AND SEMI-CONSCIOUS BIGOTRY.

THE COMMITTEE THEREFORE DEMANDS THAT YOU, ACTING IN YOUR CAPACITY AS THE SON

OF GOD, APPEAR BEFORE THE COMMITTEE
TO EXPLAIN THE RELIGIOUS SIGNIFICANCE OR
JUSTIFICATION OF YOUR STATEMENTS, AND/OR OFFER
A COMPLETE AND UNCONDITIONAL RETRACTION,
REFUTATION, DISAVOWAL AND CONDEMNATION OF
YOUR STATEMENTS AND THE RESULTANT WORLD-WIDE
HATE-FUELED SENTIMENTS, AND A PROMISE TO NOT SAY
ABDOMINAL THINGS LIKE THAT ANYMORE.

It went on for a bit longer but clearly the committee had thought long and hard about the issue. It concluded with a notice to contact the committee within 10 days to schedule an appearance, and it was signed by all 15 committee members in a rainbow of colored inks and in a variety of illegible but purposeful and indignant hands, with each signature block accompanied by the relevant email address, QR code, and URLs for their individual Facebook, Instagram, Twitter, TikTok, and GoFundMe links.

Orbin was reading the subpoena over Hertell's shoulder, "You people have this all wrong..."

The woman wasn't paying attention to Orbin, she was looking at the camera crew, "We good?" She was given a thumbs up.

Hertell was inwardly relieved to hear Orbin finally accept that the "H" in Jesus H Christ didn't stand for Hertell, but the feeling quickly dissipated when Orbin continued.

"Nazareth was His old address, from His first trip down here when they crucified him. This is a whole 'nother thing. He came from Heaven this time, and I don't know the address for that, but you can always find Him here at

Christ Resurrected Ascending Victory Everlasting Church, 777 Round Mountain Road, Bakersfield, California, 93306, and on the web at..."

The woman and the camera crew were already walking back to the helicopter and called back an acknowledgment, "Thanks! Got it!" She wasn't actually thumbing in the address, she was texting that she'd successfully served the subpoena, which she knew would help elevate her from intern to staffer. She'd been assigned the busywork task of monitoring the social media accounts of the CRAVE church and intercepted some posts, pics, and videos announcing the date, time, and location of a modest, private memorial service to be officiated by Jesus Christ Himself in the CRAVE cemetery. Since the intern was also the niece of the Joint Committee's Chairwoman, her diligence was rewarded with the privilege of serving the subpoena to the alleged Son of God, a camera crew to make it official, and a helicopter ride.

Hertell was still holding Dot as the helicopter lifted off. She waved at the camera crew as it flew away.

Chapter Forty-Two

Big Data

I t was eventually traced to a capture the flag (CTF) contest at a DEFCON hackers convention. It seems that one of the teams improperly, and in violation of contest rules, used a 9G chip vulnerability, commonly known as the cyber-vagina exploit (CVE) to penetrate, replicate, and exfiltrate (PRE) target system data. The team was immediately disqualified, but in protest released their PREbot into the wild, resulting in a massive data breach that flooded the globe over a long World Cup weekend. The tsunami of data included not only the tech titans, Google, Amazon, Apple, et al., but also millions of corporate, academic, and government websites of every hue and stripe, plus the various incarnations of the cloud.

The tech titans insisted that they had always planned on releasing all of the data from their walled gardens for the public good and commonweal, but everyone knew it was just an ass-covering, face-saving fig leaf. Nevertheless, it caused quite a stir at the time since it included browse histories, search-strings, spreadsheets, pdfs, every text, and junk pic posted, voicemails, emails, every word uttered within range of a WiFi device or a phone or a wristwatch, medical records, videos checked out from way back when there were video stores. All that plus the stealthily collected and mathematically fluffed and folded data used to recommend a movie or a book or a foot cream, and all of it timestamped and traceable to specific IP addresses and device serial numbers.

It was all pretty embarrassing too, and led to the resignation of an assortment of CEOs, governors, senators, university presidents, and a few regents, and also the implosion of a galaxy of esteemed and venerable institutions, non-profits, and NGOs: Sierra Club, NRA, NEA, ACLU, etc.

Even the political parties were affected since the data revealed levels of cynicism, hypocrisy, avarice, corruption, and deceit that so exceeded traditional and otherwise acceptable levels of such behavior, that ultimately both were engulfed, discredited, humiliated, and effectively reduced to smoking ruins. In an act of desperate self-preservation, they collectively decided to not only make sweeping changes in election laws, but also to change their names and rebrand. They even hired some marketing firms to help pick new logos and color schemes. Apples and oranges replaced donkeys and elephants, though nobody was sure which was which or why. As a sop to the aging baby-boomers, harvest gold and avocado green became the respective colors of the new parties which gave the US party maps a retro '70s look.

Hillary didn't care about the embarrassing or otherwise controversial data. She cared about the routine stuff, weather, demographic, financial, physiological, etc., which was now revealing something unusual. She'd noticed it first in the t-SNE visualizations. It was even more striking in the MSTs she'd generated. The zombie apocalypse that she'd been expecting was clearly not happening, but something else by all appearances clearly was.

She was running her archived fMRI imagery against some of the hacked data to establish the chronology of the whole Las Vegas fusiform gyrus phenomenon. The most promising strand she'd found thus far was in the consolidated failure logs from CAPTCHA—that dialog box that pops up with a grid of photos and asks the user to click on the road signs or driveways or streetlights or cliffs, all photographed at various angles and lighting conditions, so that the website knows if you're a real person that can be monetized or just a mere spambot. While distinguishing between a person and a bot might have been part of it, it was mainly a great way to collect petabytes of human-labeled imagery for free to train self-driving cars to obey road signs and pull into driveways and avoid running into streetlights and off cliffs.

Hillary wasn't interested in the road sign stuff, but rather in a subset of CAPTCHA failure data that was based on showing a person a grid of photos of random people, with one of the photos shown being of the person themselves, taken either directly from the user device camera or from an old Facebook image archive. The CAPTCHA dialog box would then ask the user to click on the image of themselves in the grid, and this is where it got interesting because, while the failure rate was initially zero, since people can always recognize their own face, over time the failure rate rose out of the random noise floor and began to monotonically increase until the failure rate was statistically 100%. At which point CAPTCHA stopped using the face grid protocol, since presumably it had successfully harvested petabytes of human-labeled facial recognition imagery for some unspecified purpose.

The CAPTCHA data (i.e., the millions of people who failed the CAPTCHA photo test) was not only a statistically valid sample of the larger population, but it was also almost perfectly correlated with her fusiform gyrus Vegas light show data over the exact same eight-year timeframe. No causality, but an interesting correlation.

It was all very promising, definitely a paper at least, and maybe even a book or a TED Talk. But then things took a surprising turn when she'd accidentally included the wrong dataset in a geospatial run. She'd always been slightly dyslexic and it was fairly common and often comical when she'd reverse two letters or numbers in a search string or parameter set and end up with spurious but hilarious correlations: Sperm counts to SAT scores, bra sizes to zip code, etc.

In this case she'd intended to use some GIS data from a USGDSM data set to plot the facial recognition data on a map to see if there were any geographical correlations, like people in legalized hemp states having a harder time recognizing their own faces or possibly a correlation with opioid hotspots. However, instead of typing in "USGDSM" she typed in "USGSMD" which was the USGS Magnetic Declination data set.

"Well fuck me dead." She sat in silence for a time, trying to make sense of what she was seeing and trying not to overreact or otherwise do anything to wake up Donnie who was sleeping on the floor next to her. This would be more than a paper. This would be big, maybe not Watson and Crick big, but big for her. The light show, the faces, the dates, the poles: all the strands were weaving a tapestry that told a story, like that one from the middle ages with guys on horses chopping each other up with swords.

She knew what she was seeing. She knew what this meant. People were failing to recognize their own faces. Not all of them and not all at once. The strands rose slowly and steadily out of the noise as millions of poor dumb slobs, each one of them clicking on the wrong photo, their fusiform gyrus going full Vegas and doing its level best to recognize its owner's face, and failing. And it all started when the poles reversed.

She looked down at Donnie, still stretched out on the floor from doing her back exercises, now snoozing on the rug, her beautiful dark face at peace, a face that she could now, by some miracle, finally recognize. She wondered if Donnie could still recognize her own face, or Hillary's for that matter since it now appeared that the whole world was slowly and steadily coming down with prosopagnosia.

Chapter Forty-Three

Lawyered Up

While Orbin's church had an aggressive and capable legal team, they were totally unprepared for a congressional subpoena since it didn't have to do with liability, taxes, mineral rights, HR, content licensing, or anything that was even remotely legal or illegal. Consequently, Orbin brought in some specialized talent because he felt that the Lord had been poorly served by His previous legal team, resulting in the Crucifixion, and Orbin was determined to not let that happen again.

The team was led by a well-connected DC-beltway rainmaker who had recently joined Orbin's church. Hertell actually remembered her since she'd once organized a presidential town hall meeting with the people of Mustard Seed in the weeks before the bunker buster incident. He'd lost track of her since then but was glad to see that she was well and had gone on to a rewarding career and become an active member of Orbin's church.

She was one of the many swept into Orbin's flock in the days following the Miracle-of-the-stopped-sun. Her conversion started at a Georgetown cocktail party at which videos of Orbin's Miracle were the laughable centerpiece. While others at the party tittered and lapped at their lemon drop martinis and tried to top each other's wry, sophisticated observations, she lapsed into thoughtful silence.

Her thoughtful silence eventually resulted in her taking a turn that no one in her circle expected, though they certainly understood it since they assumed her religious conversion was simply an act, a part of doing business, a strategic business decision, and not the lifechanging event that it actually was for her. Thus began the journey that brought Courtney to the conference room atop the fish-like Performing Arts Center overlooking the CRAVE campus. And now, here she was giving legal advice, to Hertell, AKA the Son of God.

"Okay, just remember it's not so much that you've done anything wrong, and certainly nothing illegal, but more that you have a platform and lot of visibility because half the country, maybe more, thinks you're the Son of God."

Hertell shifted in a massive, C-level executive chair, "That's Obi's thing, I never said I was the Son of God."

Courtney smiled knowingly, "Yes, and that's a very shrewd position to take."

Others in her team winked and nodded with overlapping affirmations, "Very shrewd... Totally shrewd and prudent... Very prudent given how it went for you the last time..."

Hertell shook his head, "It's not a position, it's the truth."

"Perfect, yes, whenever you speak be sure and start out like that, by saying things like 'truly I tell you...' this and that, and 'I tell you truly...' and so forth and so on."

Courtney's team chimed in, "And say 'unto' whenever you can... it is the most used word in the bible... 'unto' it has a very biblical cash... cashier...cashew..."

"I don't want to sound biblical, I'm not a biblical guy, and besides, I thought they wanted to talk about watermelon."

Courtney shook her head, "No, that's just a cover, it's just a way to get you in front of the committee and the cameras and the streaming services because every sitting member of the committee is running for president right now."

Hertell was surprised, "What, all of'm?"

"Yes, but that's just on the Joint Committee."

The others at the table contributed, "There's another 40 or so in the rest of congress... and that's down from over a hundred a month ago... it doesn't include the governors and mayors... and YouTubers and singers... and actors and cornholers and such."

While he would later learn that the traditional professional sports like basketball and football and baseball had been abandoned by fans years before in favor of non-political sports like curling, darts, and cornholing since they didn't normally start with the national anthem anyway, Hertell couldn't help but ask, "Anybody can run for president now?"

Courtney thumbed her phone, and nodded, "Yeah, once they proved anybody could be president a few years back. Voting already started, and they're all just trying to break out of the pack."

"People are voting for president? It's not time yet, is it?"

"They changed that a few years ago, it goes on for a whole year now, and only ends when somebody reaches the magic number, but the point is that half of them are gonna want an endorsement from you, and the other half are gonna want your scalp as the con man grifter fronting a bug-fuck crazy church."

Hertell nodded silently and immediately thought of dung beetles, part of his history shed reading from a tattered old *National Geographic*. And now he was commanded to appear before the human variant, with him being merely a fresh turd to be scuffled over. While there were many species of dung beetles, they generally fell into two broad categories, consumers or dwellers.

"So just pick a side and you'll be fine."

Hertell wondered which was which, consumer or dweller, "What, like Republican you mean?"

There was a dismayed groan from the team as they shook their heads violently, "No, no, no you can't say that..."

"So, Democrat then?"

Which released a flurry of admonitions, "Not that one either... My God no—uh sorry for taking your name in, whatever... Nobody's using those names anymore, they're toxic... Everybody hates them... It's the 'Us' party and the 'We' party now."

Hertell blinked a few times, "The Us party and the We party? Seriously, that's what they're called now?"

"Yeah, We and Us."

Hertell laughed, "Which is which?"

"It doesn't matter anymore. Once it turned out that illegals didn't vote the way they expected, everything was up for grabs."

Chapter Forty-Four

Suddenly Personal

I t didn't come to her in a flash. Well actually it kind of did. It was something Donnie said when she was flossing her teeth that triggered it. They were both standing at the bathroom sink.

"You remember those old Honda ads on TV where they showed how people looked like their cars?"

Hillary was still brushing and didn't want to froth over, so she tipped her head, and kept her mouth closed to answer, "Mmm Hmm."

"And that people-that-look-like-their-dogs meme from a couple of years ago, or was it this year?"

Hillary laughed at the thought, dribbling toothpaste on her T-shirt, and then spit in the sink, "Yeah, the dog with the Mullet."

Donnie continued her thought while Hillary rinsed, "Well, it's getting kinda like that with us, I mean look at this."

She was pointing at Hillary in the mirror. Hillary looked up from dabbing at her T-shirt, "Look at what?"

"Us, I mean look..."

Confused, Hillary looked in the mirror, at the first human she'd ever recognized, "What about us?"

"Oh yeah, you can't see it because of your face thing."

"See what?"

"Never mind, it's gone now."

"What is?"

"It's not all the time, but every so often, when I'm not thinking about it, it's kind of a flash thing, I look at you and I see, well... me. It's so fucking weird, but kinda cool too, it just happens whenever it does, and I can't make it happen."

Hillary stopped dabbing at her T-shirt, and then blankly offered, "Yeah, I probably don't see it because of my face thing."

Donnie laughed as she left the bathroom, "I guess we're just turning into old married folks now, like your mom and dad, like we're the same person."

Well now it was certainly striking closer to home. No longer some nameless person clicking on a CAPCHA panel, or some random skull in brain imagery. It was personal now, Donnie was officially one of those people who couldn't recognize her own face. And it was at that point that she flashed on something her dad had said. They were playing croquet when he froze suddenly. She thought he was having a stroke at first, but then he laughed, and then said pretty much the same thing Donnie just said, "I keep forgetting we're not the same person."

Chapter Forty-Five

Dung Beetles

"**M**ister Christ, would you mind walking on water for us?"

A chorus of derisive laughter filled the committee chamber which was then followed by a tempest of gavel pounding, spirited exchanges, and calls to order.

"Will the honorable sleaze bag from California and the esteemed skid mark from North Dakota and the rest of you please observe proto... procto... proctocol?"

While Hertell had been briefed on what to expect at the proceedings by his legal team, he was unprepared for the new evolved form of political theatre. Apparently like logic and miracles, political discourse itself had modulated in the intervening years and was now more akin to WWF pre-bout trash talk only with frequent F-bombs, C-words, and a variety of scatological and school-boyishly obscene characterizations to keep it real.

It had started out nicely enough. Hertell was seated at a table with a microphone, a few bottles of water, a tin of Altoids, and a title card which read, "Hertell Daggett, PhD, Son of God." Since Hertell had once been a physicist of some standing before he was shot in the head, he was delighted to see his academic pedigree acknowledged, even though it was somewhat overshadowed by the "Son of God" designation.

The Son of God had been outfitted with a Lavalier mic in case the table mic failed. However, Courtney and her legal team surrounding Hertell, cautioned that it was really there to catch embarrassing hot mic "gotcha" moments and that he should be careful not to mutter things to himself, unless they were biblical and Christ-like of course.

Seated above on a raised platform, more accurately a stage, was the Joint Committee on Sensitivity, Hate, Inclusion and Tolerance, a diverse and intergenerational admixture of withering scowls, toothy smiles, chin-tucks, and botoxed foreheads looking over their microphones and sweating water bottles at Hertell far below.

Hertell felt slightly overdressed in a suit and tie since the dress code for such affairs had obviously changed. The committee sitting above him looked more like a row of airline passengers waiting for a domestic flight, wearing an assortment of traditional suits but also Hawaiian shirts, jerseys from sports teams, cargo shorts, t-shirts, hoodies, and what appeared to be pajamas. He noticed that several wore surgical masks emblazoned with colorful graphics and wondered if the pole reversal was causing an increase in germaphobia in addition to making people forget stuff.

Like most people, Hertell had never been much interested in politics, even before he was shot in the head, and certainly not after, so he was unprepared for the attention he was now receiving by the members of the committee who commanded the high ground above him, and the phalanx of media poised at his rear.

Order was finally restored by the committee chair who was a starchy woman wearing what appeared to be an Old Glory themed surgical mask. She lowered the diminutive flag to take a sip from her water bottle, complete with label sporting the Congressional seal, and then leaned back to sit through the customary word salad served up for such proceedings. She was one of the scowlers.

"Mister Christ, Daggett, whatever, please, like, proceed with your opening statement."

Unfamiliar with the ritual, Hertell shook his head, "I don't have one, you wanted to talk to me."

Courtney and her crew leaned forward and gestured at a stack of papers in front of Hertell. Their movement was so artfully and fluidly executed that it reminded Hertell of the synchronized swimmers he'd seen in the Olympics back when they still had them.

Hertell looked at the stack of papers, shrugged, picked up the first page and began reading, "Honorable M-x Chair...they?" He looked at the team, "Is that a typo? Chair-they?"

Courtney hit the mute button, put her hand over the Lavalier mic and whispered, "No, it's correct, go ahead and read it, we MRI'd all the focus groups for the wording and we have all the I-tell-you-trulies and untos in the sound-bite text, so you're good to go."

Hertell read in silence for a moment, and then leaned over toward Courtney, "You guys need to check the settings on autocomplete, because this is totally messed up."

He set the opening statement down and then addressed the committee, "You've been calling each other the C-word and the CS-word and the MF-word and a buncha new ones that are very colorful, and you're okay with that, but you're all bent out of shape because I talked about Mexican watermelon? Why do you care what I say about anything, much less about what I say about Mexican watermelon? What's the issue here?"

The Sleaze Bag from California was sitting at the far end of the dais and went off leash, "The issue happens to be that, as the alleged Son of God, what you say about Mexican watermelon in general and all fruit in particular, has an impact on a great many things, and the American people deserve..."

"I never said I was the Son of God..."

The Sleaze Bag stopped, smiled, and then continued sweetly, "So are you denying that you're the Son of God? Yes, or no?"

The Skid Mark from South Dakota sat at the opposite end of the dais and was immediately on his feet, "What the senator from the hemp lobby doesn't seem to understand is that given the witness's history with proceedings like this, in which He was whipped, nailed to a cross and His side pierced with a spear, it is understandable that He would be low key about who He actually is!"

Several other likeminded committee members from flyover states supported the position by speaking out in tongues, "Shaaallem ballaalika... shimmy-shong shammalala... voh vodeeo doh voh..."

Which was immediately met with vigorous return fire of gavel pounding, stomping, and shouting, "Hoax... Hater... Xenophobe... Phony... Nativist... Grifter... Jesus Freak... Fascist... Nazi!"

Then, apparently satisfied that sufficient soundbites and dramatic footage had been captured, they all quieted down, and turned their attention again to Hertell, who had been observing the exchange, experiencing various states of amusement, dismay, and confusion.

"So lemme see if I've got this right, I talked about Mexican watermelon, and that makes me a Nazi?"

He could tell by the looks on several faces that the question was confusing.

"Mister Christ, or whatever, the committee is asking the questions here, not you."

Hertell nodded, "Okay, but you do know what a Nazi was though, one of you used the word so you must know who they were and what they did, right?"

There were some sidelong glances and amused smiles at the table. The committee chair leaned over to confer with the Sleaze Bag from California, who then spoke, "I'm happy to answer the question for Mister Christ, and yes we know what Nazis are."

"Good, then how do they relate to Mexican..."

"Nazis are part of a Medal of Honor expansion pack, they are a fictional construct, like unicorns and fairies, and frankly like you, the self-proclaimed Son of God."

There was laughter, the smug, snarky, knowing kind which has a distinctive sound. A committee member in an LA

Lakers jersey added to the mirthful atmosphere, "You get Nazis free in the premium version, and Orcs too."

The press was now laughing. Hertell was stunned, but he wasn't surprised. His rage rose to a low simmer as he waited for the surrounding laughter to slowly trail off. He addressed the room, "Why are you laughing?"

The room was unprepared for such a question and went momentarily quiet. "Nazis aren't fictional, Nazis were real."

Several on the committee smirked and shook their heads in disbelief at the laughable assertion.

"Mister Christ, are you like, trying to mock this committee?"

Hertell answered flatly, "No, you have that under control."

There was a ripple of laughter from the camera crews to his rear. Several on the committee offered some support: "No, he's right, there actually were Nazis... Yeah, back in the middle ages somewhere... My grandfather dropped bombs on'm I think."

The discussion continued among the dung beetles, but Hertell didn't hear it. He was thinking of something Kaye had said to him in the stacks, right before the earthquake and the water, only it was bigger this time. Actually, it was more of a sensation, it was the same feeling he had when he thought he was going to fall into the sky a few weeks before. Only this time it wasn't the sky he was falling into, it was the relentless, overpowering, undeniable beauty of an idea. He was helpless before it, helpless as a twig in a raging river as it carried him toward an inescapable and glorious revelation.

The dung beetle chattering and buzzing had gone strangely silent, and Hertell had a vague sense that something was calling for his attention.

The room was silent except for all the clicking cameras, and all eyes were on Hertell, who had risen from his seat and was now standing on the stars and stripes carpet, a few feet from the dais and the formation of dung beetles, all of them leaning back slightly in their carapaces, unsure of Hertell's intentions.

The security guard wasn't sure what to do either. Even though she knew that the Son of God had been through several security checkpoints, she also knew that they'd stopped doing cavity checks some years before when a Barbie doll shoe was found in a Senate staffer, and that a well-trained special forces operator could kill with a pencil or nail clippers, but a Barbie doll shoe probably not so much; nevertheless, she uncrossed her arms to be ready for any havoc the Son of God might wreak.

The Sleaze Bag from California was visibly uneasy, but to project an air of indifference, took a nervous sip of water which he immediately and comically sprayed out, misting several committee members, "Wine! Who put wine in my water!?"

Hertell's blink rate increased, and he thought he was going to sneeze, but instead spoke, and when he did it reverberated and echoed throughout the chamber in a very surprising and basically God-like way.

"I tell you truly, I am Jesus Christ, Son of God, and I've come back to clean up this shit hole!"

He pointed at the two opposite ends of the dais and then addressed the right side, "Fuck Us..." and then the left side, "and fuck We..." and then unsure which was which, reversed polarity by pointing with crossed arms "...or fuck We, and fuck Us..." and then, in summation with arms outstretched, "Fuck you all!"

And all were amazed.

There was a stunned silence, followed immediately by an atmosphere of general chaos, and amidst the gavel pounding, flashing strobes, and shouting exclamations that the water in every congressional water bottle had indeed turned to wine (a passable domestic chardonnay by all accounts). The Sleaze Bag from California, shortly after comically spraying out his mouthful of wine, seemed to be overcome by something. He slowly and silently rose from his seat, and then, as if in a trance, stepped down from the dais, and walked up to Hertell, and as the room momentarily held its breath, knelt before him and then, with tears streaming down his cheeks, took Hertell's hand, and kissed it.

Half the room erupted in raucous laughter at the stunningly brilliant snarky stunt, the other half gasped in horror at the mockery of the potential Son of God, and valuable political ally.

Hertell was surprised by the action, but before he could say or do anything, the kneeling man, choked with emotion, turned, and issued a stinging rebuke to the laughing chorus of committee, press, and gallery, "Hey, assholes, shut the fuck up, I'm totally serious!" He then looked up into Hertell's face, nodded his head in sanctified recognition, wiped tears of joy from his eyes, and then spoke for all to hear, "He truly is the Son of God."

The laughter faltered, and then faded with the general realization that maybe it wasn't a stunt after all.

Hertell looked down into the man's face, and then for some strange reason, was totally overwhelmed by a completely unexpected but unmistakable feeling of warmth and even affection for the asshole who, only moments before, was trying to destroy him. Unsure of what to make of the feeling, Hertell helped the asshole to his feet, patted him awkwardly on the shoulder, and then not knowing what else to say, shrugged and finally uttered, "Uh... unto."

Chapter Forty-Six

Information Justice

I t turned out that the massive library, now soaking beneath the hills of the Mustard Seed National Cemetery, had probably been the last real library in active use. The rest having long since been closed and converted into low-income housing during the virus years in accordance with the Information Justice Act so that people wouldn't have to risk going into what experts and their computer models insisted were toxic petri dishes with a book problem, and also because research determined that the only people that actually used libraries were homeschoolers and the homeless anyway.

Books didn't disappear entirely of course, like in *Fahrenheit 451*, and most people still had some: Time-Life books with lots of pictures, some coffee table travel books, children's board books, cookbooks, and such, but for the most part they were mainly home décor since there were so many games to play and streaming feeds to watch. While there were a few private libraries that were extensive, though narrowly focused on some specific topic, they were mainly props, like trophy cases, a mere backdrop to reflect erudition and sophistication on the puffy squire and their glass of ... it's a kind of fancy wine and it's also a word for the left side of a ship.

The Information Justice Act was accompanied by the much-heralded decision to migrate all the hard copy books to the cloud, before recycling the paper. The legislation was triggered by a UC Santa Cruz College of Diversity and Gender Studies monograph proving that physical books were not only exclusionary and oppressive, but were also the last and most insidious tool of the white male patriarchy, and were in fact conceived specifically for purposes of discrimination, and they had computer models to prove it. The study was well received and resulted in The New York Times' "1440 (Gutenberg) Project" which was immediately followed by a corrective and conciliatory movement that rolled through the virtue-besotted conference rooms, faculty lounges, salons, and state houses across the land.

However, while uploading to the cloud was universally hailed as a benevolent and egalitarian act which made the accumulated knowledge of western civilization freely accessible to all, it also made it accessible to a hacker in Finland. The Finnish hacker exploited a backdoor factory he'd embedded in an open source compiler that he had debugged several decades before. This allowed him to exploit a backdoor the CIA had put on top of an NSA backdoor, on top of an old BSD utility backdoor that everybody had forgotten about.

Everybody except the Finnish hacker, who used the daisy chained backdoors to give himself root privilege for the enterprise cloud, and then systematically and quietly traverse and encrypt the entirety of western civilization while the rest of the world was distracted by a massive data breach over a long World Cup weekend. It was going to be an epic ransomware play. However, unfortunately the hacker accidentally hung himself while engaged in solitary celebration of his stunning achievement, thus taking the decryption key with him into the next world and leaving the history of the world he'd just departed, permanently encrypted.

And as it turned out, it never would be missed.

Chapter Forty-Seven

I Tell You Truly

I t was streaming on all the aggregators within minutes with bold red headlines and flashing spinning beacons and dramatic photos of Hertell with Christlike arms outstretched, artfully silhouetted against the ashen landscape of shocked congressional Pharisees and Sadducees.

"It's official, we're F****d", "F-Us... F-We... F 'em all!", "Jesus H Christ, keepin' it real!", "Jesus is back, and boy is He pissed!", "Salty Talk from the Savior!", "Water to Wine miracle – 'an inferior Chardonnay.'"

Hertell was peering down from some fluffy clouds at the silent world below. Probably cornfields, or wheat fields, or cotton, or alfalfa. It was hard to tell from thirty-five thousand feet. Orbin's jet was empty except for Hertell, Kaye, Toodlah, Ginny, and Dot who were sleeping on a very luxurious leather couch. Orbin had stayed in Washington with his legal team presumably to do damage control on the wreckage the newly annunciated Son of God had left behind.

He was watching a tiny, ant-sized 18-wheeler crawl along an interstate freeway far below, and wondered what the trucker inside the tiny speck was listening to on his phone or Spotify or satellite radio, possibly Merle Haggard, possibly Enya, possibly reports of Jesus Christ returned to the earth to clean up the shit hole.

Hertell once had a job as a receiving clerk, and one day while unloading a truckload of gardening supplies, the trucker confided rather randomly that even though his name was Vern and he was from Oildale, that he was actually Jesus Christ, the Son of God. He also asked Hertell to keep it to himself since He didn't want it getting around because people would think He was crazy and such, and also for how it turned out the last time. Hertell's store was on the trucker's weekly route, so they had many conversations on the topic of being an undercover Jesus the Author of Salvation.

Vern offered that being Jesus was basically okay, except that there was so much shit you couldn't do anything about what with people being the way they are and everything. So, Vern *qua* Jesus generally just lived His life and tried to set a good example for his daughter, and to not be an asshole to His ex-wife. He figured that if there were enough people doing that and not making a big deal out of it, that eventually, in a geological timeframe of millions of years, that things would on average get better. He admitted that the first time He'd come down from Heaven, that He'd been a little too aggressive on the scheduling, and it caused the big pushback and crucifixion and whatnot.

Hertell considered the man to be delusional but harmless to anybody, including Himself. Nevertheless, Hertell considered the notion of a million or a billion unacknowledged Jesuses sprinkled across the globe, driving an 18-wheeler, hanging drywall, herding sheep, or whatever, a really sweet and almost life-affirming notion.

One of the pilots opened the cabin door, "We're gonna be coming into turbulence in a little bit so make sure you're strapped in. It's just a light chop, no big deal." He then gave a thumbs up and returned to the cockpit.

Hertell wondered what the pilots thought of flying with the Son of God in the back of their plane. He had to admit that it was kind of over the top, the whole "I tell you truly I'm Jesus Christ" thing. Not the Jesus part, that was necessary. The F-bombs were okay too since, even though he rarely used such language, they were heartfelt and sincere. It was the "I tell you truly" part that seemed excessive.

He'd always been troubled by the presence of such phrases in the Bible since the whole notion of having to preface a statement with assurances that it wasn't bullshit suggests that it was bullshit the rest of the time unless otherwise indicated. Either you're telling the truth or you're not, so there shouldn't be any need to signify which was which, especially in the Bible, and especially for the Son of God and everything. But then again, Hertell knew that the Bible had so many authors and been through so many translations, Aramaic to Greek to Latin to whatever. Perhaps the whole, I-tell-you-truly riff was just a flourish one of the translators threw in for branding, or maybe Jesus was totally down with the struggle and just trying to keep it real and "I shit you not," or the equivalent in Aramaic, didn't translate well into Greek.

They were over a solid cloud layer now, nothing but blinding whiteness as far as the eye could see, and as the earth silently hid beneath the white shroud, Hertell reflected on the revelation that had triggered his exclamation. It was a once in a million-year opportunity, literally, because it had been over 800,000 years since the last pole reversal. So clearly, for nearly a million years of evolution, our humble little human brain grew and ripened as we learned to pick up tools, master fire, hunt in groups, and honor our dead. Our little brains bulged with new lobes and ventricles, and furrowed with new folds and contours, all while bathed in the steady and soothing magnetic lines of flux from north to south as cultures were formed, wars were fought, civilizations were forged and written history emerged from grunting, hirsute prehistory.

And then the world switched from DC to AC, only people wouldn't come to a sudden shuddering stop, frozen and twitching at 60 cycles a second. They wouldn't arc and smoke and hiss and shrivel. They would just forget. The past, with all of its vexing contortions, was just so confusing and inconclusive, that it was way too much work and of little value in the here and now. It simply didn't matter as long as one could find a recipe, or the lyrics to a song, or a DIY video for clearing a clogged sink. No past in the rearview mirror to cherish or regret, no multi-lane future snaking toward some distant promised land. Instead, just a pleasant, flat eternal present stretching from horizon to horizon, unthreatening, undemanding, and indifferent.

Unmoored by the memory of how thoroughly people of the past had fucked up, people of the present were able to float on untroubled waters, confident that everything they thought or said or did was totally rational or ethical or moral or sensible or whatever self-justifying itch they were trying to scratch. History was of no further use; consequently, losing it would have a receptive audience. It wouldn't be a problem at all, but actually a relief. And now that the poles had flipped, they were all slowly forgetting that it ever even was.

Everybody but Hertell at least, and that was the beauty of the thing, the once-in-a-million-year opportunity that overtook him while sitting in the chair before the committee. He realized that when a person forgets everything, they don't forever after remember nothing, they could be made to remember almost anything. He really could start the world over again, and try to get the story right this time, and as the reputed Son of God, he might be able to actually pull it off.

He, in the role of Jesus Christ, could create a new historical age, an exo-historical epoch. He could absolve the world of its many sins by simply letting the world forget them. He could teach that it all never happened, that all the ugly, savage, dismaying, unimaginable cruelties conceived by the mind of man and inflicted by the hand, had never actually happened. Yes, it would be a big relief, like when you wake up from a dream and realize you hadn't actually killed anyone, or that all your teeth hadn't actually fallen out.

It would take some creative explaining, but he would leave all the shitty stuff out of the playbook. They wouldn't be an option anymore because they never ever happened.

He was, of course, uncomfortable passing himself off as Jesus Christ, but then again, he'd always heard that God works in mysterious ways and all that, so maybe his case of mistaken identity was part of something bigger than he could understand. It seemed almost as if all of it – the copper specks in his head, finding Mustard Seed all those years ago, going underground with them, the poles flipping, coming out of the ground again, the recycled libraries, the encrypted cloud, the fading memories, the end of history, his debut as the Son of God – all seemed to be to unfurling in accordance with some cosmic tapestry, the fulfillment of some ancient, though ridiculous, prophesy.

Maybe all the stuff in Revelation wasn't just the lunatic ravings he always presumed them to be. Perhaps everything that was happening to him right now was actually what the crazy prophet was talking about, but not getting quite right since things were happening out of order and a lot faster than specified in the Bible. Perhaps it really was the end of the world, only the wacky prophet got it backwards. The end of the world didn't mark the end of history, instead it was the end of history marking the end of the world, at least our world, the civilized human world since the rest of it would go on without much notice.

By forgetting everything that it ever knew, and did, and was, Hertell saw a chance for humankind to unbite the apple and toss it back up into that snake-infested tree in the garden, and then live in a new world of his invention without all the shitty stuff. And if he could get enough people believing it, it'd be like vaccinations and help even those people that think it's total bullshit. Only it wasn't with dead viruses, it was with empty spaces, like with homeopathy, forgetting the shitty stuff would leave empty spaces in the water that he could fill with goodness and kindness and things like that to keep people from doing shitty stuff again, because the water remembers, and we're 98% water. Perhaps there really could be 1000 years of peace, and even though he wouldn't be there to see much of it, at least he'd be there to get it started, even if it was all based on a case of mistaken identity.

He kept feeling his blink rate rise and fall, each time with the urge to sneeze just like it did when that surprising and involuntary prayer erupted from him on moving day. Only it wasn't a sneeze, not a classical one anyway like with horsehair, or the sun where he could just turn his face toward the brightness and be rewarded with a conclusive and satisfying sneeze. His nose wasn't itching, like in a real sneeze, and the itch wasn't even in his body really, but slightly above and behind and just out of his peripheral vision. And no matter where he turned his face or looked, it kept eluding him. It wasn't really even an itch but almost more like a presence—not like a person type presence or even an angel type presence or anything like that, it was almost more like a concept or a thought or maybe a memory fluttering, teasing, just out of reach.

It was at that point that he noticed that even though he was staring into the white clouds, he couldn't see the clouds anymore because he was seeing each individual water molecule inside the clouds. And they were alive, and they had hopes and dreams and desires the same way we do – simpler certainly, but still there in their own atomic versions of hopes and dreams and desires. The two hydrogen atoms desiring one more electron to fill their s-orbitals. The single oxygen atom desiring two more electrons to fill its p-orbital. They find each other, and make each other whole. Same with sodium and chlorine and all the oxidation states of iron. Why? Only the atoms know. Same as us. He laughed to himself, the copper slivers in his head were up to their usual mischief. Then he heard himself whisper, "It goes all the way to the bottom?"

The jet hit a pocket of light turbulence, and the clouds became clouds again. He looked back to check on Kaye and the kids. They were strapped in and still asleep.

The air smoothed out and an ancient DJ Snake track came into his head. He knew he probably wasn't really the Son of God, not with a wife and kids and a bullet in his head, but maybe the prophet just didn't want to mention that sort of thing, or maybe a translator cut the reference. He looked out the window again, the clouds were gone and they were over the desert now.

Kaye wasn't asleep, she'd been watching Hertell stare out the window, look around as if for a buzzing fly, but there was no buzzing fly, rocking slightly, laughing to himself, moving his lips in silent conversation with his cast of angels or demons, lost in thought, in some far away parallel world. She was watching her husband, the sweet boy she married when they were scarcely out of their teens, the cold man she divorced, the kind man she married again under very different circumstances. A damaged man, and a good man, but he wasn't the Son of God, he was the son of Hertell Daggett senior, a vinegary old bastard that she knew and loved. She knew and loved the father even before she knew his son, who was now slipping into a swirling vortex of fantasy, made up worlds and words, and heartbreaking delusions. She wiped her eyes and nose at the realization that whatever remained of the Hertell she knew and loved, was steadily and rapidly fading away.

Chapter Forty-Eight

Damage Control

T he aftermath of the Son of God's Joint Committee exit wasn't wreckage at all. Quite the opposite in fact, and Orbin was making the best of a great big fist full of miracles. Not just Hertell's clean-up-this-shithole miracle, but the Sleaze-Bag-conversion miracle, and the congressional-water-bottle-to-wine and Biblical-voice miracles as well. The last two were quickly explained as a labeling mistake by the distributor and the natural reverb caused by Hertell's Lavalier mic and the house mics, but Orbin considered them both just more logical miracles like the miracle-of-the-stopped-sun and all subsequent miracles, so he went with it.

Within minutes of Hertell's spirited exit from the committee room, Orbin's team was contacting church members in every state, plus D.C., Puerto Rico, Guam, and American Samoa to coordinate filings, circulate petitions, collect signatures, and such. Now that Hertell realized and admitted who He really was, Orbin knew that everything was in place. He knew that God had a plan for him too, because Denise was in Heaven working extended hours to get all these miracles arranged like she did with that first Easter miracle on the day she died. True, there was no angel visitant, no trumpet blast, no opening skies to inform him of his role, but Orbin figured God knew he'd be happy to help any way he could, and that it was his destiny to work the logistics of the end times. There would be no Tribulation, no Anti-Christ, not even an Armageddon in the traditional sense. None of that was necessary anymore, it had all been arranged: we would skip right to the end of the world, and straight to a thousand years of peace with a simple, almost laughably simple act that Orbin would help come to pass.

That massive data breach, in combination with several squalid and unsavory presidential elections, had also resulted in extensive changes to national elections. The consensus among all stakeholders was that since party logos, colors, and names were being changed anyway, they might as well seize the day and change a pile of pesky election laws too, and the swarm of rules, regulations, and protocols, buzzing around them. For the most part the changes were seemingly benign since they were essentially only there to serve and protect the traditional game of political pattycake so that the newly renamed, rebranded, and recolored parties could continue to alternately get their turns at the trough.

The changes, with great fanfare, addressed the usual suspects for the most part: the electoral college, undocumented guests getting the vote, electronic voting, and so on, but there were several that were intended to open up the playing field for third party and non-traditional candidates like actors, YouTubers, and cornholers. However, while the major changes were optical and inert, so as to preserve the frat party franchise, the minor changes, mere sops to placate the rabble, made the whole system completely vulnerable to black swan events, such as the return of Jesus Christ to Earth, which would certainly qualify.

It did, and by the time the black swan had completed its migration across flyover country, and Orbin's jet landed at Meadows Field in Bakersfield, Hertell Daggett AKA the Son of God, was officially a candidate for President of the United States.

Chapter Forty-Nine

An Accidental Antichrist

I t had been a day since they'd returned in Orbin's jet, and Hertell and family were walking across the CRAVE campus. They'd accidentally left Dot's little shopping cart walker in Orbin's jet, and it was too far for her to walk, so Hertell and Kaye were swing walking Dot between them on the way from their dormitory suite to the Blessed Redeemer dining commons. Ginny and Toodlah had already run ahead and were safely out of earshot, so Kaye proceeded to unload on Hertell.

"Okay there's no way to sugarcoat this, so I'm just gonna say it. Hertell you're not the Son of God.... Wheee... you've been shot in the head and Obi's been filling the hole with all kinds of End Times crap... Wheee.... and now he's got you believing you're the Son of God... Wheee... it's a delusion, you are not the Son of God... Wheee!"

Hertell nodded vigorously, "Kaye, totally agree, I am definitely not the Son of God, no more than anybody else anyway. ... Wheee!... But everybody's forgetting stuff, do you think that's gonna end well? Wheee... People, a lotta people, think I'm the Son of God, I know I'm not, but they think I am.... Wheee... God and geophysics are giving the world a do-over, and it was all your idea anyway... Wheee!"

Kaye shook her head, "What the fuck are you talking about, I never..."

"Potty mouth!" Dot shook her head in disapproval, "Potty!"

Kaye was immediately repentant, "You're right Dot, Mom did a potty mouth... Wheee!" But she quickly recovered and refocused her attention on Hertell.

"It was not my idea to promote you to the Son of God...Wheee!"

"Not the Son of God part, the leaving out all the S-word stuff part... Wheee... That was your idea, but then it was just for Mustard Seed... Wheee... But now we've got a chance to set a direction here, a chance nobody's had, at least for the last couple thousand years or so... Wheee... You think this is all some kinda accident, that there isn't some kinda plan here? ... Wheee... Don't you think we have an obligation to do something? Human nature is what it is... Wheee... but maybe we can do like you said and take a few shitty options off the table..."

"Potty!... Potty mouth."

"Oh, yeah... sorry... wheee!"

Kaye walked in silence as Hertell continued with an occasional, but spiritless "Wheee!" as they walked across the AstroTurf past Orbin's Prayer Tower. He could tell by the way she held her head, and looked straight ahead that she was praying. She finally nodded to herself, "Hertell, what if you're the Antichrist? ... Wheee!"

Hertell was surprised by the question, since he'd never really had a clear handle on the concept and was never sure if the Antichrist was an actual person or a vague demonic boogeyman. He certainly didn't feel like one of those. "Can a person be the Antichrist and not know it? Or by accident maybe? Wheee!"

But before Kaye could answer Hertell, they both felt a sharp electrical jolt just as Dot's feet touched the dirt path. And it was at that moment that Dot released their hands and ran toward Ginny and Toodlah who were waving to her from the far end of the quadrangle.

Hertell and Kaye stood silent in the shade of Orbin's Prayer Tower as what they'd just beheld sank in. Dot had never been able to walk more than a few hundred feet on her own before, and even then, it was slow and labored. She was never ever able to do anything even approximating a run, but now by some miracle, she was nearly a football field away, and she was running.

Hertell watched Dot catch up to Ginny and Toodlah and then disappear with them into the Blessed Redeemer dining commons. He was stunned and speechless, trying to comprehend what he'd just witnessed. It was then that he heard a soft, almost kitten like mewing sound, it was Kaye.

Kaye watched her daughter trot, then skip, then run across the fake lawn, running like a broken toy, arms flapping awkwardly, legs flailing like a puppy, but she was running. It was a miracle. Kaye crumpled and sank to the ground in one fluid motion, first to her knees as if praying and then to all fours as if playing. She curled in on herself and buried her face in her folded arms and quietly sobbed as waves of joy and then guilt and then redemption and then joy again and then every other emotion she'd ever felt, and probably ever would feel, washed over her.

Hertell was quite undone at the sight of Kaye face down on the gravel path, her shoulders heaving with each soft mewing sound, and he didn't know exactly what to do. He instinctively knew how to comfort Dot or Ginny or Toodlah when they needed it, but he had no idea what do for Kaye, partly because he was in shock himself and also because he'd only ever seen her cry once before that he could remember.

Not knowing what else to do, he knelt down beside her and patted her awkwardly on the back.

Kaye could feel Hertell patting her on the back, and hear him repeating again and again, "It's okay, it's just a miracle... yeah... that's all... just a miracle."

She felt herself nodding. Yes, indeed this was a miracle, a joyous, glorious, undeniable miracle. But it was a miracle with implications. What if Hertell actually was the Son of God? And if he was, was he the Son of God this whole time? If not, when did it start? Was he the Son of God back when they were teenagers and he felt her up, or the first time they made love on his Boy Scout sleeping bag out on Whisper Hill during a meteor shower? Was he the Son of God when he abandoned her and left her heartbroken and scarred, or when he got shot in the head? Should she start treating him differently, more obedient, reverential, worshipful, whatever?

She noticed that she wasn't sobbing anymore. She could feel Hertell's arms around her now, and his chest against her back, and it felt like he was shivering. Only he wasn't shivering, he was crying. Would the Son of God cry? Or laugh, or fart or do the stuff any other person would do? He was still a man after all, a person.

And if God had wanted her to treat him any different, He certainly would have let her know by now. But there was never any angel visitant appearing before her, or in a dream even, telling her to not give him shit for anything, even if he deserved it, or telling her to be more deferential or humble or anything like that. No. God must have been okay with how she was with Hertell, and probably wanted her to keep on doing what she was doing, keeping him grounded, keeping the Son of God from getting too full of Himself.

Yes, she would go on as she had, no special treatment for the Son of God.

They helped each other to their feet, and then stood and hugged each other for a time. Hertell felt Kaye take a deep breath, the kind you take when you're going to dive under water. He felt her hug tighten, and then tighten some more, and then more. He never realized she was so strong.

And then she spoke to him in an urgent, almost desperate whisper, "All right, maybe you're not going crazy, and maybe you're not the Antichrist. Maybe you are the Son of God, at least a little bit, but only for this, so watch your language, and don't do anything to embarrass God, or me, and don't forget, that you're still just the sonovabitch I married. Twice."

Hertell stood in silence for a moment, and felt Kaye's bear hug loosen slightly. He then took a deep breath and whispered, "I tell you truly, I am blessed that way."

It would later be determined that the electrical jolt was merely the discharge of static electricity collected on the shuffling swing walk across dry AstroTurf with Hertell and Kaye serving as capacitors. Dot's miracle sprint was traced to exposure to natural full spectrum light (including critical wavelengths that were missing in the artificial light of their former world below) which triggered her hypothalamus to gradually release an inhibitor enzyme that prevented generation of several deleterious proteins that suppressed musculoskeletal development. A perfectly logical miracle.

Chapter Fifty

Operation Blackjack

H ertell's presidential campaign was late to the party but nevertheless had a number of things working in its favor from Team Orbin's perspective. The team was assembled in the conference room of the great copper fish lodged in a CRAVE campus hillside. Courtney had once been chief strategist on a presidential campaign early in her career, and even though that campaign had been spectacularly unsuccessful and the incumbent lost in a humiliating defeat, she was anxious to put her shoulder to the wheel and give the Son of God the benefit of her hard-won political experience.

Orbin and Hertell were seated at the conference table opposite the wall-sized HD display showing a dazzling assortment of demographic maps, charts, timelines, and bullet points that Courtney was stressing.

"Okay, we have, three strategic advantages: number one, Hertell is a fresh face, He's never run for office, He has no voting record to apologize for, He has no social media footprint so there aren't any jpegs of His junk in some teenager's inbox or tweets to be embarrassed about and blame on hackers, none of that. He is a clean slate, and on top of all that, He is the Son of God."

She pointed at a world map and pie chart, "Two, there are about 2 billion Christians, in a variety of denominator... dominio... flavors all over the world, and a lot of them are in the US, and like 70% of voters identify as Christian or Christian leaning, at least around Christmas and Easter, and are very likely inclined to vote for the Son of God returned to the earth. Just in case."

Orbin thought of his wife up in Heaven helping God move the levers of the miracle before them. He thumped his finger on the tabletop, "We've had generals, politicians, a cripple, an actor, a minority, a game-show host, and even a guy with a nose that looked like a male penis, and now here we sit with the next President of the United States, the Son of God! That's what I call progress, the Kingdom of God starts right here in the good ol' USA."

Hertell wasn't really hearing any of this. He was hearing Kaye's voice in his head and wondering if he could actually be the Antichrist and not know it. He thought perhaps there might be some kind of test he could take just to be sure, like a vampire looking into a mirror, to find out one way or another if he was or wasn't.

Courtney was now pointing at a US map that appeared to be a patchwork of harvest gold and avocado green states, "Three, all the new laws they made up: write-in laws, so even if we can't get You on the ballot in every state, You can still win; negative voting, so people don't even have to vote for You, they can just vote against the other guys, which makes You bubble up to the top."

She pointed to a bar chart, "And as soon as anybody hits 21% of the vote it's Blackjack, immediate shoot out with the top five, and as You can see, and You've already got 19% of the vote, You're already leading the pack."

"What do I say?"

"You're the Son of God, You can say whatever you want, but maybe not 'fuck you all' again. That works once for making a point and establishing a policy position, but You don't want to overuse it."

Chapter Fifty-One

Expansion Packs

But there was one more advantage that Hertell had that nobody knew about, at least not consciously. While it was true that Hertell had a number of things working in his favor, they were all merely logistical, the biggest one was personal, emotional, and internal. It was flying under the radar, following the contours of the subconscious terrain. It wasn't the Son of God religious stuff, it was bigger than that. It was a game.

The Mustard Seed Duck-n-Cover MMORPG had more devotees than any single religion on Earth, over 3 billion downloads worldwide, with over 300 million in the US alone. And nearly every person of voting age had played it at one time or another, some more than others; nevertheless, it was part of the internalized cultural landscape, like Dorothy in Oz, or Santa at the North Pole, or Hobbits in Middle Earth. Only this game was populated not with fictional characters in an imagined world, it was populated with real people who had once actually lived in a real world below, and then above, the surface.

In the game, the lost civilization of Mustard Seed wasn't concluded with a bunker buster, but instead the good people of Mustard Seed continued on with various adventures and quests on the surface in an assortment of expansion packs in which they emerge in various alternative versions of the present age: one in which Nixon had been elected President instead of Kennedy, another in which the Roswell UFO landed safely on the White House lawn, and so on.

The initial version was basically a factual retelling of the actual Mustard Seed saga: from the discovery of the civilization beneath the pet cemetery, to their interactions with SWAT teams and such, and their excursions and escapades on the surface, all in the form of an addictive, OCD-inducing game with compelling graphics and a whimsical but haunting soundtrack. It was developed by a disillusioned former civil servant with direct and personal experience with the Mustard Seed civilization in the days after their original discovery.

Rusty was the child of an EE and a software engineer and had grown up with all three volumes of Knuth's *The Art of Computer Programming* on his bookshelf along with *The Adventures of Tintin* and *The Way Things Work*. He had been part of a team responsible for closing the DD254 file on the formerly classified and top-secret program, code named "Mustard Seed." He had mapped the entirety of the underground complex, cataloged, and dispositioned all relevant documents, and debriefed the adult population. He also spent a lot of time beneath the earth with the people of Mustard Seed, playing miniature golf with Hertell and others, setting up a LAN and IT infrastructure, and joining a bowling league in those few, blessed halcyon months before things were complicated by SWAT teams and such.

The game was Rusty's response to the way the people, and the miracle, of Mustard Seed were treated. However, he didn't do it as a coping mechanism, or as a way of working out any emotional issues, grief, survivor's guilt, remorse, or any of that. He'd been the one that actually provided the specific targeting information programmed into the GBU-28 that, over ten years before, had penetrated a dusty hillside on what would become the Mustard Seed National Cemetery, at precisely the correct angle and velocity to detonate in the first void encountered and thus conclude the Mustard Seed saga, with extreme prejudice.

Only the GBU-28 didn't actually conclude anything because Rusty had provided targeting coordinates to an abandoned pressure buffer buried in the most remote corner of Mustard Seed and separated from the Mustard Seed core by several miles of lava tube chambers and tunnels. He then proceeded to hack the BDA sensor network and patch the binaries with some notch filters so that, for all appearances, there were no survivors and that the entire Mustard Seed saga was therefore definitively ended.

Knowing they were safely considered dead and therefore of no further interest to the various government stakeholders, and knowing he would keep their secret and take it to his own grave, he then left public service claiming long term psychological damage due to his role in the Mustard Seed tragedy, and was given a generous separation package to thank him for his service.

With the separation package providing the funding, his first project upon entering the private sector as a one-person technology start-up, was the Mustard Seed Duck-n-Cover game. He did it because even though he knew them all to still be alive, he nevertheless missed them, and their world, so the game was his way to be with them and share it while still preserving the fiction that they all lay safely dead beneath the hills on the outskirts of Bakersfield. It was his way of creating alternative endings to their story and continue his life in that world with the people he knew, but could no longer, and never would again, see.

It had a theme song, a really weird version of "What a Wonderful World" that sounded strangely like dogs howling even though it wasn't dogs, it was just a weird tune that he'd found on Archive.org, but it was perfect. He created characters for players to choose from based on the real people hidden below: Garner, Lox, Travis, Dannon, Sanford, plus the usual non-player characters, SWAT teams and such. But there was one character that every single player who ever played the game, wore at one time or another, the avatar that the player would assume as they explored the world of Mustard Seed below the surface, led the people of Mustard Seed on quests in the wondrous and often dangerous, mystifying, and dismaying world above, protecting them from enemies and threats of all kind, and rescuing them when needed.

It was Hertell. He was everybody's favorite character. The copper specks let players pick various powers and skills and knowledge they wanted to possess. He was a familiar presence because he had been inhabited by virtually every

Duck-n-Cover gamer the world over as they played his role: discoverer, leader, protector, hero, and savior. And even though they didn't realize it, they all to some extent recognized themselves in him, and him in them. And it was that, in addition to the other logistical advantages, that would put Hertell on stage with five other candidates for President of the United States.

Chapter Fifty-Two

Small Price

The presidential campaigns for both Sleaze Bag from California and Skid Mark from South Dakota got needed shots in the arm from the Joint Committee meeting-of-many-miracles, and both alternately surged to the head of the pack for a few days. However, they were quickly eclipsed by the Son of God, AKA Hertell Daggett. The Sleaze Bag quickly dropped out of the race since he truly believed Hertell was the Son of God and didn't want to blow a chance for a good cabinet position. Skid Mark drifted down in the rankings and stabilized somewhere in a high single digit percentage.

Things kicked into high gear with Orbin and his team, and they'd done a great job managing Hertell's presidential campaign and keeping it about the Kingdom of God and such and above the trifling domestic and international policy issues. However, complications arose when, first the 'We' party, and then the 'Us' party, approached Orbin about Hertell coming over to their side.

They were each eager to have him in their respective camp since the polls indicated that the Son of God would really help down-ticket candidates and have a net positive impact at the state and local levels since it was going to be a redistricting year and it would really advance their gerrymandering and bribery efforts. However, each had some demands, wanted some concessions, and had aggressive fundraising expectations since both were eager to expand their brands, now glossed with new names, logos, and colors.

Orbin politely told the 'Us' party delegation to go piss up a rope. The news of which greatly relieved the 'We' party who presumed that they now had a lock on the Son of God and their fortunes and futures were assured. However, when Orbin politely told them to piss up the same rope, both parties, now faced with a threat to their two hundred-year grifter franchise, decided to join forces and fix their crosshairs on the big bullseye tacked on the alleged, and obviously counterfeit, Son of God.

Thus, Hertell found himself on the Town Hall stage, surrounded by a scowling audience and enduring a merciless crossfire from the 'We' and 'Us candidates: one a severe woman with a big Adam's apple and wearing a harvest gold scarf, the other an agitated man with a bad comb-over and a ponytail. Hertell also shared the stage with a champion cornholer in his ACL jersey, and a viral podcaster with a soul patch and Celtic neck tattoos, both of whom watched in stunned silence as Hertell was peppered with alternating volleys of 'We' and 'Us' accusations, allegations, and denunciations. Even the moderator got into the fun.

"Mister Daggett, is it true that you were shot in the head and left with severe brain damage? You have twenty seconds."

"Well, yeah, but I wouldn't say 'severe,' no more than anybody else up here anyway."

The audience erupted in involuntary laughter but quickly resumed a sullen aspect and demeanor since the whole affair had been jointly arranged by the two rebranded parties, and the audience had a crucial role to play in the process.

Specifically, that Hertell, the cornholer, and the podcaster were a distracting carny freak show that had to be endured but ultimately dispensed with by the more experienced and serious political professionals that stood at the 'We' and 'Us' podiums. Except for Kaye and some cornhole fans, the audience was curated and comprised almost exclusively of 'We' and 'Us' operatives, speech writers, bundlers, consultants, journalists, bloggers, and think tank analysts in various disguises (Tommy Bahama shirts and such) to obscure their obvious sophistication and project a just-plain-folks image. They were arranged in an intersectional pattern that would delight any HR VP or Diversity manager.

"The doctors got the bullet out, and some of my brain too, so I forget some stuff from my own life, but they thought I was gonna die anyway so they didn't bother to get some little specks of copper, and they're what make so that I can remember a bunch of other important..."

"Next question, Mister Running Deer."

The bad comb-over cleared his throat, "Would God allow his only begotten Son to get shot and have brain damage?"

"You have twenty seconds ..."

Hertell shrugged, "I don't see why not, He let the other one get nailed up on a cross."

More suppressed laughter from the audience. The cornholer and podcaster laughed out loud too. "Is it true your father shot you in the head?"

"Yeah, but it was an accident, it was New Year's, he was shooting his Luger up in the air..."

"So, God was shooting a gun in the air?"

Smiles at the 'We' and 'Us' podiums, now they had him.

"My dad was shooting the gun, not God, come on man..."

The scarf woman raised her hand to her mouth in mock surprise, "Oh wait, I thought God was your dad."

Hertell looked at the scarf woman, and thought for a moment, "Well, yeah He is, just like He is yours and hers and his and everybody else, that's the beauty of the thing."

He then turned to the moderator, "Can I ask a question?"

The moderator seemed annoyed, "Uh, okay, you have twenty seconds."

Hertell turned to the champion cornholer, "Why is it called 'cornholing'?"

The champion cornholer was surprised by the question, but quickly warmed to it, "Well... it's because the bags, if they're adhering to ACA regulations, are 6 by 6 inches and they're filled with between 15 and 16 ounces of whole kernel corn, dried. So, when you're playing the game and you toss your bag, and it's not as easy as it looks, and it swooshes right in the hole, which is a great feeling, you've literally got 'corn' going in the 'hole'. Which is how it gets its name, 'cornhole,' plus you got the whole anal sex connotation thing which is kinda funny too... Is it okay to say, 'anal sex'?"

Unable to stop themselves, as if driven by instinct or reflex, the 'We' and 'Us' party candidates got busy trying to out-inclusive each other with an escalating and overlapping litany of anal sex affirmations, "I wholeheartedly support anal sex... I do not merely support it, I embrace it... I co-sponsored a bill establishing a national day of..."

And it was while the scarf and bad comb-over continued their rhapsodic praise of the sexual practice that had an undeserved association with a popular sport, that Hertell was overcome with a strange but wonderful feeling.

"And what about the Son of God? What's his position on anal sex?"

Liking where it was going, the moderator pitched in, "Yes, what is your position on the policy, Mister Daggett?... Mister Daggett?"

Hertell wasn't really hearing what they were saying anymore, their shrill voices had faded away and he was just looking at their faces as they demanded an answer – forehead veins bulging, teeth bared and clearly quite outraged. He looked out into the audience. Same there pretty much, except for Kaye and a few of the cornholers. The rest was a sea of dark and angry faces. Faces that he knew hated him, who saw him as an enemy and wanted to destroy him.

He could feel his copper specks stirring, connecting things. It started out as a random flicker as his gaze moved from face to face, but the flicker got progressively faster until it finally faded away to reveal what seemed like one continuous face to him, a face he recognized, and it was softening. And somehow, he couldn't hate them back. Quite the opposite in fact, and for some reason he cherished them.

And it was at that moment Hertell understood what was happening, and if it was what he thought it was, it changed everything and forgetting history would be a small price to pay. He smiled to himself as a happy moment started to rise within him. He could feel it radiating from his chest, down his body into his legs and feet, out into his arms and hands, up into his head. It was wonderful, but it was different, it wasn't a mere echo of some earlier 'true' happy moment in accordance with his theory-of-happy-moments. This was a brand new one and would normally qualify as one of his 'true' happy moments, but it was more than that somehow. It felt more like it could be the source of them all somehow. It didn't rise, and then peak, and then fade away as all the others had, it just kept growing.

He thought perhaps he was dying, or was already dead since he felt so connected to everything that ever was and is and ever will be, a connection from the smallest quark and boson to every person who ever lived, or ever would live, to the dim galaxies at the edge of the cosmos. But there was no bright light beckoning him forward, there were no long dead relatives waving hello. He could look around and see the audience sitting in front of him, the lighting grid above, the TV cameras, so he knew he wasn't dead, or dying either for that matter. But then he noticed that all eyes were on him, and it was strangely quiet. The moderator had trailed off in mid-question, the scarf and bad comb-over had fallen mute, and silence had descended over the entire audience, even the people in the production booth had stopped making snarky comments as they all observed a halo slowly form around Hertell and ultimately engulf him in what can only be described as a warm golden light. And it wasn't just a mass hallucination in the studio, it was seen by millions as it happened via live streaming, and then billions virally through YouTube and such.

Time stood still in witness to the miracle as it unfolded. And then a cell phone went off.

The cornholer awkwardly fished around for his phone, "Sorry, forgot to turn this off..."

Hertell's halo was holding steady as the audience began to stir.

"Hell yes it's real!" It was the cornholer on his phone, "I'm standing here looking right at it! It's everywhere, it's the whole room, it's all of us!"

The cornholer was indeed correct, the entire audience was now aglow along with Hertell, and some were patting at their clothing to watch the glow ripple and shimmer.

The moderator's blink rate was clocked at over 100 BPM while trying to salvage the debate and restore some level of control, "Closing comments Mister Running Deer."

The 'We' and 'Us' candidates were quite stunned by events, but managed to pull it together enough to mouth their pre-rehearsed assortment of focus grouped bullet points and sound bites. But since the glowing halo was filling the room, their closing comments would have no impact.

However, the closing comments from the champion cornholer and viral podcaster definitely would.

When it was his turn, the champion cornholer stood quietly for a moment, then smiled, nodded, and pointed at Hertell. He finally spoke, "I think... I think I'm gonna vote for Him."

The podcaster nodded vigorously and wiped his eyes, "Yeah, me too."

Chapter Fifty-Three

The Golden Trim Tab

I t started out as a modest monograph in the *International Journal of Neuro-Cognitive Imagery*.

Geomagnetic polarization reversal effects on the fusiform gyrus: an fMRI investigation of a global phenomenon

Hillary Mull[1]

[1] *University of California, Santa Barbara, Neuroscience Research Validation Institute (NRVI)*

ARTICLE INFO	ABSTRACT

Keywords:
  Geomagnetic reversal
  Facial recognition
  Identity convergence
  Instinct suppression
  Coalition agility
  Prosohypergnosia
  Empathy amplification
  In-group expansion
  Out-group attenuation
  fMRI
	The recent reversal of the earth's magnetic field was considered to have no detectible impact on the biosphere; however, analysis of geophysical data, historical fMRI imagery, experimental fMRI imagery, and statistical models indicate significant correlation between the field reversal and increased activation and sensitivity of the anterior, right-lateralized fusiform region representing a new cognitive modality: *prosohypergnosia*, in which test subjects consistently perceive their own image when shown images of random strangers. This study describes the methods, data, results, and areas for additional research for this new and potentially global phenomenon and its resultant social/cultural/financial implications.

The abstract was initially rejected by the triage panel when the screener emailed Hillary to ask her where she got the photo of the screener himself in Figure 4.A and also to state that he was incensed that his likeness had been used without his permission. She explained that the photos were randomly pulled from over 200k celebrity images in the CelebA dataset, and that the image in question in Figure 4.A was actually Margaret Thatcher and not the screener.

She went on to explain that the prosohypergnosia phenomenon was ephemeral and was usually only consciously observable (when noticed at all) for the first 500-2500 milliseconds of exposure, and that the image would gradually morph back into Margaret Thatcher after staring at it for a few additional seconds (as described in the Results section of the paper); however, the screener would probably never feel the same way about Margaret Thatcher again since the phenomenon was largely subconscious (as described in the conclusion section of the paper).

The paper was quickly accepted and published, and went on to a much larger audience in an expanded form in *Science Magazine*. The web version included an app allowing the reader to directly experience what would normally be a subconscious event. Hillary also used an AI model to make the subject more understandable to a general readership unfamiliar with neuroscience. She'd once dabbled in machine learning when it was all the rage, but it was just simple matrix math when she got down into the details, and it wasn't very interesting. The only part of it that was interesting to her were the GANs since they were a pair of neural networks in which one is trying to fool the other one. They were great for generating deepfake images since they could digitally morph faces of people into other people, familiar faces, random strangers, movie stars, or completely non-existent, imaginary but real-looking faces. In the case of prosohypergnosia, the hyperactive fusiform gyrus was performing the neurological deepfake equivalent by turning the faces of total strangers into that most familiar face of all, the observer's own face, and while the effect was largely subliminal, it nevertheless had far-reaching behavioral repercussions.

She explored the repercussions in a very successful TED Talk that eventually went viral, "Fusiform Trim Tab" with lots of compelling graphics and such and using a metaphor she'd picked up from Donnie.

"There's a thing called a 'trim tab' which is a small control surface that's attached to a bigger control surface, say on the rudder of a big container ship." She focused her laser pointer at a blueprint of a container ship projected on a massive adjoining screen.

"And this little trim tab... this little rudder on the big rudder..." She squiggled her laser pointer at a tiny spot on the rudder of the container ship, "...by moving just a little bit, moves the big rudder, that's twenty times the size of this teeny, little trim tab back here." She then circled the laser pointer over the whole ship, "And the big rudder moves the whole ship, thousands of times the size of the rudder, and a hundred thousand times the size of the measly little trim tab, which is able to cause a change in direction far in excess of what its size would suggest."

The screen image changed to a blueprint of the human brain, "The most recent polar flip has made everyone's fusiform gyrus overactive." She squiggled her laser pointer on the brain, "And it's slowly making it so that everyone recognizes their own face in the faces of strangers, everybody sees themselves in everybody else, not an enemy or a threat or prey, but as themselves, at least parti... pareto... particulate... a little bit."

The screen changed to a grid of tiled bar charts, scatter plots, Kiviat diagrams, histograms, and all manner of pie charts. She swept her laser pointer across the collection of screens, "Something significant is happening. Crime rates have fallen, there aren't as many wars as had been customary, there is still shitty stuff going on of course, but for the most part things are really good."

The screen changed to a slowly turning God's-eye-view of slumbering Earth with its web of delicate points of light, "We are now 8 billion tiny little trim tabs on the rudder of human behavior. And it's pretty easy to follow the golden rule, when, even if you don't know it, you can still see a little bit of yourself in the other guy."

She put down her laser pointer and walked to center stage, "And of course the cynics will reject all this and say that they think it's a fantasy, a laughable delusion, a childish, ridiculous, naïve fantasy. And all I can say in response is, fuck the cynics, who cares what those negative assholes think."

The audience erupted in laughter and applause, but then for a moment Hillary seemed distracted as if listening to something far away. She put her hands on her swollen belly, laughed, and looked across the crowd, and then looked down at Donnie seated in the front row and cackled, "They're kicking!" And then softly, as if to herself, "They're kicking."

Chapter Fifty-Four

A Confused Look

It was later determined that the miracle-of-the-halos presidential debate was a transitory phenomenon caused by an interaction between fumes from the recently shampooed carpets and the LED stage lighting system which, when exposed to XG chip frequencies, resulted in bioluminescence emitted by the plankton-infused antibacterial textiles used in modern clothing; however, the logical explanation had no effect on the election, and Doug played the bagpipes at Hertell's inauguration.

The first few years of the Daggett administration were pleasant enough and thankfully uneventful, except for a spike in UAP sightings which had become fairly routine, and most people saw the darting and diving Tic-Tacs, that seemingly defied the laws of physics, as a benign curiosity and non-threatening.

It wasn't like things got perfect all of a sudden since human nature was still what it always had been. There was avarice, wrath, hubris, the usual, but their practical application was generally buffered by seeing a little bit of oneself in the other guy, and it gradually and subconsciously became a way of navigating the world, and as intuitive and instinctive as balance or breathing.

There was still enough self-contempt out there to keep the world mostly recognizable. There were still crazy people, and cruel people, and evil people: the occasional active shooter felling total strangers for no particular reason in spite, or perhaps because he could see his own face in theirs as the trigger is pulled.

Nevertheless, Hertell knew that the perfect was the enemy of the good, so that on the whole, there was a gradual change in the day to day behavior of people. It was hard to say how much, perhaps an order of magnitude or just a simple multiple. But whatever it was, it was noticeable, and only required the slight adjustment provided by Hillary's fusiform gyrus trim tab so that people weren't constantly fighting human nature. Plus, they were forgetting history and all the shitty stuff, so those options were falling off the table, and there was a chance to start history all over again, and maybe even get it right this time.

Hertell was on the way to Sweden where he was to be awarded the Nobel Peace Prize. He wasn't sure why, but he figured the committee wanted to be on the right side of things just in case he really was the Son of God.

Hertell looked out the window of Air Force One. He was visiting the cockpit with Toodlah who was reciting the international phonetic alphabet to the flight crew.

"Alpha, Bravo, Charlie, Delta..."

The staff on the flight was minimal since they were always a pain in the ass to Hertell, forever running around trying to look busy and indispensable. So, it was just the crew and some cooks, and the doctor and some secret service guys plus Kaye and the twins who were still in the dining room having pizza. Hertell left his staff in DC and put Vice President Stubbs, the cornholer, in charge of things. The 12th amendment had been repealed as part of the post embarrassing-data-breach housekeeping some years before, so the 2nd place winner served as VP just as they had over two centuries ago. Stubbs was also a great guy and fully able to handle things while Hertell was getting his Nobel Prize.

"Echo, Foxtrot, Golf..."

Hertell listened to his son and looked past the pilots, out the windshield. They were somewhere over the ocean now, and Hertell's ears were ringing. It wasn't an annoying buzz but was more like the shimmering radio stations heard late at night driving across the desert.

"Hotel, India, Juliet..."

He reasoned that it must be his copper specks picking up some random satellite radio signals.

"Kilo, Lima, Mike..."

It was actually quite comforting as he looked down at the water far below and his thoughts wandered.

"November, Oscar, Papa..."

What if the latest pole reversal wasn't making some special clump of brain tissue overactive? Perhaps it always was active, active before that reversal a million years ago. What if people had always seen themselves in other people, but the reversal a million years ago made it so that we couldn't anymore? Maybe that reversal made it so that we started seeing faces where there actually weren't any, like in dark clouds and forest shadows and granite counter tops and knotty pine so that people started believing in demons and spirits and devils, and acting accordingly.

The copper specks were fluttering and the ringing in his ears was now almost like a choir, distant, faint, shimmering and unseen but getting closer.

"Quebec, Romeo, Sierra ..."

Perhaps people weren't slowly changing into something new, but just the opposite. Perhaps they were returning to an original, natural state. What if the way we are now, is the way we're supposed to be, maybe that's our natural state, and always has been, from over a million years ago? Perhaps the way we've been for the last million years was the exception, the anomaly, what if that was our curse? Maybe paradise and the garden of Eden was more than just a silly fable. Maybe it wasn't a snake and apple that got us kicked out of the garden, but just a routine pole reversal.

"Tango, Uniform, Victor..."

And everything being forgotten, all the holes left by the poisons and pain that people were forgetting, maybe those holes are being filled with something new, something that we didn't know we knew.

Precious memories, unseen angels
Sent from somewhere to my soul

Something hidden in a part of our brain we didn't know about, and the reversal is making it so that it's all starting to seep back into those empty spaces and fill them up with something new.

How they linger, ever near me
And the sacred past unfolds

Only it's not new, it's old, from more than a million years ago, and it's turning us back into who we once were, people who saw themselves in every other person they ever set eyes on.

Precious memories, how they linger
How they ever flood my soul

The choir faded away into a soft hiss as Hertell found himself staring at an ancient whiskey compass dangling from the overhead console.

In the stillness, of the midnight
Precious sacred scenes unfold

"Whiskey, X-ray, Zulu."

The entire flight crew was very impressed and began giving Toodlah a detailed explanation of the cockpit and all of its digital wonders.

Hertell continued to stare at the only surviving vestigial analog device in the otherwise entirely digital flight deck, and watched the compass card swing randomly back and forth, as if confused.

Hertell stiffened, "Do you ever use the compass?"

The co-pilot, Zak, who was a level 40 Mustard Seed Duck-n-Cover player, responded professionally, "Yessir, it's on the checklist, and it's been recalibrated for the pole reversal, so we check it during taxi and when we line up on the centerline. That's pretty much it, we don't really look at it after that since there's not much use for it with GPS and the Flight Management System."

"Are we... turning?"

The pilot responded, "Negative, straight and level." She pointed at the FMS, "046 on the nose."

Hertell pointed at the compass, "Then why is it doing that?"

They all looked at the primitive artifact of an earlier age, when it was all people had to keep from getting lost once they went beyond the sight of land and darkness engulfed on the open sea.

They silently watched as the compass cycled hesitantly back and forth a few times, and then slowly and resolutely swing all the way around from north to south.

One More Thing

(Actually two)

I hope you enjoyed reading *Water Memory*, and if you did, **please** leave a review. Reviews really help, and they can be as short as you want (longer too if so inclined). Since you're reading the print edition, here are QR codes for your smartphone or tablet that will take you straight to the appropriate *Water Memory* review page...

Amazon Review Page

*Barnes & Noble review
page*

Apple review page

Kobo review page

WATER MEMORY

GooglePlay review page

That Second Thing

And if you haven't already read *Dog Logic* (the first book in the Dog Logic Triptych) or listened to the audiobook, point your smart phone or tablet camera at the QR Code below...

Dog Logic Audiobook

Hertell Daggett has just discovered a time capsule. Only this one is full of people, and they've been living beneath his pet cemetery since 1963 due to some bad information they got about the end of the world. Hertell leads the duck-and-cover civilization into the glorious, mystifying, and often dismaying modern world. What could possibly go wrong?

About the Author

Tom Strelich was born into a family of professional wrestlers and raised in Bakersfield, California. His plays include *BAFO (Best and Final Offer)*, *Dog Logic*, and *Neon Psalms*. Honors include National Endowment for the Arts grant for playwrights, Kennedy Center Fund For New American Plays award, and Dramatists Guild/CBS New Play Award. Strelich has one screen credit, *Out There* (Showtime). His first novel, *Dog Logic*, (loosely based on the play - same setting, same characters, epically different story) has won several awards. *Water Memory* is his second novel.

Acknowledgments

Cover Design by Brittany Ragan

Author Photo by Alison Strelich

Special thanks to Steve Johnson and Thom Petersen who gave me some truly and astoundingly insightful notes that greatly helped the characters, the story, and the book.